OF SILVER & SIN

KAYTALIN PLATT

Published by Duskbound Books, Ohio
duskboundbooks.com

Cover design by: Kaytalin McCarry
Interior design by: Kaytalin McCarry
Edited by: Cari Dubiel
Digital Formatting: G.A. Finocchiaro

ISBN: 979-8-9897478-4-9

First Edition

Published in the United States of America

For Soran Nightblade
(aka Kathy)

Dedicated to the twenty years of
friendship that forever changed the course
of my life for the better.

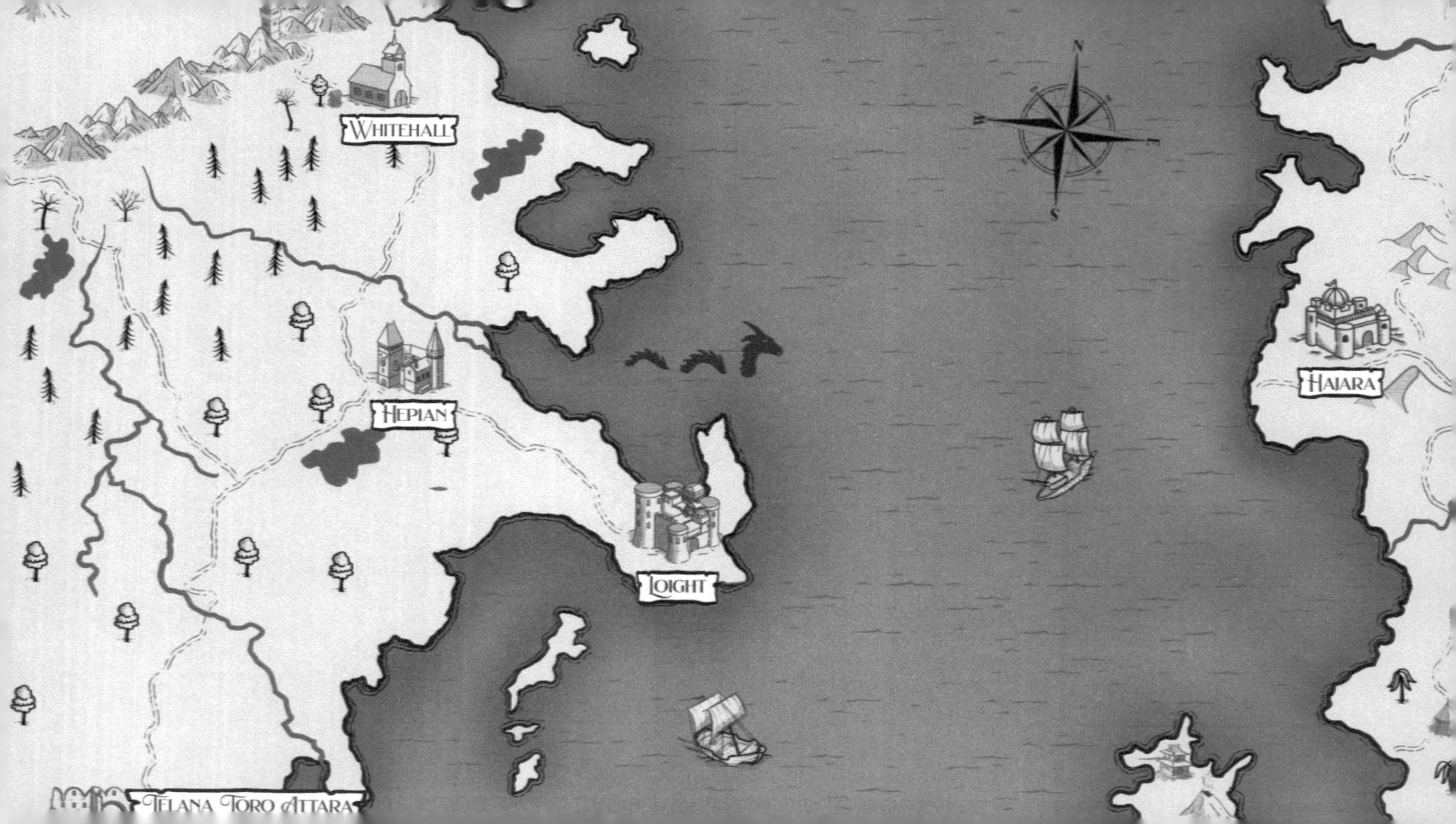

WHITEHALL
HEPIAN
LOIGHT
HAJARA
TELANA TORO ATTARA

ITHA LOLIN

"BLESS THE MOTHERS, for they bring the future. Bless the Sick, for they are helpless. Bless us Mortals, for we are the needy. Bless us Attara, Goddess of First Breaths and Healing, for we are damned. In your light, we are sheltered. In your love, we are saved."

Itha Lolin finished her morning prayers as the High Priestess's incessant bell rang in the hall. She was late, per usual, and she knew if she didn't hurry, the stern-faced woman would drag her out for her duties, dressed or not.

She donned the loose gray robes of a novice, pulling a drab cowl over her mossy hair. Itha didn't bother brushing it. What was the point when it stayed hidden beneath a sheet of muslin?

The Sisters of First Breaths were already gathered in the hall outside her room, filing out of the dormitory towards the cathedral. She fell in line with them, crossing the courtyard garden and adjusting the heel of her shoe as she left.

The cathedral doors parted and a wave of music filtered out. The Sisters of Last Breaths signaled the end of their night's watch with joyful song, flowing out from the cathedral and nodding to the Sisters of First Breaths as they went. It was a pageantry changing of the guard, a tradition as old as the monastery itself.

As the Sisters of First Breaths entered, Itha's gaze swept over the aged granite forming the arched door frame. Once, carefully carved figures and ornamentals had decorated the molding, and now they had weathered to barely discernible ridges along the stone. The monastery was old. Nearly forgotten by most of the world.

Three hundred years ago, the Goddess Attara would have had shrines all along Ighten's coast. People would have traveled for weeks to make pilgrimages to her churches and temples, to ask for blessings on their families and healing for their sick loved ones.

But a jealous god killed Her, robbing the world of the watcher of mothers and the sick.

Attara's temples and monasteries slowly shuttered as prayers went unanswered until only *Telana Toro Attara—Remember the Goddess Attara*—was left.

In the old days, the monastery was called *Belina os Toro Attara—Home of the Goddess Attara*. It was said to be her first true temple, and so Itha thought it made sense to also be her last.

Where there had once been hundreds of Priestesses, there were fewer than sixty now. Thirty to watch the day and twenty-five to watch the night, and if not for the vague interest of tourists, there would be no need for those either.

In fact, these "priestesses" who watched the monastery day and night were mostly all for show. This ritual of going back and forth was for the few people who still made the pilgrimage—who dropped their coin-based offerings into collection boxes at the center of the great cathedral and whispered their prayers on deaf ears. Those poor desperate fools who longed to have children and couldn't, or whose loved ones were near death with plague and sickness. They came seeking a miracle, unwittingly surrounded by non-believers.

The priestesses weren't holy. They were widows and whores and lost girls looking for refuge. They were paid in food, protection, and a safe place to sleep far south of the raging war at Ighten's border.

Their prayers weren't even real. Their bowed heads were often empty or pondering what might be on the kitchen's menu that day. When they weren't pretending to worship a dead goddess, they did chores. They mopped and scrubbed the floors or tended the garden by pulling weeds and reining in the thick vines that threatened to swallow the crumbling brickwork.

Itha realized she might be the only one, other than the High Priestess, who actually prayed when called to worship. As they entered the church and went to their respective rows, Itha watched the novices and priestesses kneel before the altar to their Goddess and bow their heads and close their eyes. But there was nothing. No whispered prayer. No creased, earnest brow. She did not need to see their eyes to know their minds were vacant. Was she really the only one who believed gods and goddesses could not die—not really—and that Attara would return to the world someday?

She had to believe there was a reason—other than convenience for the local economy—that *Telana Toro Attara* still stood as a functioning monastery. It was, after all, the source of Attara's final, most wondrous miracle.

The story was told in tapestries hanging on the library walls, in the spaces between rows of bookcases and shelves. A fable woven in gold thread and blood. Of how, on the day Attara was slain by a vengeful god, a virgin novice grew and birthed a child in a single day.

To Itha's great disappointment, that was where the story ended. The tapestry laid unfinished.

Three hundred years ago, a goddess died, a child was born, and no one knew what became of it. Itha liked to think the child was Attara, reborn in human form. Everyone assumed Itha was crazy, and no one thought the child had existed at all.

After morning prayers, Itha continued to the garden house and grabbed her basket and clippers before heading to the rose bushes growing along the courtyard walls. She spent the hour clipping the dead heads and placing their browning petaled bodies in the basket. Summer heat bore down, a sweltering pressure that soaked her robes in sweat.

The garden was quiet. In fact, the whole city was little more than a tomb for bodies lost far north at the border, never to return. Most of the men had gone, conscripts to a seemingly endless war. The war had been going for so long, in fact, most had forgotten how it even started. Itha knew, though. Verin, the God of Monsters, had gifted Ighten's northern neighbor, Alykith, a horde of beasts, and Alykith had used them to invade.

Itha snipped her skin while clipping off a drooping purple rose. She hissed at the bead of blood swelling on the edge of her finger, bringing it to her lips to suck the copper taste into her mouth and soothe the wound. She was always so wrapped up in her thoughts, always half in the world and half with legends.

A thunderous boom rattled the earth, a single clap without the continuous rolling clatter afterwards. Those standing in the courtyard looked up at the blue, cloudless sky before returning to their duties. A second later, a burst of air blasted over the monastery, blowing limbs and trees to the ground and sending all the priestesses and novices to their knees.

When the screaming died, Itha dragged herself up, a nervous flutter in her belly. Her heart raced in her ears as the flutter turned painful.

She wrapped her arms around her stomach, groaning at the pressure building within. Her abdomen grew, swelling as her skin stretched beneath the drab cotton. She screamed, belly bulging bigger by the second, until she felt it might burst. Several of her sisters gathered around, their faces drawn with horror.

This morning she had been a frail, idealistic girl, and now she was swollen around her middle, heavy with what looked to be a child…

But that wasn't possible.

Itha had never been with a man.

Her bones and muscles strained, her joints popping and stretching by the second. The Sisters pulled her to her feet. A terrible throb wrenched through her. Itha doubled over, screaming. A minute later, it appeared again, and as they led her into the cathedral, before a collecting gaggle of witnesses, water rushed down her parted legs, spilling across the marble floor.

Itha choked on a cry. She felt the thing inside her roll, felt it wiggle and shift. She saw its form ripple grotesquely beneath her dress. Pressure and pain compounded and built until Itha knew she was being torn in half from the inside.

Something told her to stop. To squat. To reach down, and so she did. She pushed, a throaty groan cracking into a piercing cry as she curled her hands beneath her and caught the blood-soaked child as it came free, taking its first, screaming breath in the world.

CASIMIR DROWSKY

150 YEARS LATER

CASIMIR DROWSKY HAD been alive one hundred and fifty years, at least as far as he remembered. But who knew how long he'd lived before? He couldn't say. His first memories were of waking on a battlefield during the Queens War—his clothes tattered and covered in blood—and then Ighten soldiers threw him in the dungeon far beneath their gleaming shore-side castle. They'd offered him no explanation. No trial. *Nothing*. Leaving him to be forgotten—a man without a past or a future—and for fifty years he'd lived in the dark until escaping.

Casimir Drowsky wasn't even his name. He'd stolen it. He'd taken Casimir from his cellmate, who lasted two weeks in Ighten's prison before being executed for murder. Drowsky, he'd borrowed from a merchant in passing.

Now, it seemed, he'd steal a job.

Father Olrin Peeble dusted an ornamental altar to Thar— the God of Light and Life, and the patron god of Ighten— while humming a hymn to himself. Casimir sat in an empty back pew. The church was old, all sharp carved stone, weathered and chipped. The ceiling stretched two stories high, covered in wooden rib vaults and slate tiles in need of repairing. Detailed stained-glass windows stretched floor to ceiling in height, with broken panes replaced by rippled clear glass. The missing pieces had caused one of Thar's perfect, angular jaws to go missing.

Casimir suspected this hovel to be one of the oldest churches in Ighten, and it sat forgotten in a minuscule town called Whitehall, a half-day's ride south of Ighten's border with Alykith.

"Are you looking for guidance, my son?" asked the priest without ceasing his busywork. He'd left Casimir alone when he entered, continuing his dusting, likely hoping Casimir would go away on his own and leave him without further work to do. "Just passing through?"

Casimir stretched his weary legs, clasping his hands in his lap as he settled further into the pew. "Has Thar ever spoken to you, Father?"

"Of course," said Father Peeble. "All the time."

"Does he ever give you dreams? Visions?"

"Yes."

"What do they mean?"

Father Peeble stopped his dusting and turned. He wore old green robes with a strip of gold cloth bunched like a scarf around his neck. Casimir would dress better.

"Are you having dreams, my son?"

Casimir stiffened. For a moment, he saw ghastly visions of beasts emerging from darkness. He saw blood and bone and agony, and it called to him. A voice, a longing, a need...

"I dreamed of this church," said Casimir as he stood and stepped toward the altar, turning and facing the priest.

"Then Thar has led you here." Father Peeble gripped his shoulder, the kind of touch Casimir assumed a father might place on a son.

He frowned. "Something has… Though, I don't think it's Thar."

Father Peeble's head tilted in the confused way most people looked at Casimir as he killed them. He hated killing, but it was the easiest way to get what he needed when he needed it.

Father Peeble's eyes widened, and he looked down at the dagger buried in his gut. Casimir only vaguely remembered driving it in. The priest crumpled to the ground at his feet, gasping and coughing and begging for his god.

"I don't think Thar listens," said Casimir, kneeling and running his hands over the top of the priest's head. "Don't worry, though, I'll tend to your flock until a god that listens comes along."

When the priest was dead, Casimir dragged him out back to a patch of grass near the forest's edge. A shadow moved and warped and formed into a physical being standing seven feet in height, with great gold horns swooping either side of its head.

"Jyn," said Casimir. "Make a spectacle, would you?"

Jyn smiled. His charcoal skin glinted in the faint warm light falling through the open church door. Gold eyes shimmered with amusement. Jyn brushed a lock of black hair behind his pointed ear and stooped to grab the priest's body.

With Whitehall being so close to Alykith, a land ensnared by dark magic, strange and evil things happened there in varying frequency. Now and then, untethered Shadows or dark sorcerers found their way over the border and into town limits.

So, when the residents of Whitehall woke to find their priest in several indiscernible pieces at the edge of town, they were not surprised. However horrifying, it wasn't rare to find someone half-devoured after defying curfew, and Father Peeble was known to sleepwalk.

A day later, Father Casimir Drowsky arrived. Some remarked it seemed too soon for the Church of Thar to send another priest, but they welcomed him. They couldn't afford to be suspicious, and if anyone needed the blessings of Thar, it was Whitehall.

TENELE RAIDER

"THIS IS A *stupid* plan," growled Maiden Klane as she passed the heavy circular shield to Tenele. Tenele slipped an arm through the straps at its back and gauged the weight with a frown. Almost too heavy, but it would do. She slipped her arm out and moved the shield to her back, hooking it over the hilt of her sword. Hopefully, it would stay.

Tenele adjusted the leather straps of her armored bracers and chestplate in a ritualistic fashion. Her pulse beat in her ears, her heart hammering its way out of her chest. She forced a smile. "Of course it is, but what choice do we have?"

"It's coming back around!" cried Maiden Ora several stairs above them.

Tenele glanced up through the wooden doorway to the roof of the tower. She ran her hands over her braided silver hair, down her face and neck. She was stalling.

"We could let it go by," said Maiden Klane. "Track it until it sleeps. It's been a long time since we faced one this big."

"We can't let it pass. It'll decimate a village." Tenele's jade eyes sharpened on the pale morning light breaking through the roof hatch above her. She nodded. "This will work. Get everyone to the valley."

The floors and walls shook, raining dust and ash. A keen screech broke the air and the morning light dimmed. Fire blew across the roof above their heads, pouring through the hatch in the ceiling to fill the air above them. Tenele and Klane ducked. Above, Maiden Ora's screams faded as sharp and fast as they'd begun.

"Blessed Thar," prayed Maiden Klane. "Keep her in Your merciful Light."

The fire dimmed and the shaking floor rattled to a lulling tremor. Tenele met Maiden Klane's watery gaze. Her brown eyes were warm—trusting but afraid. It wasn't like Red Court Maidens to fear, but Maiden Paelae Klane was still young. New.

"To the valley," said Tenele, standing and rushing up the burning steps. The palms of her hands blistered against the heat, but she burst through the fiery opening and crossed the tower roof to a wooden trestle connecting one tower to another. It was, surprisingly, unscathed.

Tenele scanned the horizon in quick, focused glances.

Hundreds of sharp craggy mountains made up the northern border between Alykith and Ighten. Lastower was one of the oldest forts along the border, built into the mountains and hovering on the brink of collapsing into a deep, snow-filled valley between two ranges.

The fort protected Ighten from remnants of a war which had ended over a hundred and fifty years ago. Creatures who didn't care—or perhaps didn't know—the war was over still clamored over Ighten's mountain walls, eager to claim it for the dark god who had abandoned them.

A flash of gold caught Tenele's eye. She whirled to where it glinted against the morning light. The shape of a man hovered in the air—far too large to be human. He stood four stories high with six feathery white wings. His skin was pale, iridescent white and almost translucent, revealing hard, gold bones and a golden skull with sharp pearlescent teeth. He wore a crown of white hair, and two wide gold horns stretched out to curl at either side of his head. Pale white-blue, glowing eyes burned into her.

He looked holy, as if he were born of Thar, but the Dark God Verin's fire boiled faint in his translucent belly. It trailed up his chest and spilled from his mouth. No, this was not a Glory—a holy, faceless servant of Thar—but neither was it a Shade, the strongest of Verin's monsters.

Shades were intelligent. They could speak many languages, even had a language all their own, and used both to twist, manipulate, and feed on mortals. But this creature was sophisticated in appearance only, moving and thinking like a common low-born monster—a Shadow.

The beast careened toward Lastower with a horrible screeching cry. Tenele pulled the hatchet from the loop on her belt and the dagger from the sheath at her back.

"This is a stupid plan," she said as the creature approached, its gaze fixating on her, its teeth bared. And just as she thought it would breathe its monstrous fire upon her, it passed beneath the trestle she stood on, treating her as if she weren't even there.

She leapt from the wooden support and landed with a hard scraping thud on the Shadow's back, digging the dagger in as an anchor. It wailed, twisting and arching in the air to throw her off.

"Stupid, stupid plan!"

She hacked at the base of one wing, a sturdy feather-covered bone connecting the three articulating wings on its right. The Shadow screeched and reached with long translucent arms, dagger-sharp golden nails grasping at her while it moved. It tried to grind her against the mountains and plowed its shoulder into the cliffs, knocking boulders into the valley below.

With one final hack, the massive wing tore away, and they plummeted to the craggy, snow-laden earth. The creature landed, skidding against rocks, sand, and snow until it crashed against a mountain and slung Tenele into a boulder.

She wheezed, struggling to breathe and see through the rush of dust and snow. Fire glowed behind a fog of floating particles, beginning as a bud of orange behind the gray and growing into a stream of lapping flame. Tenele dragged the shield from her back and cowered behind it as a scorching river of fire spread, singing her hair and skin. Then the heat disappeared, the air growing dull and cold again. She drew her sword and stood.

A battle cry echoed off the granite mountains. Fifty warrior women descended on the creature from a narrow passage beneath Lastower. The Shadow breathed fire and thrashed as they swarmed it like ants, hacking and slicing. Arrows bathed in holy fire lodged in its eyes, blinding it. After several failed attempts at flying away, it collapsed dead beneath them.

Rich blood, the color of liquid gold, leaked from its wounds to pool on the desolate earth. The ground hissed and popped and sizzled where its heat met ice. Tenele caught a Maiden's hand as she went to run her fingers through it, shaking her head and pressing the feathered end of an arrow into the liquid until it caught flame.

Maiden Klane barreled toward Tenele and hugged her too tight. "You didn't die!"

Tenele winced, feeling the twinge of bruised ribs beneath her armor. "You were right, Paelae, that wasn't my best idea."

"But it worked!"

It had, but only because the Shadow had done a peculiar thing—ignored her on the trestle.

Tenele limped back up the long, winding road leading to Lastower's heavy iron gates. They laid the wounded in the medical ward, a narrow room lined with cots. Medics tackled the easiest cases, but Tenele hesitated in helping the worst. She paused at the ward door, staring at one Maiden writhing in pain as they tended burns covering her lower half. If she didn't succumb to her wounds, infection would likely take her.

Tenele caught sight of High Maiden Lindor standing across the room, giving marching orders to the medics. The old woman met her gaze and gave a stern shake of her head, as if she could read the thoughts brewing behind Tenele's eyes.

"They'll heal," said Paelae, appearing at her side. She urged Tenele forward, pressing her hands into Tenele's bruised back, but she winced away from the touch. "You have your own injuries to worry about."

Tenele glanced down at her scuffed, dirty hands. Though she ached to ease the other Maidens' suffering, Paelae was right. While healing another would take its toll, it wasn't a matter of health. The High Maidens—even the queen herself—had urged her, since she was a child, to hide her healing gifts. *"Only in the direst circumstances,"* they'd said.

This felt dire. Though, it seemed High Maiden Lindor thought otherwise. Tenele wondered what would happen if she waltzed in and healed every injured girl in the room. Tenele was quite certain it might put her in a coma. The few times she'd used her power, it had been draining.

Paelae knew of it because Tenele had broken the rule to save her life. She'd found Paelae bleeding out during a Shadow swarm five days after arriving at her posting, fresh out of academy. Tenele had healed her wounds only to immediately collapse next to her, and, for reasons Tenele still didn't understand, the woman hadn't spoken a word to anyone.

When night fell, the Red Court Maidens feasted on roast and wine and made up songs about the silver-haired, half-Grela madwoman who'd flown on the back of a towering demon. Tenele laughed… and regretted it, rubbing a hand over her ribs. They ached when she enjoyed herself, so she drank more wine to dull the pain, and when she'd drank so much she couldn't stand, Paelae helped her off to bed.

Tenele woke before dawn, a common occurrence after indulging in too much red wine. It filled her chest with a nagging anxiety she could never place. It made her over-analyze every conversation to see if she'd said or done something foolish, even if, normally, she couldn't give two shits what anyone thought.

The Maiden tossed and turned. When it seemed she wouldn't find sleep, she rose from her bed to put a whetstone to her sword. The blade glinted in the dim candlelight. Engraved threads of gold runes were set along its pale steel length. It had been hers since taking her oath as a Red Court Maiden over a hundred years ago. It would be hers until her long half-Grela life ended.

Maidens were orphaned girls—educated, battle hardened, and required to serve until age twenty-five. It wasn't a long sentence, but not many survived, and those that did often stayed to serve longer. Not many knew what to do with themselves when they weren't fighting or thinking about it.

Maidens were given insensible rules around chastity and marriage to keep them focused and childless—all of which the Court thought easily maintained by stationing them miles from the nearest males. But, group a hundred or more women in a cold fort for months on end—with little to do other than fight and sleep—and no one remained chaste for long.

The thought pulled Tenele's lips into a smile, and she fell down a rabbit hole of blurry, patchwork memories lurid enough to color her cheeks and stir a longing for something other than cold steel in her hands.

A soft knock sounded against the door, and the whetstone slipped from Tenele's grasp, clattering along the floor. It was too early for anyone else to be up, save maybe a Watch Maiden making her rounds.

Tenele found Paelae on the other side, clothed in her dressing gown and rubbing sleep from her eyes. Her dark skin glowed warm against the hall's shadow.

"I saw candlelight under your door on my way back from the kitchens," she said. "I heard the scrape of a whetstone."

Tenele smiled. "I couldn't sleep."

Paelae nodded. She glanced into Tenele's room, to the sword and her disheveled bed. Paelae's brown eyes lifted expectantly as she stepped forward. "I could keep you company." Her fingers curled in Tenele's dressing gown, warm against her hip.

Tenele wrapped her hand over Paelae's, fingers flexing, grasping, trailing over the soft skin of the girl's wrist. "I'm too old for you."

It was both true and a joke. Tenele was half-Grela. She was nearly two hundred, but less than thirty by human standards. Grela aged slowly, and Tenele had aged as a human until her twenties. Then, time turned sluggish.

She felt an ache in her heart as Paelae looked away, fingers uncurling from Tenele's gown. Tenele thought about Meredith and Robert—two people she'd known in more ways than the Court liked. Both were dead.

The people she loved always died, and Tenele lived on, by genetics or sheer luck. She mourned them. Missed them. Longed to feel their touch. Loneliness curled heavy in her stomach. As Paelae turned to leave, the ache cut into Tenele so deeply her lips parted and a word spilled out before she could pull it back in. "Wait."

Tenele grasped Paelae's gown. The young woman paused, turning as Tenele tugged her into the room and closed the door behind her.

TENELE RAIDER

THE WAILING OF Lastower's many warning bells woke Tenele at morning. She cracked an eye open, her arm stretching across the empty portion of her narrow bed where Paelae had curled next to her in the night. She was gone, which was for the best given what would happen if the two of them piled half-dressed out of the same room.

Tenele moved as fast as her aching body allowed, thinking of Paelae's soft lips on her skin as she tightened the straps of armor over her torso. Tenele was still deciding whether it had been a mistake to bring the woman into the room, to lie with her in the bed and taste her. The memory of it brought an ache of longing to her center.

High Maiden Crayl was in the dining hall when Tenele entered, speaking with others of her status in hurried, hushed whispers. Tenele paused in the doorway, watching them closely. They were worried, and that unsettled her because the Red Court rarely worried about anything.

"That could be you up there," said High Maiden Lindor as she stepped next to Tenele. "If you'd ever accept any of the promotions I offer." She was nearing her sixties, but Tenele remembered her as a child coming into the Court. Tenele had trained her, and now the woman gave her orders.

That was the unfortunate side effect of aging in slow motion.

"I don't like clerical duties," said Tenele with a smile, brushing a rogue strand of silver hair behind her ear.

"So we've gathered," mused High Maiden Lindor as she left to join the others at the front of the hall.

As the last Maidens filed in, Paelae rushed to stand next to Tenele. She was still adjusting her armor as Crayl called the room to attention with a hard rap of her cane against the floor.

Crayl was another Tenele remembered training. She'd become an old crone now, her hunched back straightened by the trappings of her armor.

"Maidens," said Crayl, lifting her hand to hush the young women. "We received word this morning that Eastower has fallen. Overcome by a swarm of Shadows… too many to count. Someone sent a bird, but we have seen no sign of survivors."

Murmurs fluttered through the room.

"Has Alykith abandoned the truce?" someone asked.

"There's no reason to believe they have," said Crayl.

"Then, why has the fort fallen?"

"Because a bunch of men were guarding it."

Laughter rolled across the room in a wave.

"Enough." High Maiden Crayl cracked her cane against the floor. "People have died. Respect them." The room fell silent. "A dark sorcerer has called Shadows over the mountains. The closest town to us is Whitehall, and we must protect the residents. I'm sending Maidens to guard them until we understand the full force of this threat."

"They overran Eastower. What are a handful of Maidens going to do in a town of civilians?"

High Maiden Crayl frowned. "We can't afford to send more than a few. There could be more Shadows approaching the border, and we need fighters here to stop them. Maiden Raider, gather nine Maidens and head south to Whitehall. Maiden Raider, are you listening?"

Paelae nudged Tenele, and she winced at the pressure against her ribs.

"Listening," said Tenele. "I'll take Maidens Klane, Wool, Shire, Laftry, Holda, Rol, Ingress, Trei, and Mako."

Crayl nodded. "Pack up. You leave before noon."

Beneath the great mountains lining Igthen's border with Alykith was a forest born of fire and death. Once, long before the Queens War, it had been filled with magic and Grela—long-lived beings with lithe figures and a penchant for earth magics. The forest thrived under their watch, making it a dense line of defense until it burned to cinders in the early days of the war, taking the Grela with it.

Now, they called it Ashwood. A hundred years of peace had allowed the forest to grow back thick and strong, though locals whispered the Shadow blood spilled on its soil had cursed it. A heavy fog always lurked near the feet of travelers, and some found themselves lost in its depths, following voices of loved ones long gone.

Small villages dotted the forest—nameless and unknown to most mapmakers. They barely had enough residents to justify the title of "village." Most were clusters of families who formed small communes after the ravages of war. None of them heeded Tenele's warnings as they passed on to Whitehall.

Night hung heavy in the air as they neared town. It was well past the point of needing to camp, but Tenele didn't call the company to stop—though Paelae urged her to.

"We're only a few minutes from Whitehall," said Tenele.

She knew better. The forest became treacherous at night, and more so with Shadows lurking nearby, but Tenele saw the faint flicker of lights in the distance—a warm amber beacon against the misty black.

"We can go a few minutes more." She smiled at Paelae, hardly able to see her in the dark. Paelae didn't smile back.

A terrible, pain-filled squeal broke the night's silence. Tenele recognized the shape of a Maiden's horse as it reared and then something tore apart. A monster, darker than black, rose to loom over them.

"Shadows!"

The group formed a circle on the narrowed road. Horses snorted and stomped, shifting beneath their night-blind riders. A terrible quiet settled around them. Nothing moved—not the leaves, not the crack of a limb. Even the hooves stomping against packed dirt deafened.

"Torches," whispered Tenele.

Several Maidens with HolyFire torches struck flint to their pre-oiled sconces. Fire roared bright against the night, illuminating the dark breaks between trees. Monstrous Shadows lurked in the gaps. They blended together in a wall of eyes and teeth. Too many to count. Too many to fight.

Tenele reached for her sword, dragging it from its sheath

slowly, as if any sudden movement might bring the wall of writhing eyes and gaping maws crashing down on them. "Make a hole and head to Whitehall. Ride as fast as you can," said Tenele, her gaze settling on Paelae. "Don't look back."

The other Maidens drew their swords.

And the wall came crashing down.

HolyFire torches were the first to go. They snuffed out, one by one, in screams and gurgled cries of pain until one torch remained. It fell to the wayside, flickering faint and forgotten while Shadows cut through the Maidens in less than a minute.

A great mangled hand of gnarled bone and broken skin ripped Tenele's horse out from under her, dragging the wailing beast into the forest and silencing it. She clamored to her feet, cutting through the mass of shapes. They danced and slashed and bit—too fast for her to identify faces or figures. Her back pressed to Paelae's, and they hacked at the beasts together.

Then, Paelae was gone.

The massive hands of gnarled bone returned, lifting Paelae and pulling her apart like an insect. Tenele reached for her—for a part of her—as they rained heavy and hot and many.

Pain split across Tenele's back. She whirled on the Shadow, but a heavy hit sent her flying into a tree. The bruised ribs from the day before cracked and she crumpled to the ground, wheezing panicked breaths into her burning lungs. She rose, shoving the blood-laden hood from her head to see better.

A fist—more like a spike—drove like a knife into her side. Tenele stiffened, sucking in a shocked breath as she felt along the fleshy stump impaling her. It lifted her into the air. Pain ripped through her, and she screamed, bringing the sword still in her hands down, severing the massive claw.

The creature shrieked, shrinking back.

Tenele fell, collapsing on the messy, wet earth. She grabbed at the claw still lodged inside her and ripped it away, knowing it wasn't the right choice—that she'd bleed out faster. But she was dead already, and she couldn't stand the feel of that monster's twitching appendage inside her.

Hot blood ran over her fingers, soaking cloth and earth. The creatures clung to the dark, inching forward with every sputtering flicker of the last HolyFire torch. A Shadow crawled forward, its mouth gaping and wet. Drool fell like a fountain over the HolyFire torch, and with a sharp hissing last breath, the dark swallowed Tenele.

Here it is, she thought. The end.

Tenele fell back into the heap of death, laying beneath a cloudy sky and listening to the slow creep of beasts towards her. They chewed through parts of girls still large enough to find, munching and slurping. The sound made her wish she could bleed out faster.

She took slow, quiet breaths, feeling the warmth of her life spread over her hands and into her clothes, into the mud at her back. Then, the clouds parted, and the moon unveiled itself in a wash of pale blue light glinting against the strands of her silver hair.

The moon's light swelled, and the shine on her hair turned diamond bright. The Shadows closest to her retreated with horrific, gravelly murmurs in a language she didn't know.

The edges of the world grew faint and dark. Her head swam and her vision blurred, but just as she knew death was taking her, she caught sight of two shimmering gold eyes glowing against the dark. A tall shape approached, this one humanoid. She grasped along the earth for her sword, wrapping her hand tight around the hilt and swung up. The blade lodged in the being's forearm, blessed gold hissing in the flesh. The Shadow didn't flinch or howl. It tilted its head at her, shaking off her attack in such a way that the sword was knocked from her slackening grip. Then, he was over her, a black shape against the moon. She saw the glint of a smile set into charcoal-colored skin.

"You're dying, *Minka'nes*," said the creature, and Tenele swallowed at the sound of his deep, silvery voice.

A Shade. A *real* Shade.

She fumbled for the dagger sheath at her back, grasping the hilt. A breath, and she lunged up with it. He caught her wrist and throat and forced her to the earth.

The Shade loomed large and menacing over her, snuffing out the moon and the sky. He wrenched the dagger from her hand and tossed it over his shoulder, careless and amused. Fisting the leather armor on her chest, he ripped it free before tearing the fabric of her blouse open, baring her chest and waist to the chilly night air.

Tenele let the dark edges of her mind drag her down, lulling her towards unconsciousness. Better to be dead than alive for whatever he had planned.

Then, he lifted his hand as if to show her something, and a white-hot glow caught her attention. The gold in his eyes brightened. He lowered his flaming hand to her waist, to the wound at her side pouring out her lifeblood. She felt the heat before the burn, but then it was all she knew. Agony—hot, molten pain pressed against her bleeding side. She screamed,

screamed until she lost her voice and the world went dark.

Tenele woke with a start. She lay in a small stone room with a warm fire crackling in a narrow hearth. A lumpy straw bed pressed into her back. Her body burned and ached and screamed with pain, while her hands fumbled over herself beneath the wool blankets, finding rows of bandages and nothing else.

Her vision blurred in and out as she struggled for the strength to lift her head, managing a quick glance around the modest room. A single bed. Several bookshelves. A small writing desk and two wooden chairs. The remains of her armor and shredded clothes draped one chair.

It was not a room in Lastower—at least not one she had ever seen.

Tenele's shaking arm dragged back the sheet to study the wound on her side. She tried to sit up and her chest screamed with pain, her breath coming short and tight.

The door clicked open, and then at once slammed shut. Tenele dragged the blanket back over her as a knock rattled through the wood. "Can I come in?"

A man's voice.

This was definitely not Lastower.

Tenele's lips parted to answer, but a strangled sound slipped out. She cleared her throat and tried again, managing a groan that sounded enough like "yes" for the door to open.

A young man dressed in black robes slid in. He carried a silver tray balanced on one hand, loaded with bread, cheese, and a glass of water, and set it on a small table near the bed.

"I'd hoped to find you awake," he said. "I'd begun to think you wouldn't. That you might have lost too much blood…"

Tenele winced. "How…"

"My church is at the edge of town. I heard screaming and rounded up a few men. We found you and brought you here."

"Church?"

"A Church of Thar, in Whitehall… I'm Father Casimir Drowsky."

Tenele appraised him. She bit back the desire to remark how, for a human, he seemed too young for his own parish. He was in his early thirties, with shaggy brown hair and deep brown eyes—and he wasn't built like a priest, either. The Church had likely sent him to the middle of nowhere to stop the priestesses and prioresses from breaking their vows.

"Father Drowsk–"

"Call me Father Casimir," he said, smiling. Thar's Mercy, he was beautiful.

"How am I alive?" Her throat was dry. Raspy. She wanted the water but couldn't imagine finding the strength to sit and drink. Her fingers flexed out for her clothes. "My shirt."

Father Casimir turned for a narrow wardrobe tucked in the corner. "I'm afraid there wasn't much left of your shirt, so you can have one of mine." He handed her a black tunic. She fumbled into it as best she could without sitting up while he stoked the fire. The fabric swallowed her, smelling of lavender and thyme.

"You've got a Shade's Mark," said Father Casimir casually. He rolled a log over before standing. The fire cracked and hissed, framing him in light.

Tenele flinched at the news. Bracing herself on a quivering elbow, she shoved the blankets away and dragged the shirt up, peeking beneath the bandages. A messy, burned circle of flesh replaced the gaping, ruinous hole the jagged spike had left behind. Laid over it, like a large black stain, was the shape of a handprint, the fingers curling around her side.

Father Casimir leaned against the wall. "It cauterized your wound and saved your life."

Tenele swallowed and sank into bed. "Shit."

"It's not all bad," said the priest, amusement dancing in his voice. An odd thing for a priest to say to someone cursed with a Shade's Mark.

"It's like putting a tracking spell on a deer," muttered Tenele. "Except it comes with mind games, too."

Father Casimir smirked and dragged a chair over to her bed. "I've heard they only claim you so other Shadows won't eat you—to save you for themselves. It essentially tattooed 'mine' on your stomach." He gestured to her belly. "Shades are strange, temperamental beings, and sometimes they collect people. I think the mark is temporary, though. It should fade."

Tenele pursed her lips. She'd rather the creature kill her, and why hadn't it? Why save her? Worst of all, why mark her for later?

"You're worried," said Father Casimir. He held the cup of water out and slipped his hand beneath her head. His fingers curled in her soft silver hair and he helped her drink. "Don't be. You're on sacred ground. As long as you're here, nothing can harm you."

"I can't stay. I have to return to Lastower and tell them what happened…" Tenele pushed the cup away and struggled to sit. She stretched her hand towards her clothes again, and

Father Casimir dragged her pants from the pile without leaving his chair. He placed them in her lap and frowned so grim and dark her stomach turned cold.

"Lastower's fallen." He put his hands together, palm to palm, and breathed a prayer into the air. "You've been asleep for three days. The night we found you, I sent riders to alert the High Maidens. The fort was in ruins. There were no survivors. You… are the last."

Tenele felt dizzy, struggling to sit. Father Casimir pressed a hand to her shoulder. His other brushed fingers through her hair, tucking strands of silver behind her ear—too familiar a gesture for a priest. But he was young. He hadn't yet learned to be a distant mouthpiece for the Gods.

Flashes of Shadows and blood and screams filled her mind. She couldn't swallow. Couldn't breathe. A heaviness settled like a brick on her chest and her throat constricted with sorrow. Paelae's face appeared, and then she was gone. *Gone.* Torn apart.

They were all torn apart.

Why am I still alive?

Why was I saved?

Tears fell down Tenele's cheeks. "I have to go," she said. "I have to get to Loight and speak to the queen."

"It's dangerous," said Father Casimir, his fingers curling in her hair. "Our town, in particular. You'll never make it out."

Tenele sat up with a sharp, painful cry, urging him to turn away so she could dress. She wiped tears from her eyes, rage replacing her sorrow with every aching heave of air into her lungs. "Luckily, a Shade wants me for a snack later. I'll make it through to Loight with his Mark."

"Unless he snacks on you first?"

Tenele paused as she struggled with her pants. Dressing while wounded was one thing. Dressing while wounded and legs as heavy as lead was another. Her hands trembled. "I'll make it through."

Father Casimir glanced back, and, realizing she wasn't ready, looked away. "Need some help, Maiden?"

"Isn't touching a half-naked woman against your vows or something?"

"Wouldn't me, touching you, be against your vows, too?" She could almost see that perpetual smirk through the back of his head. "If touching a naked woman was against my vows, you'd be dead. I did undress you, stitch your wounds and bandage you, after all."

Tenele struggled a second more and then sighed. "Help. Please."

The priest turned, still wearing that very unpriestly smile and hoisted her up with an arm curled around her waist. She sucked in a breath as wounds stretched against their sutures and her ribs screamed. Tenele cursed him in two tongues.

His devilish smile softened. "I forgot to mention, your laundry list of injuries includes a few broken ribs."

"I know," she said, glaring at him as he settled his hands on her waist, just enough pressure to steady her balance. He guided her hands to his shoulder and then grabbed the trousers trapped at her knees, drawing them up and over her hips. His hands rested there, lingering too long.

"Look at us, one celibate helping another dress." Based on the glint in his eye, Tenele suspected he was as celibate as she.

"Are you sure you're a priest?"

"Last time I checked. So, how do you intend on getting all the way to Loight? You can't even put your pants on without help."

"If you put me on a horse with some food and water, I'll make it."

"How will you get off the horse?"

"I won't."

"All the way to Loight? That's two weeks or more."

Tenele frowned. He was right… it made no sense. She wasn't thinking clearly. Salarus, she wasn't really thinking at all.

Father Casimir eased her back to bed and sat across from her. His brown eyes appraised her with a distant, thoughtful look. "I'll get you a horse, a wagon, and a driver. He'll take you to Loight. It'll give you time to heal."

"The town's surrounded. The Shadows won't eat me, but they may eat the driver."

Father Casimir smiled. "By Thar, I'll bless the driver. We'll cover the cart in runes. Can I ask what you'll do when you get there?"

"I'll tell the queen what's happened. Maybe Alykith has broken the truce. There's a reason Shadows swarmed the border… We'll figure it out."

Father Casimir nodded, sitting quietly for a long time. Then, he rose for the door. "I'll see about your wagon and driver."

5

CASIMIR DROWSKY

IT WAS LATE evening when Maiden Raider and her driver departed. Casimir watched from behind his church at the edge of town as the flatbed wagon limped along the bumpy road. A deep frown creased his youthful face. He folded his arms across his chest and didn't turn back for the church until the wagon, and the woman it carried, disappeared around the bend.

Jyn stood in the shadows of the forest, leaning against a tree with his eyes closed. He seemed bored, which was a change from the Shade's usual maniacal playfulness. "Do you want me to stop her?" His golden eyes opened, his gaze flicking towards Casimir.

Casimir glanced back over his shoulder as if he could still see her. A thought nagged him, scratching at the back of his mind. A warning? No. That wasn't it.

"Why did you save her?" asked Casimir.

Jyn's eyes brightened. The boredom slopped off of him as he stood straight and stepped into the afternoon light. A broad, frightening grin spread across the Shade's charcoal face. "Do you want me to kill her?"

Casimir glowered at the Shade. "No."

"Why not?"

"I don't know." Casimir's jaw tightened. He didn't like not knowing.

He knew he should tell Jyn to go after her—to get rid of her—but the order wouldn't leave his lips. Instead, he thought of her silver Grela hair, her green eyes, and her pain—of all the tiny wounds littering her body, and the hand of his Shade staining her skin. Casimir wanted to touch her. Comfort her. Shield her. All those feelings were the reason he should order Jyn to kill her, and also why he couldn't.

Jyn's dark laugh filled the small clearing, and Casimir's hands clenched into fists. This was a game. The creature had no intention of killing her, or Jyn would have. So why save her?

And why did she feel familiar and warm to Casimir, like he knew her? While she was half-Grela, he doubted she was old enough to know the man he had been 150 years ago.

The pretend priest pinched the bridge of his nose. This, like so many things, was another puzzle... and he had so many to solve already.

"Do you want me to stop her from leaving?" asked Jyn, his voice lowering an octave, growing seductive and powerful. "Do you want me to bring her back to you? You could nurse her. Coddle her. Taste her..." The image of him tangled with her in the sheets of his narrow, stolen bed flourished in Casimir's mind, and he shook his head to rid himself of the desire before he did ask Jyn to bring her back.

People believed Shades could walk you off a cliff with their words alone. If Casimir were any other man, he might have been tempted by them. But he was different. Whatever that meant.

Jyn's grin widened. "Or I can kill her. It's whatever you desire, Master."

Casimir shook his head, feeling tired and hungry. "What's one Maiden going to do? Let her tell her queen. Nothing will stop this. All I have left is to find the door and the key. Then this will be over. I just need time, and there are plenty of ways to occupy or kill anyone who comes searching."

TENELE RAIDER

A SALT-TINGED BREEZE tickled the loose strands of hair along Tenele's neck as she looked over the side of the cart and out at the city stretching along the coast of the Ongore Sea. For the first time in years, she was home.

Loight was a shining port city—a hub for arts, culture, and commerce in Ighten. The palace, the seat of power for both their sorceress queen and the Church, was built with pearly white stones harvested from a desolate island just off the coast. Spindling towers of gleaming white stretched up towards a blue, cloudless sky, the spires tipped with slate blue tiles. It glowed like a holy beacon in the center of a gray, granite city.

Across Tenele's lengthening life, home had become an increasingly confusing place. In Loight, there was nothing to do but attend court or banquets or parties. While she enjoyed fine dresses as much as the next girl, mingling with people— especially nobility—proved difficult. They were hollow and stuffy, knowing nothing of real hardship, pain, or loss. A century without war had made them soft. Tenele couldn't hold a conversation without falling into battle stories or showing off scars, which tended not to go well with lords who wanted her silence and smile.

Her townhouse lay forgotten. With no maintenance and no visitors, she suspected the roof had fallen in. Not that it mattered, and not that she cared.

Their peace was ending, and Tenele knew she'd never see that little house again once Queen Sinead learned what had happened to the Red Court Maidens at the border.

Tenele swallowed and hunkered down against the wagon wall, feeling along her side for the Shade's Mark. It had acted as a shield on their journey, but not without a price. She turned her sharp gaze on the forest, half expecting the beast to burst out and gobble her up now that she was close to safety. She'd looked over her shoulder for almost two weeks, but he never came for her… at least not in the waking world.

He occupied her nightmares, slipping in to torture her in unspeakable ways while she slept. When he opened his mouth, commands spilled out, serpentine and constricting, forcing her to commit terrible acts against her will. Sometimes he ordered her to gut herself, and she did. Sometimes he told her to make love to him, and she did. Her will didn't matter in the world of dreams, only his.

The palace guards had tripled their usual presence, which set Tenele on edge as she turned her wrist up to them. The barely-noticeable, iridescent white tattoo glinted in the light, revealing a conjoined sun and moon—the mark of a Red Court Maiden. When they saw it, the world collided into a flurry of joyous shouting. A guard grabbed her arm, apologizing as he ushered her into the courtyard, behind the iron bars, and to the grand staircase leading to the main doors.

A horn blared as a burly man clamored down the steps, almost tumbling to a stop at her feet. "Maiden!" He looked at her—really looked at her—and his eyes brimmed with tears. "Maiden Raider. Merciful Thar… you're alive."

Hours later, Tenele waited in a quiet room, smoothing restless hands over a borrowed violet gown. She'd hurried through her washing, forgetting vital steps—like drying off. Her hair hung stringy and wet over her shoulders, dampening the violet satin to a dark purple.

She glanced at the wood doors leading to Lord Byron's personal study, her teeth grinding. She resisted the urge to kick them open and force herself into the conversation. Was Sinead in there? Had they alerted the queen while she bathed?

Perhaps she should have waited on the bath. What was one more hour compared to two whole weeks of stench? But the advisors she met on arrival couldn't stand the smell of death on her clothes. They'd listened politely, at first, while she stood before them, wearing cloth blackened by Maiden and monster blood, before sending her away to wash.

They hadn't stopped on their way to Loight save to eat and sleep before starting again. Her message had felt more important than the comfort of inns and baths.

Lord Byron's study door opened, jerking Tenele from her thoughts, and he emerged looking wearier than usual.

"Maiden Raider." He crossed the room to her side and offered her a somewhat brusque bow. The lapel of his velvet robe unsettled in the process, and he fussed with it as he straightened. It was rare to see Byron in such finery outside the monthly congregation of the High Court. Up close, she could spot more than just exhaustion in his drawn expression. "I am to escort you to the throne room."

Tenele hesitated before following him. Her hands twisted together in front of her, fingers clasping and unclasping. The throne room meant seeing Queen Sinead. She glanced sidelong at Lord Byron. "Has there been any word? Is it Alykith?"

Byron's austere gaze settled on the path. "It would be best to hear it from them."

Tenele and Byron breezed through the council chambers, and two stationed guards allowed them through the side entrance to Sinead's throne room.

For centuries, the focal point of this hall had been the heavily carved throne at the head of the room, crowned by four stories of stained-glass windows at its back. The throne itself was a sight to behold but seldom occupied. Even now, Queen Sinead was not seated there, but at her usual place at the end of a long mahogany table tucked into an alcove off to the side. Her azure gown drew the blue of her eyes out like gemstones, and she looked almost ordinary seated at the table. Nothing about her screamed of magic, of the power that had once killed a god.

It was a familiar sight to see the monarch poised behind a pile of documents. What was not at all normal were those seated around her. Every one of the eleven members of the High Council were in their place, and every one looked at Tenele with dread in their eyes.

"Tenele," Sinead greeted her. The woman's strong, clear voice did little to settle the near-physical tension in the air. "I must apologize for pulling you in to meet with us so abruptly.

I have heard that you yourself are injured."

Tenele curtseyed, scanning the room one more time. A sick feeling curled in the pit of her stomach. "I was able to heal on the trip here, for the most part. I can get back to the border as soon as you wish. I just... I needed you to know about Lastower. I wasn't sure how soon word would get here if I didn't come myself."

If the entire council had been staring at Tenele a moment ago, not a single eye met hers now. A darkness that looked entirely foreign on Sinead's face stopped time. "It is a blessing, and a testament to your skill, that you were able to return at all."

Tenele stiffened. Her hand skimmed her side, smoothing over the Shade's Mark. Skill hadn't saved her. Not even luck. Something darker had let her live while all the others died.

I shouldn't be alive, she thought.

Tears burned her eyes, but she blinked them away. "I was lucky," she said. "I would have died if a priest hadn't found me. He's the reason I'm alive. Lastower fell and I don't know how long before the others will face what we saw. We need reinforcements at the border."

The queen smoothed her hand over Tenele's arm. "Your luck has delivered back to us a priceless resource..." A pain dimmed the light in Sinead's eyes. "Messengers from across Ighten have brought us terrible news, one after another... Tenele, you are the first to return to us in person. The only one to make it back to us alive... from any outpost."

"The first..." Tenele's chest tightened, breath quickening as a wave of nausea rolled through her. She looked away to the windows, the ceiling, the floor—anywhere to keep from meeting their eyes. She felt the gazes like fiery flames on her skin.

There were seven outposts. Seven. All of them, gone.

She was the last Maiden of the Red Court.

I should be dead. I should be dead. I should be dead.

"Alykith? Is it Alykith?" Tenele finally leveled her eyes on the table, her gaze hardening. "Have they broken the truce?"

"We don't know. For a group of Shadows to manifest and act together, with such speed… This level of organization requires a powerful summoning. Someone with skill we haven't seen since the war, and a massive amount of dark magical energy."

The seated council members cast careful glances at one another. Their skepticism wasn't uncalled for. Killing Verin, the God of Monsters, had ended the war and cut back such energy to a whisper.

Finally, Lady Nyris gave voice to what they all seemed to be thinking. "It can't have been a summoning. Only Verin could call these beasts from his dark realm, and he is gone. These demons were already here, and a powerful sorcerer is controlling them. The only one powerful enough is Lyra, Alykith's queen. It has to be Alykith."

Another noble cut in, "We can't be certain. Our relations have been stable. There's no logic in breaking the truce now. And besides that… the brands—"

"Who else would have Shadows like this just lying around? Their culture hasn't changed. They still worship Verin!"

Murmurs around the table proved this debate was not a new one.

"There weren't any sorcerers," said Tenele. "No one guided

them, at least that we could see. They were a horde." Tenele thought about the wall of eyes and teeth, the mass of Shadows clustered together—all different kinds and strengths gathered around that little town in the forest. She doubted anything would be left of it if she returned. "There was a Shade." Tenele's eyes unfocused at the memory of his tall form emerging from the forest, golden eyes and sharp white teeth gleaming in the moonlight.

You're dying, Minka'nes.

She rubbed at the Mark on her side.

They were devilish, smart, brutal creatures with power beyond her understanding, and hard—if not impossible—to kill. If there was one, there could be more, and if there were more...

"If it's the work of Alykith, then what's controlling them is already in Ighten—"

"How did *you* survive a Shade?" asked Lady Nyris, a dark brow arching as her lips pursed together. Tenele had wondered when the nobles would turn skeptical.

"I got *lucky.*"

"You know," Lord Cillian mused, drumming his fingers against the table. Tenele's gaze settled on him, his angular face and sharp blue eyes. They'd never seen eye-to-eye on anything, and she curled her hands in her dress, bracing to keep from thrashing him. "They say Shadows never hurt your mother, either. Like they were forbidd—"

"A *Shade* killed my mother. So obviously, before that, she got lucky too." She itched for a blade. Itched to cut the smirk from his face. "And, as you can see—" she held out her arms, revealing faint pink scars and still-fading bruises—"Shadows had no problem chewing me up with the others."

She didn't have time for these people, people she'd bounced on her knee. She'd watched their parents age and die as years passed her like sap from an old pine. Now she was left to debate *children* over why she'd lived and others died.

But if they found out about the Mark, she'd be compromised. Questioned. Detained.

And that would get in the way of vengeance.

"How I survived doesn't matter. I did. Someone called them here. I'll find them and I'll stop them." Tenele turned her gaze on Queen Sinead. "With your permission."

"With all respect, my queen," Cillian said. "We should be sending an army to the front, not a single wounded girl."

Sinead looked over the group. "Lady Raider is not a *girl*. She's a Maiden of the Red Court, older than you by a hundred years. She's a specialist in killing monsters, and the only one qualified with finding who called those things over the mountains or why they left those brands behind."

"Brands?" asked Tenele. She almost felt the one on her side buzzing beneath her dress.

"Black runes blistering the corpses or the earth near what might have been bodies. As if marking… locations or people… like they were searching for something and noting where they'd already looked," replied Lord Cillian.

"Whoever is controlling these demons just decimated the entire Red and Black Courts in a matter of hours. Our infantrymen are well prepared for mortal battle, but if confronted with Shadows, they will be worse than defenseless," added Sinead. "That is why we made the Courts to begin with…"

And to deal with your influx of orphans, thought Tenele.

The Red and Black Courts were homes to orphaned girls and boys, where they were tended and taken care of and made useful so they could repay their debt to the kingdom in blood. Now, their blood and bodies dotted the mountain range to freeze and rot, having paid their debts in full.

Lady Nyris rose to her feet and placed her palms firmly on the table. "This hesitation is exactly what they want. These Shadows are a distraction. We should be marching our troops on Alykith right now, before they make another move."

The queen raised her eyes to the flustered advisor. Sinead didn't need to stand to be intimidating. This was a woman who had killed a god. A woman who had seen the kingdom through war and ruled for three centuries. Her ice-blue gaze may as well have been a blade at Nyris's throat.

The whole council watched tensely as Nyris slowly returned to her seat. Silence pinned the room still.

"Please forgive my outburst, my queen. It's just that I'm very concerned," Nyris spoke quietly.

Sinead took a deep breath. "I know this, Nyris. Your love for our country is steadfast, and you may yet be right about Alykith. But I will not dissolve our hard-won armistice without proof."

"What more proof do we need? Who else but those depraved heretics could possibly control such monsters?" demanded Lord Cillian. The skepticism made his too-high eyebrows stretch even further upward, until they threatened to tumble over the top of his head.

Sinead smiled—a hard, sour display of teeth. "It is not just Alykith or her people who can call such beasts, Lord Cillian, or have you forgotten that I control one myself?"

Cillian stiffened. The room went painfully quiet as disgust battled with embarrassment in his eyes.

They never discussed the queen's pet nightmare openly. It was an ugly stain on Sinead's otherwise immaculate leadership. Among the populace, it was a black rumor—a bogeyman used to ensure children were always home before dark. And Sinead had not mentioned it by accident.

"My queen… Please, do not make these matters worse than they already are."

"Weapons exist to be wielded, Lord Byron. If my surrogate daughter is willing to fulfill her mission alone, I will not send her unarmed. Or would you have me send one of your daughters?"

Tenele stiffened at the word "daughter." She glanced to Sinead, who never referenced their closeness aloud. It was a conflict of interest in more ways than one, and the reason Tenele was sent to the Red Court to start.

Tenele had spent her childhood within the palace walls as an orphan, true, but not just any ordinary one. She'd been the daughter of the queen's best friend, and, as such, Sinead had felt some responsibility for her. She'd taken Tenele in, treated her as a daughter—until the High Council made assumptions.

Queen Sinead being long-lived and willful, had no intentions of ever marrying. Thus, she would have no heirs. The High Court had believed Sinead would adopt Tenele and name her the heir to the throne of Ighten. Sinead had squashed those rumors with an iron fist by sending Tenele to the Red Court.

"My queen," Lord Byron muttered. "Send Maiden Raider,

if you must… but not the monster."

Tenele only possessed vague memories of the monster from her childhood, and she wasn't certain any of them were real or simply nightmares. She knew the legend enough— Queen Sinead's magic subdued and bound a Shade during the Queens War to help her and the Alykith queen kill Verin, God of Monsters.

An uneasiness settled in the pit of Tenele's stomach.

She turned her attention to Sinead. "How would… how would I keep a thumb on him, should you… should you let him out? If you're here, I mean. How will I control him?"

"The matter of control we will discuss in private." Sinead's blue eyes ran a cool patrol around the huge council table. "And on that note, I have words for Maiden Raider alone. Thank you all for your council. You are dismissed."

The High Council quietly disassembled. They filtered out in twos or threes, drifting into conversations too quiet to make out.

One councilman did not leave with the others. He made his way to Sinead's side, disapproval creasing his forehead.

"Yes, Lord Byron." The queen and her oldest advisor were well accustomed to disagreement, but it was Sinead's policy that the council speak freely.

"This is a callous choice, my queen."

"It is our best chance at success."

"Her sisters are gone. Those monsters took them, and now you would ask her to work alongside one?"

"Anyone else will only slow her down, and you know this. You and I both know Alykith didn't bring those monsters here or leave those brands. Someone *else* did." The way Sinead said this made Tenele think the queen almost knew who the *else* was, but that couldn't possibly be true. Why wouldn't she say?

"Even if it makes sense, using *him* will further divide the council."

Sinead's expression softened into a regretful smile. "You speak the truth. Thank you, my friend." She turned to Tenele. Her eyes were warmer now, and the formality dropped from her tone. "Well, Tenele, I'll let you make your own choice after you've met him."

Byron grimaced. "*Meeting* him would hardly improve her impression."

Sinead smirked.

Tenele clasped her hands behind her back and knotted them in the folds of her dress. "Of course," she said while her heart thumped in her chest. She trusted Sinead with her life, as all Red Court Maidens did, and if Sinead thought it best to ally with a beast, then she would do it. Even if the hairs on the back of her neck stood up and her stomach rolled. She thought of the Shade in the woods, his scalding hand on her side, his Mark on her skin.

How bad could this one be?

7

TENELE RAIDER

THE GLINT AND majesty of Loight's palace disappeared behind a heavy wooden door. Plaster walls and gold filigree were replaced by heavy granite blocks lined with iron sconces every five feet. Tenele followed Sinead, who followed a guard leading them to the iron dungeon door.

The dungeon consisted of three floors. The first belonged to those who had committed menial crimes—theft and vandalism. The second belonged to murderers and rapists— those to never see the light of day, unless, of course, for execution. To Tenele's knowledge, only one person had ever escaped in five-hundred years. The third floor had only one room at the end of an ever-tightening spiral hall, and only one occupant—Ranemir Stroud.

They'd given it a name, she thought, glancing at the back of the queen's head. *Why?*

At the end of the third floor's spiral hall was an iron door sitting ajar. There were no guards. No bars. No series of locks. Tenele assumed it to be the door to the room in which all those things would be found, a door leading to another, stronger one, covered in holy runes. Instead, it led into a room populated with sparse furniture. A bed tucked into an alcove, a desk, a narrow dining table, and two chairs. There were no windows this far down, but there was a painting made to resemble one with a view of the Ongore Sea.

"You're early," a flat voice mused from the bed in the shadowed alcove.

"I brought someone for you to meet," said Sinead, nodding for the guard to leave them.

Tenele's nerves jolted. No locks. No guards. Just how far under Sinead's boot was this monster?

An amused chuckle rumbled out of the dark. "I've already eaten today, but I might be able to find room for dessert." The voice was smooth and deep, like the warm, lulling comfort of too much whiskey. There was movement in the alcove, a shadow rising from the sheets, and two dull, glowing magenta eyes pierced the blackness. His legs slipped out, and then the rest of him, and he rose to stand over six feet in height. Broad-shouldered, clad in finely tailored black clothes.

No rags and no chains. This wasn't a prisoner at all.

His skin was tinted the color of her hair, dull silver like the glint of moonlight on snow. His face appeared human-like, handsome and sharp, with swirling tattoos of iridescent white stretching up his neck and along his brow to fade into the ebony hair he wore long around his shoulders. Two matte black horns stretched out of his head, curling back and over his ears to nearly brush along his jaw.

The glow in his eyes faded into dark burgundy as he appraised her, his gaze dropping to her side. Tenele placed a hand over the Shade's Mark, as if she could hide it from a creature that could smell it in the room like a fine perfume.

He met her eyes with a knowing smile. "Not a meal for me, I suppose."

"No," replied Sinead.

Tenele glanced at his silver-tinged hands and the long fingers sporting dulled black nails. No claws? As if to answer, he flexed his fingers, and his nails stretched to needle points. He reached up and tapped his chin thoughtfully, smiling to show off his sharp teeth.

"What do I owe the pleasure," he said, the words rippling through the room like a caress. Tenele felt woozy, hot longing thrum through her.

"Enough," said Sinead, scowling at him. "Stow your tricks, Stroud."

Ranemir's grin turned maddening, and then he shrugged and slinked off to a chair at his dining table. He sat, plopping his boots across the top.

Sinead slipped into the chair across from him. "You're getting out of your cage, Ranemir."

He chuckled, the sound like dark music. "And who do you want me to kill this time? A duke? A queen? A peasant who painted an unflattering caricature of you? Don't you have guards who can do these things?"

Sinead turned her gaze on Tenele. "He's jesting. I've never sent him to kill anyone."

Ranemir nodded in agreement, his smile slipping. "Not that I can remember, at least." The air in the room shifted, and then so did he, his boots slipping off the table to clonk against the floor. "Well, where are you sending me, then?"

"Your brethren attacked Ighten," replied Sinead. "All our

outposts along the border were decimated, my Red and Black Courts gone in a night, and the dead branded with this…" Sinead reached into her pocket and produced a piece of parchment. She unfolded it and pushed it across the table. Tenele peeked at the black emblem scratched across the paper, expecting to see a handprint, much like the one she wore. This was different. It was a rune—three jagged lines, like claws, with a single black circle off to the side.

"What does it mean?" asked Sinead.

The Shade leaned forward, appraising the paper. His lips curled with a grin. "I haven't the slightest," he said, flicking his gaze at Tenele. "Do you?"

"It's your language," replied Sinead.

"It was my language. But then you burned it out of my mind, rather like you've burned most of everything else. What would you like me to be, Sinead, a monster or your monster?"

Sinead sighed. It had been a long time since Tenele had seen her that exasperated. "You will go with Maiden Raider—"

"I thought your special Courts were wiped out."

"She is the last," replied Sinead, impatience hitching her voice. "You will go with her to the border and you will hunt for what brought your kind here, and find what this brand means, and then you will deal with it."

Ranemir's burgundy gaze flashed to Tenele, then to her middle. Again, she felt as if he could see through her clothes to the Mark on her side. "How did you become the last?"

"Luck."

He grinned, sharp teeth glinting in the candlelight. "You didn't bargain with a monster, did you?"

Tenele snarled. "No."

Ranemir reached up to his collar and thumbed at a gold chain beneath his black shirt. "Not coming, Queeny?"

"You and Tenele will lead this expedition alone. I already have very few supporters with this decision. It will be a secret. Only my council knows."

Ranemir laughed. "Well, then, the whole kingdom knows."

"And how will I control him?" Tenele asked. She knew Sinead had a leash for her monster, but she had never seen it.

"Kneel, Ranemir." The Shade's eyes glowed, and Tenele wasn't certain if it were from rage or the power the queen had over him. He knelt, dropping to both knees hard enough to crack a mortal's bones. The impact did not seem to faze him. "Place your hand on his shoulder."

Tenele stepped forward, fingers flexing at her side. She placed her hand on Ranemir's shoulder as Sinead instructed, and the queen took from her wrist a gold chain with a single ruby connected between its two links. She looped it around Tenele's arm. Tenele did not see a clasp, but somehow the chain links connected again and the bracelet was whole.

"It has taken years to refine the spells that keep Ranemir in check," said Sinead, placing a hand over Tenele's. "I am not a dark sorcerer, so tuning holy magic to control a monster has been… tedious, though not without its rewards. I am proxying my ability to control Rane to you."

The Shade snarled and pulled the gold chain around his neck from beneath his shirt as if it burned him. The chain held a matching ruby, and it glowed a searing, hot red.

"You can control him, if he proves to be more of a problem than a help, but I still ultimately hold the keys to him. If you are injured or incapacitated, he is not free."

The red in their twin rubies cooled, and Ranemir glared up at Tenele. If not for her hold over him, or the Shade's Mark on her, she imagined he would have gutted her.

"Get some rest, Tenele," said Sinead. "You should leave in the morning."

Rane stood and went to his table, to a game board and pieces strewn haphazardly across the top. He picked up a piece, twirling it in his fingers, black nails scraping against the ivory. "In the morning, then," he said, and tossed it to Tenele.

She caught it, just barely, and opened her palms to see the pawn inside.

CASIMIR DROWSKY

CASIMIR RAN HIS hands over the soot, dust, and shredded pieces of wood covering the floor, clearing them from the stone as he admired the symbol he'd found. It wasn't what he was looking for—at least, he didn't think so. He still wasn't sure exactly what he was looking for. The voice in his head told him he'd know when he found it. This one, a series of circles, did not feel any different than the other brick.

He dusted his hands on his trousers and climbed out of the narrow space he'd made between the floorboards of Father Peeble's old bedroom, drawing planks of flooring over the hole and tapping them down with the curved edge of his crowbar.

"Anything?" Jyn's voice called from the window. The creature stood close enough to peer in but far enough that the church stone didn't touch him.

"You can come in now, you know," muttered Casimir as he stripped the dirty shirt off, tossing it into a pile of clothes he desperately needed to find time to wash.

Jyn sneered and looked around. "I don't trust it."

"I desecrated the church," said Casimir. "What bound it

to Thar is no more. Though he'd hardly notice."

The Shade stroked his charcoal chin. "Still… It makes me uneasy." He watched Casimir clean up the mess. "Why do you do that?"

"Do what?"

"Fix everything like it was before?"

"Someone may come in here and wonder why I've ripped the flooring up. The less people ask questions, the easier my life will be."

It was easy to remove wooden floors and replace them with minimal sign of disruption, but he would have a harder time explaining the upheaval in the central cathedral where he'd started chiseling up stone bricks to see what lay beneath. He'd started in the back rooms on purpose. They were easier.

But Jyn thought he was stalling.

And maybe he was. Casimir couldn't tell anymore.

"She's dreaming about you tonight," said Jyn with a toothy smile. "I mean, I may have nudged her there…"

Casimir settled onto the edge of his bed. "How often are you snooping in that woman's dreams?"

The toothy smile turned into a wicked grin.

"I don't want something drawing her back here," said Casimir, pointing at Jyn. "Do you understand me?"

Jyn's wickedness dampened. "If she comes back, it won't be because I gave her nightmares."

Casimir ran his fingers through his hair and fell into bed. His back ached from the church's nightly destruction and reconstruction and he hadn't taken time to rest, save for the spare moments he had to listen to the confessions of towns-people or give a stirring sermon at weekly Mass. Thankfully,

Father Peeble had a stack of prepared sermons, and Casimir hadn't needed to write his own. He had a few weeks left before that torture became his responsibility too.

Casimir stared at the flicker of firelight glinting on the stucco ceiling. "You should have let her die."

Jyn hesitated before resting his arms on the stone window seal. There was a glimmer in his gold eyes that unnerved Casimir and always had. It spoke of knowledge Casimir didn't have. A secret Jyn wouldn't share. Not even the strongest, sternest commandment tore it from his lips, which was strange, as Jyn was bound to obey.

"Perhaps I should have," agreed Jyn, but even that sounded like a lie. "Old habits die hard, though. Verin ordered us to never kill a silver-haired woman."

Casimir cracked an eye open. "Why?"

Jyn shrugged.

"But you harmed her…" Well, the Shadows had harmed her and Jyn healed her, and now the Shade was haunting her…

The Shade frowned. "Details are murky, and He's gone now. Gone because a silver-haired woman distracted him. Just because he ordered us never to kill one doesn't mean I can't make her wish she were dead."

"The Shade's Mark won't last forever."

Jyn disappeared in the dark. "It doesn't need to."

9

TENELE RAIDER

TENELE CAME AWAKE with a sharp gasp, heaving air into her lungs, eyes darting wildly around the dark room—searching for the gold-eyed Shade. A cold sweat slicked her skin, and she raked a hand through her damp hair, shoving the stringy wetness away from her shoulders.

Moonlight bathed the unfamiliar space in pale blue. This was a far finer room than the one she had at Lastower, and finer still than the home her mother had left her on the north side of town. It was all smooth walls, gold ornamental molding, and marble floors. The bed could fit six people and was so soft it swallowed her. She swam to the edge of it and rolled out onto the floor.

Her bare feet met the cold marble and padded to a window, drawing it open to let the brisk, salty air wash over her. Each breath drew the ocean's taste into her mouth.

It was late. Most of the city lights were out. The moon bathed Loight in blue. A few blocks from the palace, the grand Church of Thar rose from the midst of granite houses and cobblestone streets, looming over the city like an overbearing father. Its gold-tiled steeple glittered like diamonds beneath the stars.

Tenele settled there against the window, arms crossed with her chin resting atop them. The world felt peaceful, a sharp contrast to her dreams. Those were nothing but blood and gore and… other things.

She shivered.

She knew it was natural for the memories of her dead friends to haunt her—to see Paelae die over and over. Horror stayed with you—that was undeniable. But she'd seen horror. She'd lived it on more than one occasion yet hadn't had nightmares this vivid. She felt pain and pleasure and sickness. She could still feel it, even awake, like the faint, lingering burn of whiskey after swallowing.

The glint of the gold chain around her wrist caught her eye, and she stretched her arm out, watching the moonlight reflect against the ruby. It looked like such a delicate piece of jewelry, but as she tried to pull it free from her wrist, it wouldn't budge. She turned her gaze to the white pawn piece sitting on the table near her bed. She grabbed it up, pinching it between her fingers, squeezing and hoping to crush it, but she wasn't strong enough for that. The memory of Rane's mad eyes and wicked smile sent a shiver down her spine.

She'd dealt with hundreds of Shadows, but Shades… She'd only ever faced a handful of them, the encounters horrifying enough to leave imprints and nightmares behind for weeks.

The beast could smell fear. He'd use it against her. Perhaps it would be easier to think of him as something other than a Shade—but there were the horns, glowing eyes, and towering, imposing height to contend with.

She'd killed so many of his kind, she should have been used to the unsettling feeling they gave her, but… each monster was different. You never knew what powers they possessed or how twisted their imaginations were. They were unpredictable, and Tenele thrived on order.

The faint sound of talking drifted up from outside her window, and she bent forward to see what was going on. Odd that people were out so late at night but, then again, she was the one wide awake staring at a demon's ominous gift.

Three men were down below, spreading a line of white powder along a walking path bordering the castle's inner wall. Her brow wrinkled with a frown.

Salt?

Were they worried about Shadows invading the castle?

She'd heard no warning bells. No one had banged on the door to tell her they were near. Why would they spread so much salt if a threat wasn't imminent, not when it might rain and melt?

Tenele twisted the pawn in her fingers, trying to shake the uneasy feeling worming in the pit of her stomach.

A sharp knock rattled the door, snapping her focus on those below. "Maiden Raider!" an unfamiliar voice begged from outside. "Forgive me, you've got to come quick!"

Tenele went to the door, drawing it open enough to peer out, but not so much that it didn't act as a shield. She braced her foot on the bottom of the door as flickering candlelight blinded her.

"Yes? What's wrong?"

A stout woman on the other side was red-faced and

breathless. "Maiden Raider…" She shifted from foot to foot, like she wanted to run and was forcing her legs to stay in place. "Someone's attempted upon the queen—there's been made upon an attempt—" She stammered, searching for the proper etiquette to convey such an awful message at such an improper time. "I don't know who to trust, but surely you… Please, please come quick!"

Tenele was out the door before the woman finished, running down the hall and up the stairs, winding through corridors she'd once traversed as a child with her eyes closed. Sinead's room was at the end of a long hall lined in stained glass windows.

It was a place for bedtime stories and kissed scrapes, of cuddles and comfort. At least, it had been a long time ago, before Sinead had sent her into the Red Court, before their bond changed from motherly love to cold shoulders and distance.

Tenele rushed for the open door. Gold light spilled across the marble floor, painting a path into Sinead's bedchamber.

Sinead had never needed guards, but they were usually there, more ornamental than anything. Now, they were gone. Tenele stopped. A sick feeling twisted in her gut. Instinctively, she reached for the sword at her hip and grasped air. Her hand smoothed along the silk of her nightgown.

"There, she's inside, oh heavens!" the maid heaved, actually crying now. "She said not to bring anyone, but she's bleeding awfully bad." The woman went to the heavy, open doors and looked back pleadingly, tears shining on her cheeks.

Tenele braced herself and eased her weight forward, planning a step. A pair of hard palms slammed into her back, knocking her forward. Before she could stop, she tumbled into the queen's quarters. Sprawled across the floor, she tried to gather her balance under her, to maneuver away, but a blow lit the back of her head. Pain shrunk her vision into narrow, black funnels.

"I'm sorry, my Lady. It's for the best," the maid's fluttering voice spoke, seemingly miles behind her. The last thing she heard was the chamber doors latching with a heavy clank of wood and iron.

Tenele wasn't sure how much time had passed. She woke, dizzy and nauseous, feeling at the splitting ache in the back of her head and drawing her hand away with a sharp hiss. Blood stained the tips of her fingers and matted her silver hair.

She stumbled to her feet, taking in Sinead's chambers in a blinding, spinning blur. Sinead wasn't there. There was no body, no pool of blood, absolutely no evidence that she'd ever been there at all. Tenele's vision warped as she stumbled to the door and attempted to draw it open.

Locked solid.

She knew better than to break her shoulder trying to ram it open.

Tenele worked her way around the room, feeling along the windows and attempting to open each one until she tripped over Sinead's writing desk.

The queen's bold, cursive handwriting caught her attention, drawing her eyes down to the desk. Letters, scribbled hurriedly across parchment, seemed to dance across the page. For a moment, she wondered if she'd been concussed far worse than she knew. But their swirling waltz solidified, and the first word came into being.

Tenele,

Enchantment. These words were only meant for her.

They've dispatched troops to Alykith.
Don't trust the Church.
Get Rane. Run, before

The sentence broke off, unfinished.

Get Rane. Run, before… Tenele glanced out the window and froze at the sight of men still pouring a line of salt around the castle.

Get Rane. Run, before they kill him.

A salt circle meant an exorcism, a purge of all dark magic. Essentially, a charred Shade or, at least, an untethered one in the dungeon.

Neither were good.

Neither would happen.

Tenele tried not to think about the amount of power needed to subdue Sinead, one of the most powerful sorceresses ever to live, and who might have such. Until today, Tenele didn't think anything could slow the woman down, short of killing her. The Maiden immediately shoved the thought from her mind. There was no time to contemplate impossibilities, or to wonder why they'd lured her here at all.

Why not kill her? Why the ruse…

"Sorry, Sinead," said Tenele as she lifted the monarch's antique desk chair and smashed out the glass balcony doors.

Sinead's balcony sat several floors above the next. Tenele didn't have time to make a rope from expensive bedding, so she hung from the railing, shimmying to the lowest point before swinging and dropping to the balcony below it. She landed on her side with a harsh crack, the air rushing out of her lungs. The ache of her barely-healed ribs splintered across her chest, and Tenele didn't want to contemplate whether she'd fractured them anew.

A second later, Tenele was on her feet and through the glass doors, still struggling for air as she passed a noble rousing, bleary-eyed and sleep-drunk from his bed.

The hall outside was quiet. One could hardly tell there was a coup going on. The only curious indicator of anything decidedly wrong was the line of salt running center through the corridors, leading to the dungeon doors.

Tenele had years of experience finding her way in and out of places without detection, but trekking through Ighten's prison halls in little more than thin silk commanded more attention than desired. She ignored the leering eyes and lewd calls, the outstretched hands vainly trying to take hold of her as she passed. Inmates emboldened by the lack of guards.

The Red Court Maiden didn't knock on Rane's door. She went in, breathless and angry.

The chamber, previously lit with torches, now sat dark as pitch. A pair of burgundy eyes flashed on her from the cavernous darkness. Fire roared up, hot and angry, in the stone hearth centered in the room. Rane stood next to it, regarding her with a cool gaze. "To what do I owe this honor?" The polite words scathed from his lips like a curse.

"We're leaving. Now."

"Oh, are we?" His neon gaze eyed her up and down, taking in her silk nightgown. "Well. This is unexpected. Weren't Red Court Maidens trained to abstain from this sort of thing?"

Laughter tickled at the end of his voice, but his eyes were pure, inhuman rage.

Tenele scowled. "Look, unless you enjoy a fiery death, I suggest we hurry. I mean, I'll be fine, but…" Her shoulders slumped. She hadn't the time to bicker with him, though bickering was a gift she enjoyed. "Someone has staged a coup. They want you dead. Sinead told me to get you out. Let's go."

The Shade straightened, suddenly even taller against the firelight. His frown descended into a full-on, bestial snarl. "Where's Sinead?"

"Occupied. Likely beating her advisors into submission." Tenele stepped further in, straightening taller as he had before. She was short for a half-Grela, having taken after her mortal father. She appeared delicate, like silk flowers in a fragile vase—if vases could kill with a smile. "She ordered us to leave. We leave."

"If she is under attack, I will deal with the threat." There were whole paragraphs of chilling subtext to the way he said "deal with." He strode to the doorway and walked past her. When he reached the door, however, his body tensed up and drew to a halt. "Release me," he growled.

"You're coming with me," Tenele replied. "The only way you go out that door is with me, following her orders to leave." She didn't like the idea any more than he seemed to, but she knew Sinead could handle herself. At least, she needed to believe that.

The command sent an almost imperceptible shudder through the Shade's posture that maddened him further. He turned in a too-smooth movement, radiating menace as he waited, silent, but at least no longer protesting.

On the way out, Tenele grabbed a cloak a guard had left behind and tossed it to Rane. "I have a house across town. If we can get there, we can gather what supplies I have and head out."

The Shade's attention focused mercilessly on their surroundings. He took the cloak she handed him without comment and looped it over his arm.

They made it as far as the central corridor before being stopped.

"Lady Raider," a guard called as they bolted past. "I need to ask you to stay within the castle. Something's not right, and we're still investigating—"

He broke off as he took notice of the tall demon standing beside her. The guard's eyes sprang wide with fear, and he lurched a step back. "Stroud," he said, recognizing the Shade. "Maiden Raider, what's the meaning of this?" He phrased it as a question, but he was already drawing his sword. Two more men noticed the commotion and approached from the hall behind them.

Again, Tenele reached for a sword she didn't have.

"Orders from the queen. Top secret and none of your concern. She needs Stroud at the border." Tenele took a step forward. "I outrank you. All of you. So never question me like a common thief again. Understood?"

The man's face dropped several shades paler. His stance weakened, even as his arm seemed unwilling to lower the sword. "Forgive me, Maiden Raider... But the captain wants no one in or out until we have this sorted."

Tenele smirked. "Lucky for me, I outrank him, too." She grabbed Rane's arm and stepped past the guard.

When they were around the corner and well on their way to an exterior door, Tenele released Rane like he'd scorched her. She stepped ahead of him to exit through the smaller courtyard passage.

"Seems the captain is part of the coup," she growled. "We need out of here before they activate that holy circle and fry you like an egg."

Rane smirked. "Your concern is touching, Maiden." If he was concerned by the impending spell—one that could conceivably reduce him to ash—it didn't show. He matched her pace with a long, somehow predatory stride as they cleared the front entryway. No one was in sight—a sure sign of how disjointed the castle's command was at the moment.

A few more yards, and they would cross the outer gates.

Rane's legs missed a stride, hesitating. A new tension pulled at the corners of his expression.

"What are you waiting for?" She noticed the stance he seemed frozen in—a half step—like he couldn't go any further. She lowered her eyes and found a line of salt just before him, which should have been useless. Unless… they'd completed the circle.

"Shit."

Tenele ran back to him and went to drag her bare foot through the salt when an arrow buzzed her leg, then clattered across the cobblestone.

"Maiden Raider," a voice called from the wall surrounding the castle. "Come back into the palace."

Tenele sneered, her attention drawing up to the Captain of Guards.

"In all my years, I never thought you would side with a

Shade and betray your queen. You, who she raised like a daughter." He lifted a hand above his head, and the telltale creak of bows being drawn served as a stark warning. "Come back inside, Maiden."

A bow tightened somewhere, putting truth behind the threat. The castle itself held its breath.

Rane laughed. The rich, searing sound resounded up the walls of Sinead's fortress and across the courtyard, rolling through the pre-dawn shadows.

Tenele shivered. "Captain, I didn't fight for this kingdom a hundred years to die in this courtyard…" She looked at the salt line with a frown. "But it seems I may."

Tenele drew her foot across it.

The captain's hand cut down sharp. A chorus of pops sent arrows into the sky, and Tenele braced herself for the strafe, hoping to avoid the bulk of them.

Something cold and hard hit her from the side and shoved her backward. She heard the distinct, dull thump of arrows meeting flesh, and a flurry of movement. Brilliant pain laced up her left ankle.

When she looked up, the Shade was standing with his back to her, facing their would-be firing squad. An aura of dark power rolled off him like smoke, gathering, preparing. He glanced back with a manic smile, eyes too bright with power to make out any expression behind them. He ripped an arrow from his shoulder like he was plucking a dart from a board and threw it easily back toward its owner. There was a pained shout from the castle wall.

"Go!" Tenele shouted, slinging her arm towards the gates. She stood. A tight cry burst from her and she sank down, turning a betrayed glare on her ankle. Blood poured from a gash where an arrow had narrowly missed driving through her heel.

She looked up to the menacing Shade, anger boiling in her belly. There was absolutely no way. No. She wouldn't even think of asking. The idea of his arms around her drove a cold line of fear and revulsion down her spine. Tenele clenched her teeth and stood. "Stroud, the penalty for treason is death. Isn't it?"

His demon eyes met hers and flared. He canted his head at her as if she'd confused him. Or *amused* him. Whatever the case, his teeth spread into a sharp, mad smile. Claws like black knives split the ends of his fingers, and the power swirling around him tightened close to his skin like a focused flame.

She didn't actually see him run for the wall. If she weren't so experienced with Shades, she might have sworn he teleported up to the palisade. Then the screaming started. Blood splashed down, droplets clinging to her face.

Commotion at the front entryway called her attention away from the carnage. Two men entered, their swords shining. They wore the white cassocks of Gold Clerics, and between them stood a tall woman shrouded in blue-green robes. A Priestess of Thar. She approached the smudged salt line, her right hand carrying a gold staff carved in holy runes.

Tenele tested her ankle, curling her lip into a snarl as she lunged, unarmed, at one of the Clerics. His blade arched towards her and she rolled under it, coming up next to him. She grabbed the dagger at his belt and drove it in. As he fell, the second Cleric sliced at her, grazing her arm. She spun to avoid another sweeping arch of steel, throwing the dagger at him as her injured ankle struck the earth wrong and sent her down. He dodged the throw, and the dagger clattered uselessly off in the distance. The Cleric snarled, stomping towards her as she scurried back.

The Priestess reconnected the salt line and drove her staff down. Feverish white light blasted up, beaming into the sky like a wall of shimmering glass. Tenele looked up for Rane, taking her eyes off of the swinging sword.

Two bodies fell from the palisade. One landed with a wet thump at the base of the wall. The second figure hit hard in a black-clad heap. The Shade rolled to his feet, breaking into a sprint toward Tenele and the salt line.

Tenele caught the glint of a sword blade and stretched back across the cobblestones, watching it pass over her. A blood-slicked fist slammed into the Cleric's face, knocking him sideways. The Cleric stumbled, shaking the dizziness from his head as he sized up Rane.

The punch had been strong, but it had been human-strong. Tenele knew the gruesome strength of Shades, and this was the first time she'd ever seen one throw a good old-fash-ioned slugger.

Which meant…

She twisted, watching the circle of light close, creating a dome above them.

The brilliant light in Rane's eyes fizzled, and the power humming off his skin snuffed out. If not for the black horns arching from his temples and his silver-gray skin, she might have mistaken him for mortal.

"We have to go. Now." Tenele hobbled across the glowing salt line for the gate. A harsh clank echoed from the gatehouse and the chains rattled, the gate lowering.

Rane moved to follow her and stopped short of the circle. The Priestess on the other side offered him a victorious smile, grinding her staff deeper into the stone and singing her incantation to the heavens. The salt line was no longer a simple barrier one could sweep aside. It had become a true seal, blistering with holy energy that grew brighter by the second.

Rane snarled, shoving against the invisible cage entrapping him. He shouldn't have been able to touch the wall at all. That alone should have turned him to a pile of crisp cinders. A cold line of fear danced down Tenele's spine, but, for once, she was thankful he appeared stronger than any other Shade she'd come across.

Ranemir appraised the holy wall of light and settled his dull, angry eyes on Tenele. "Command me."

Tenele's gaze darted from the Shade to the Priestess. She'd spent her life trapping monsters and slaughtering them. Helping one cross a holy circle went against everything she'd ever been taught—against her very nature. And, yet, she *would*. Because her queen had commanded it.

Tenele limped back to the circle as the last Cleric charged Rane from behind. She thrust her hand through the barrier of light, grasping for the Shade. "Ranemir Stroud, take my hand… and step out of Thar's Light."

Her words frightened the Cleric to stillness, or maybe curiosity. Nothing could leave a holy circle once charged, and even if it managed to, it would never survive the crossing.

The very air around them chilled.

Something twisted inside Tenele. Something cold and wrong and… freeing. The band around her wrist glimmered, the ruby glowing bright. She flexed her fingers, beckoning him to take her hand.

The demon glared at it, but took it anyway. His monstrous claws, now no more than a mortal man's dulled hands, crushed around her as a thrum of energy passed between their skin.

Tenele tugged, and Ranemir thrust against the barrier. It tore his skin and clothes like razor wire, shredding him as her command stole him across. When she finally hauled him free, the hand she held was slick with translucent black fluid.

Behind them, the iron gate had closed.

"Let's go," he said without releasing her hand. He pulled her tight against his chest.

An icy cold poured into her, and the surrounding space went dark. When the light returned, they were several hundred feet outside the castle gates, and her ankle burned worse than before.

Tenele tore herself away from him, withholding the urge to pat herself down as one would after finding a spider. She fell against a brick wall, shivering and disoriented, smearing the black fluid on her hands along the length of her silk, stained gown.

Dizziness assaulted her. Pain traveled up her ankle like a searing nerve while the Shade's Mark on her side tingled… as if a hand pressed against her. Fear clawed its way through Tenele as she realized she was feeling the one who'd made it. Could he sense what happened? Was he making sure she was alive or that this Shade hadn't tampered with his property? Tenele wanted away—both from the Shade before her and the one from the woods. She took a step and choked on a cry, nearly crumpling if not for the steadying wall.

A frustrated growl rumbled out of her.

With clenched teeth, Tenele slowly made her way down the alley, holding the wall with one arm and wiping at the Mark with the other. She glowered back at Ranemir. "What the fuck was that? You… took us here? How?"

He ignored her.

In the pre-dawn quiet of the surrounding town, there was almost no activity. The quiet wouldn't last. "We need off the street," she said. Somewhere, she heard the shuffling and stomping of a merchant and his horse, preparing their wares for travel.

Horses… there was a thought. But they couldn't select mounts from the queen's stables.

"This is unlocked," came a cool voice from her left.

Rane had proceeded down the alley ahead of her and was holding open the hatch of a root cellar. He looked like a nightmare, skin dripping with dark fluid, monstrous eyes bright with anger. He studied her for a long moment, measuring her reaction to him.

"You stay here. I will find something nearby."

Tenele hobbled to the cellar door, frowning down into the darkness. She didn't like the idea of Rane walking the town. He didn't exactly blend in… but then again, neither did she.

"You aren't free. Don't think of wandering off." She stood a few inches from him, sizing him up. "I'm good at tracking your kind."

The Shade crossed his arms and smirked at her, his damaged face making the expression grotesque. "You are full of surprises, Maiden."

"You have no idea," she replied, slowly descending, step-by-agonizing-step, into the shadowed cellar.

It didn't occur to her until she made it to the bottom that trusting him and going alone into the dark was a bad idea. The cellar door slammed shut above, the only light coming from the pre-dawn glow spilling through the slats.

"Fuck!"

She would have banged on it. Screamed to be let out. But all of that would draw attention, and attention would draw guards.

So she waited, sitting with her back to the wet stone and plotting how to get out of the mess on her own. The Captain of the Guard and the Church would paint her and Sinead as traitors. Terrorists. If Sinead were safe, morning would vindicate them… but if she weren't…

Tenele wasn't sure what would happen to an Ighten without Sinead or a Shade without a permanent tether. While every fiber of her begged to find Sinead and ensure her safety, Tenele's duty was in following the orders the queen had given.

Somewhere in her plotting, she drifted to sleep.

RANEMIR STROUD

RANE STARED AT the cellar door, lips curling with a snarl. He sank down to a knee, hating the way his body felt after being trapped, even a second, in that holy circle. It had been a century since he'd felt holy magic brush his skin, since Sinead let her little minions test all their spells and traps on him to either make him stronger or them stronger. At least, after all of that, he'd had a hot meal waiting for him. Right now, he just had a virgin with a Shade's Mark in a fucking basement.

He rose, weaving his way through the back alleys, tearing clothing from lines and stealing a pair of shoes that *might* fit the half-Grela he'd trapped in the cellar. He wasn't even sure why he was gathering these items, preparing for a trip he didn't wish to go on, other than Sinead had ordered him to do it and he had no choice but to obey. Was it the thing around his neck making him do this, or was he so conditioned he did it automatically?

A few hours before dawn, he threw open the cellar door. The woman jerked awake, her black-stained hand rising to shield her face. He expected protesting, shouting, cursing. He expected her to order him to his knees and to beg her for mercy. Instead, she lowered her hand and blinked at him. He appraised her blood-soaked gown, a mixture of red human blood and black Shade blood. He felt a twinge of hunger at the site of the silk strap slipping off her shoulder, but he pushed that down to the furthest depths of his being.

Not the time. Not the person.

But if he didn't feed soon…

He shook his head, and stepped away from the opening. A second later, she climbed out, limping on her injured ankle. "Bandages," he said, tossing a wad of coiled cloth to her. She caught it. "Hurry."

She sat in the alley and he passed her a canteen of water. She poured it over the wound, hissing as the water washed the dirt and blood away. It wasn't hygienic, and mortals were so frail, so prone to infection…

"You came back," she said, taking the cloth and wrapping her ankle.

"I didn't have much of a choice, did I?"

"We should get to the docks before daylight, while it's empty. We can follow the shore to the forest and cut back towards the border from there. If we go now, maybe no one will notice," she said, glancing up at his horns. She was no less inconspicuous with her shimmering silver hair.

"And the queen?"

"We stick to the plan. Sinead will handle the conspiracy. The woman killed a god, for Thar's sake. She can handle a few headstrong nobles," the Maiden said. "We head for the border and find out who brought those Shadows here, before the

High Council sends an army to Alykith."

"You don't think it was Alykith?" Rane didn't care either way.

"Alykith helped end the war. They signed a treaty. They suffered as much as we did under Verin's wrath. It makes little sense for them to rekindle that bitter conflict when they haven't even rebuilt from the last one."

Rane appraised her.

"Something brought those *things* over," she continued. "It's in Ighten already."

Rane grinned. "One of those *things* has you in their sights, Maiden," he said, glancing pointedly at her waist. He felt the power in the Mark, radiating as a beacon and a warning.

Mine, it said, though Rane couldn't fathom why the creature hadn't come to collect.

He reached down for the pile of clothes he'd gathered and dropped them over her head as he passed. "Change so we can go."

Sun peeked through the cracks in the pier above Rane's head, its piercing glint breaking with the thundering steps of people coming and going above. Salt water washed in heavy waves around them, sweeping up his hips and soaking into the holy wounds still healing on his back.

Ships swayed in the port, groaning against the waves and bumping along the rope fenders lining the docks.

There were no bells. No signal to the public that a coup had taken place, that their queen was no longer in a position of power, or that a Shade had been set loose into their streets.

It meant many things. Either Sinead had regained her power, or her High Council didn't want anything to be amiss. It changed nothing, either way. He still had a jailer. If he could somehow get that bracelet off his warden, he might finally, after one hundred and fifty years, know freedom.

He eyed the Maiden's back as she waded through the waist-deep water ahead of him. She limped each step, until they came to the pier's end, where their choices were to risk being seen by running from the water to shore and into the forest, or swim further out before heading inland. Rane wasn't a fan of swimming, so he turned his gaze down on the Maiden. "Can you run?"

She tested her weight on her injured ankle, nodding. "Go ahead. I'll catch up."

Rane shrugged and ran until the shadow of trees enveloped him. He cleared the distance in a quarter of the time it might have taken a mortal and turned to see the Maiden charging after him. His gaze went to the docks. When she was close, he spotted a port guard making his rounds to the pier's end and grabbed her by the arms, dragging her behind a tree and pressing her into the cypress bark.

Her panting breath washed across the skin of his neck and he clenched his eyes against the feel.

He was so fucking hungry.

Rane peered around the tree at the docks, and, realizing the guard had not spotted them, released her. He eased away, turning to go deeper into the woods. The Maiden followed.

The terrain was not easy, least of all for someone with an injured foot, but she didn't complain. He had expected her to order him to carry her eventually. Instead, they continued until sunset, when she waved at him to halt. "We should stop for the night."

It almost sounded like a command, but he suspected most of her will was in her feet, moving them forward against the pain and exhaustion. Mortals were so frail.

She sank against a tree, sliding until her legs stretched across the root-covered earth. "I need a fire," she said, pulling a short dagger from her stolen trousers.

He blinked.

He hadn't pilfered that for her, which meant that somewhere along the way, she'd picked it up somewhere. He hadn't noticed, and it wasn't like him not to notice. He was either very far gone in his hunger, or she was very good.

He eyed the dagger and thought of her request. He knew what she needed the fire for, but the Maiden didn't seem resigned to the pain which came with such a choice. *Interesting.*

"A moment," he said, stepping away to collect some twigs and small logs. He returned with a bundle in his arms and poured them out on the mossy earth near her legs. He could have easily started the fire with a wave of his hand, but he needed to conserve his energy or he'd devour the mortal woman before she could limp away. He rubbed the sticks together with some dry leaves and spindles of pine straw until there was smoke and, eventually, flame.

When the fire was bright, the Red Court Maiden dug into the pack he'd snagged for her, pulling out her bloodstained gown. She ripped the cleaner parts into strips and laid them in her lap. Then, she poured water from the canteen over her wound and warmed the blade in the fire until it glowed hot and red. She shifted, leaning on a thigh and tucking her ankle near her, and then she pressed the red-hot blade to the wound.

A scream tore from the Maiden's throat, and he felt a bolt of rapture ripple through him before she dampened it behind clenched teeth and drew the blade away. Her hand shook.

Rane knelt, tilting his head as he admired her pain. His eyes flashed with a burgundy glow, and, for a second, his hunger felt quenched.

She pressed the blade into the fire again, turning it as it heated.

"I could fix it," he said, sporting a wiry grin. "If you like."

She scoffed. "The last thing I need is another Shade staking a claim." She passed him the dagger. "You do it. I cannot hold it again."

Rane arched an eyebrow, taking the dagger in his hand. He admired the blade's glow. Well, he *was* hungry. Why not feed on her pain?

He pressed it to her ankle, and she clawed the dirt, throwing her head back with a cry. His eyes went to the long line of her throat, and the urge to cover the soft flesh with his lips nearly tore a groan from him. He focused on the task, on her pain, and let that be enough.

When finished, he stabbed the blade into the dirt and left it there.

"I'm sure that was fun for you," she said, her voice tight. "Thrilling."

She slept not long afterwards, either driven into it by exhaustion or shock. In her sleep, she whimpered and cried and begged for someone to save her, and while she did, he inspected the bracelet around her wrist, trying to pry it free. If he removed it... But no amount of tugging, at least not enough that wouldn't wake her, aided him.

Eventually, she woke, gasping and lashing out with the stolen dagger.

"Trouble sleeping?" Rane asked, adjusting the cloak over his shoulders.

The Maiden sat up, wiping cool sweat from her brow. Sweat dripped across her skin, down her neck and chest, between her breasts. Again, he fought to urge to drag his tongue across her flesh.

"I found you some drakeroot." He reached beneath his cloak for the weed's pale threads. It helped with pain, but it also induced a deep sleep, one that might be deep enough for him to worm that bracelet off her wrist.

"How kind of you," she said, her voice dripping sarcasm. She eyed him for a second and then held out her hand.

He gave an acrid smile and leaned over, plopping the strands of root into her palm, one by one. She admired a sliver in the firelight, frowning. "Maybe I won't dream…"

A peculiar thing to say, he thought.

She tossed them into her mouth and chewed before lowering herself to the leafy earth again.

The fire cracked and popped, but the rest of the world turned silent. He waited, watching the steady, even rhythm of her breath and the way the fire glowed along her skin and hair. She was a beautiful thing. Pretty and delicate looking. Silver and porcelain. If he got the bracelet off her wrist, he could break her in half and be on his way.

He slipped over, grabbing her wrist again as she began to twitch and moan. Another nightmare. He pinched the bracelet between his fingers and jerked, trying to rip it off, not caring if her skin came with it.

Rane had never done this to Sinead. Besides never having the opportunity to try, he likely wouldn't have. His relationship with the monarch was a complicated mess of obedience and respect. Even after almost two hundred years, he didn't fully understand it.

He tugged a few more times before concluding that a failsafe likely kept him, of all people, from tearing it off. Perhaps if he severed her arm…

Her breath turned panicked, and he half expected to find her eyes wide open, staring at him in utter terror, but he found her sleeping still. Tears leaked from the corner of her eyes. Her brow creased, a flinch of pain—pain too real to be a dream. He smelled it in the air around her, terror and agony, like sweet perfume.

He tilted his head, releasing her wrist. It dropped heavy to the earth.

Something was… wrong.

Rane admired her again and then his gaze drifted to her side, his hand going to the ill-fitting blouse he'd stolen for her. He lifted it, taking a peek beneath the fabric at the Shade's Mark staining her skin. The Mark shifted, moving of its own accord, stroking along her side like a caress.

This wasn't a nightmare. Something was feeding on her.

TENELE RAIDER

AMID A CLEARING, surrounded by a dark, brutal forest, sat empty church pews lined in two rows, facing a stone altar. Pale white flowers sprinkled the aisle like carpet, glowing beneath the moon. The scene might have been beautiful—romantic even—if the flowers closest to the altar were not splattered and stained red.

The Red Court Maiden knelt on the altar's top, naked and smeared in blood. Her silver hair twinkled, a cascade of diamonds spilling over her shoulders, and her skin glowed, bursting with holy light. Blood pooled beneath her, so thick and heavy and rich it flowed over the altar top, dripping to the floral floor.

She wasn't wounded. At least, not anymore. She glanced at the dagger clutched in her trembling hand, fearing the threat of sharp steel against her skin, cutting over and over.

The wound had healed, but if he ordered her to do it again, she would. She had to. Commands spilled from his lips, compelling her to drive the blade in, to watch her own guts spill out over her legs, until it reset, and the pain eased, and he said…

"Again."

His rich, dark voice came from the front pew. She didn't know his name, but he'd saved her in the forest and now haunted her every night. Sometimes, he was kind, or as kind as one could be while making love to her against sharp rocks. Even if she didn't want it, he told her she did, and it was so. Some nights, he pulled her apart, piece by tiny piece. But, most nights, she was here, gutting herself before him on this woodland altar.

His charcoal-colored skin tugged with a pearly white smile. Long, flowing black hair spilled over his shoulders, with gold horns curling from his brow, back behind his head. A tragically handsome face framed his liquid gold eyes.

Tenele shuddered and shook her head. Her hand quivered with the effort of resisting his command. "Please…"

The Shade rose, stepping to the altar. "Again, *Minka'nes.*"

She sobbed, tilting the blade and pressing the point to her belly. Her hand shook, scraping the tip along her skin. "I—I can't. Please. Please don—"

The Shade leaned against the altar and cupped her face in his hands. "Poor thing… You have to." He wiped her tears with his thumbs and pressed his forehead to hers. "Would you like me to help you?"

Tenele choked on a sob.

"Tell me you want me to help you."

Her lips pursed and jaw clenched, struggling to hold the words back. They tumbled out anyway, shaking and stained with betrayal. "Help me."

The Shade peered into her frightened eyes, his hand curling around hers, over the dagger's hilt. He pushed forward and drove it into her gut, guiding her hand across her stomach. She screamed as they carved an opening together, blood spilling out, down her thighs and over the altar's edge again.

"Do you want it to stop?"

Her head drooped to his shoulder, and she nodded against his warm skin, her tears wetting his neck.

"Tell me," he said.

"Please..."

"Say the words, *Minka'nes*."

"Please, make it stop."

Almost instantly, the pain knotting her features eased. He pulled the dagger away and the wound closed. Tenele sank wearily and heavy against him. He took her chin and turned her face up to the moon. "Better?" The words blew across her neck, so pleasant compared to everything else.

He would have her now, as he always did, in a pool of her own blood.

The Maiden nodded because she would take his body over the knife in her gut. Her gaze swept the pews behind the Shade and paused on the figure standing in the aisle. Bewilderment clouded her dizzy mind. "Ranemir?"

The Shade holding her stiffened, confusion tearing his gaze to the figure behind him. A cold pale gray swept over the Shade's charcoal skin. Clawed hands tightened over her shoulders as he tilted his head. "Ren?"

Tenele stretched her hand towards Ranemir. "Please..."

"Oh, *Minka'nes*," cooed her tormentor, brushing her hair back. "He can't save you."

Rane walked towards them fiercely, emerging from the

blackness until he seemed solid beside them. His posture eased, as though he'd been fighting through a storm to get there. He surveyed the scene with a hard tension in his eyes. "Maiden," he said. "What the fuck?"

Tenele tightened her hand around the dagger and drove it towards the gold-eyed Shade's charcoal neck. It disappeared and her fist struck instead. She planted her knuckles into him before reaching out to claw at his eyes.

"Stop," snarled the gold-eyed Shade.

She did, hands frozen, clawing at the air around him.

"Wake me up," Tenele begged Rane. "Wake me! Wake me up!"

"I'm trying!" snapped Ranemir. He turned on the other Shade. "So, you Marked her? Now I've found you." A wicked smile spread across his face, his eyes suddenly too bright to look at. "Withdraw it."

The other Shade grinned. "I'd be happy to share with you."

Tenele grasped for Rane, desperate. "Mark me. Override him! Do something!"

Her nightmare captor sneered. "That's not—"

"Mark me!"

Rane looked at her with rabid, burgundy eyes. Then, he reached out and grabbed her torturer by the throat. Purple flame spread from Ranemir's feet, washing across the ground and licking up the walls of her nightmare. He smiled handsomely at the other Shade, holding him up like he was admiring a jewel in the sunlight. "I claim her. She is mine. Unless you think you can stop me."

The Shade's charcoal lips curled up with a snarl, ready to

fight. Then, the tension coiling his muscles subsided. "Take her, then."

It felt too easy. Wrong.

The dream eroded, and the Nightmare Shade turned to mist in Rane's grip. Purple flames swallowed the podium, the pews, everything around them until they licked painlessly at her own form.

Rane's shape blurred into focus. He was over her, his body straddling her hips, his weight crushing her against the earth. His hand was under her shirt, pressed over the Shade's Mark.

"Breathe," he told her, warm fingers curling over her skin. He was frowning, covered in sweat.

She stared at him, searching his face and the woods, waiting for the world to ripple into a different night terror. Tenele breathed, as he asked, until the tension in her limbs eased.

She clutched his clothes. Her fingers squeezed the fabric, ensuring it was real, even if everything before had felt just as solid and sure. Tenele released him, knotting her hands across her chest, now aware of being awake and what he'd seen and where he was over her.

"Almost done," said Ranemir. The place beneath his hand burned like ice against her skin until it almost became too much, but just before she shoved him off, he removed his hand. He slumped as he did, his other hand pressing against the dirt near her head, his form becoming a shield against the night.

The sloppy handprint of the former Shade's Mark was gone and, in its place, a black circle—so deep and true it felt akin to peering through starless space. Her burned scar was still there, circling the black brand like the aura of a solar eclipse.

The magic flaring in Rane's eyes faded to a near mundane red-brown. "How long did you have the other Mark?" he asked, his voice low.

Tenele ran her fingers over the new one, swallowing. She tried not to think of all her nightmares, but they flared up with a vengeance. "Almost three weeks."

He looked away but still didn't move to give her space. "You're going to be dizzy for a while."

That was the first time she noticed his horns were missing.

He looked... almost human.

"Are you okay?"

His gaze shot back to her, lips curling with a snarl. "A thank you would suffice."

Tenele tugged her shirt down sharply, hiding his Mark away. "Thank you," she said, pressing her palm against his chest and shoving him off. She sat up and immediately swayed back down to the earth. The world spun, like she'd drunk too much of Maiden Klane's homemade whiskey. "You won't go snooping in my dreams, will you? Or does yours come with a different drawback?"

"I have no interest in your dreams," he replied, looking distracted as he sat back in the dirt and closed his eyes. He took a deep breath. "There will be some side effects... For us both."

Tenele narrowed her eyes on him. He seemed just as dizzy as she was... She reached down to the back of her knees, the only place she was even remotely ticklish, and began to graze the area with her fingers.

Ranemir blinked at her. He watched her hand, confusion clouding his expression. Then, he threw his head back and laughed. "No. That's not enough. But you're very intuitive, Maiden." He tapped the side of his head with a long finger.

Tenele shrugged. "I guess it's for the best. I'd spend this entire trip tormenting you." She eased back down against the earth, using the blanket he'd packed as a pillow. "It fades... right? Eventually, I'll be free of you?"

There were benefits to having the Mark. Shadows didn't eat Marked humans for fear of a Shade's wrath, and if they came up against a horde like the one near Whitehall, it would be useful.

"Fade?" Rane's hand cupped his chin reflectively. "Maybe. Eventually. Who knows?" He gave a teasing grin. "I've never Marked someone."

Tenele groaned. "Wonderful." She settled in, knowing she needed to sleep but not really wanting to. Some part of her was afraid she'd get stuck with that thing manipulating her dreams again. But the cool tingle of Rane's Mark promised otherwise. She curled on her side and stared at the fire. "What does *Minka'nes* mean?"

Rane twitched, his gaze focusing on her. His expression became placid and unreadable. "Where did you hear that?"

"That's what he calls me," she replied. "The first night I saw him and every night after. *Minka'nes*." She still didn't understand why he'd saved her and Marked her and tortured her.

Ranemir stared into the woods. "I don't remember," he said. "Probably something silly. A pet name."

RANEMIR STROUD

RANE EYED THE cloaked form of the woman limping ahead of him. He sensed her in the back of his mind—every painful step she took was a slash to his achilles. He was unaccustomed to pain, and being weakened. *Hungry.* Normally, he could feed off the sensation, but that would require hurting her more, and he couldn't do that. So, if not pain, could he feed on…

He shook his head.

"You should rest that," he called as they came to the edge of a small town. At least here they could get some supplies. Rest. Eat. Be on their way. Such human things. He almost wanted to slit his own throat at the desires bleeding over from her.

"Thank you for your concern."

"I was able to track him, you know. The one who marked you. Through that dream. If you want your vengeance, you're going to need to let that leg heal," he said, watching her back stiffen.

"Will finding him lead us to what we're looking for?

Otherwise, I have no interest in finding him," she said, continuing into town.

He grinned. "Are you afraid, Maiden? Oh devout—"

Fear washed through their link. Rane saw her tortured and screaming like a kick to the teeth. What she'd felt hadn't been imaginary pain or ordinary pain. It had been bone-chilling misery, and she'd somehow existed with that monster living in her dreams every night for almost a month. The Maiden had been in such a state of fear and agony she'd begged him—him, of all things—to Mark her.

"I'm not afraid of him," she hissed. "I'm just not eager to experience his fantasies in the real world."

Rane scoffed. "It matters little what his fantasies were. As if I would let him—" He stopped. Their link, coupled with his hunger, was driving him to ruin.

"Let's get our shopping done and find an inn," she said. Rane snarled as the Maiden tugged his hood further over his head, as if that would hide the fact he was something other than human.

They found a supply store near the edge of town, and she flashed the insignia on her wrist to the shopkeep. News of the Red Court slaughter hadn't made it across Ighten yet, so the exchange went about as normally as he assumed it usually did. She gave the shopkeep her order, and he filled two packs with supplies, agreeing to have two horses ready for her come the morning. Surprisingly, the shopkeep had paid him very little attention, so Rane's otherness hadn't been noticed. He suspected they would not be so lucky at the inn.

They headed across town to an old weathered building with a sign hanging over the door reading *The Muddy Hag.*

The inside smelled of stew and sex. A few men were gathered at the bar, more were clustered around a table. An orange glow hugged the space, the light spilling from a crumbling hearth at the center of the far back wall.

The Maiden stepped to the counter, rolling up her sleeve to show the Red Court emblem on her wrist. The innkeeper smiled. "So pleased to have you joining us, Maiden. How might I help?"

"I need a room. Preferably with two beds."

"We've only got room Three left. One bed. Missy and Scarlet have customers in the other two." The innkeeper glanced at Rane's impossibly tall form. "Leah's free if you're so inclined…"

He was. But that was the hunger talking. He placed a moon-gray hand on Tenele's shoulder. "Afraid she's the jealous type."

The innkeeper arched an eyebrow, likely because Maidens were celibate, and the man finally realized what she'd dragged through his door.

"Who did you say you were again?" asked the innkeeper, threads of fear snaking into his voice.

She hadn't said, but the Maiden replied politely and unflinchingly, "Maiden Paelae Klane."

The innkeeper hesitated, glancing around because he could not seem to focus on Rane. "I don't serve Shades."

A rippling, bitter silence spread through the tavern.

The Maiden waved her hand dismissively. "There's no choice. He's my ward. He'll stay where I can keep eyes on him."

"I. Don't. Serve. Monsters."

She frowned, appraising the innkeeper a minute more

before exhaling a frustrated growl and turning for the door. "Fine. What's another night in the woods?"

"She's injured," said Ranemir. The Maiden's head twisted towards him, a look of surprise and rage mingling on her pretty face. "Let her stay. I'll wait out in the woods."

"Eh, no…" The Maiden smirked. "Not happening. You won't be running off." She turned to the innkeeper, going back to him and leaning across the counter. "Look. He's like a pet cat. Really. There's nothing to worry about. I have control of him."

The men hunkered at the bar boiled over with laughter.

"Control of a Shade?"

She nodded. "Yes."

"Prove it."

Rane glowered at her. "Maiden…"

She pulled out a chair and placed it behind him before stepping around in front. Her green eyes rose to meet his. A defiant stillness calcified the hardness in her gaze, and with a confidence born of someone who had not been disobeyed often in her life, she said, "Sit."

Rane was going to ignore her, but then his knees buckled and he dropped clumsily into the chair against his will.

The room filled with applause, like she'd breathed fire into the air or juggled a collection of rusted saws. A single word and he was locked on his ass. His lips curled with a snarl, a low, rumbling growl itching to break free.

"That doesn't prove nothin,'" someone said. "Maybe he wanted to sit. Make him kneel."

"Yah!"

"Yeah, make him kneel!"

Rane looked up, meeting the Maiden's eyes. He didn't say it aloud, but he knew the disgust and rage passed through the link between them because she flinched.

She glanced towards the crowd. "Really, I think one demonstration is enough…"

"Make 'im kneel!"

The Maiden frowned, but he could see the gears turning in her mind. His comfort mattered little to her, just as hers mattered equally as much to him.

"Kneel."

The order was certain, and he slipped out of the chair, dropping to his knees with a hard crack. Rane steadied himself, hands and claws digging into the floor. He glared at the graining in the wood, shaking as he lifted his head. He wanted to rip her throat out. Drink in her pain like wine. How *dare* she order him to *kneel*?

He tried to stand, and the thought sent the metal around his neck white-hot.

"Alright," said the Maiden, turning to the innkeep. "Can I have the room?"

The innkeeper laughed as he reached beneath the counter, tossing her a brass key. "Room three. Up the stairs and to the right. Last door."

"Come," she said, turning for the stairs.

He rose in a slow, elegant movement, following her without a word. He barely paid attention to her as she unlocked the door and led him into the cramped room with its modest bed and separate lavatory. She closed the door, and a second later was before him, her worried gaze focusing on the chain around his neck, her hands rising to grasp it.

"I'm sorry, I didn't know…"

The anger flared higher in his molten mood. "I'm not averse to a little pain, Maiden." He snatched her wrist before it could reach the chain around his neck. His thumb gently grazed the heavy vein just below her palm, a fang-like nail scraping her skin but not quite breaking it. "But what about you?" His fury bit through him. "If I slit your wrist right now, will you order me to stop?" His grip tightened, trapping her. "I wonder if you'd have time?"

Her free hand wrapped around his arm and hand, her fingers prying at his grip, fear flaring in her eyes. "You wouldn't." Not an order. A challenge. Or maybe she did believe he wouldn't harm her. Foolish mortal.

Her fear had a primal effect on him. Satisfaction and hunger heated his veins. "Oh. You believe you know me." He frowned. Pity glowed into his voice as he squeezed her wrist, crushing down until he felt the bones flex under his grip. "Did you think I gave you my Mark to save you?"

She bent like a willow, melting closer to him as if that would relax his grip. Her feet shuffled against the floor. A stab of pain as she placed more weight on her ankle. The sensations rolled into him, and his mouth watered for more.

Her eyes misted, but there was a defiant hardness in her gaze, a resolve in the way she clenched her teeth, refusing to cry out or beg as her skin bruised and bones strained. "Why give it, then?"

He twisted her in toward his chest, close enough that he could have kissed her. Her eyes widened to saucers as he bent his head low, lips brushing hers. "A Mark is not a gift, Maiden. It's a weapon. If you used Sinead's little toy against me right now, which of us do you think would give in to the pain first? Should we find out?"

The Maiden stilled, anger and fear flourishing in her eyes. It was hard to tell which of those emotions won out when she thrashed, seemingly willing to break her own wrist to get out of his arms. "Let go. Let. Me. Go." She clawed at his hand. "Did you conspire with him to make me so willing to trade one chain for another? Let me go."

The words were angry, but she wasn't invoking the command. She was asking. Begging. Intention, it seemed, was the difference.

"Not going to use it?" He released her, and an invisible force struck her in the chest, knocking her backward onto the bed, pinning her there. He scowled down. "You have no idea what I am. Next time you show off your pet monster to your friends, it will bite you."

The fight bled out of her, and she no longer resisted the force holding her in place. She settled into the softness of the bed and looked away from him, like he no longer existed.

The sudden quiet bled the anger from his bones. He withdrew his power, removing the pressure from her chest. It had been a long, long time since he'd been that furious. His muscles already missed the anger like a lost lover.

"Let's just sleep," he said, retreating to a corner. Halfway there, a shudder went through him that had nothing to do with anger. He sucked in a breath, touching his chest. Hunger grabbed at his insides with tiny teeth, and he knew she felt it too when she wrapped her arms around her belly.

13

Tenele Raider

TENELE WOKE WITH a start from her first dreamless sleep in a month. But the second her mind drifted into consciousness, she remembered where she was and who she was with. Her bruised wrist ached, a harsh throb that brought the devastating knowledge she'd fucked up by letting him Mark her. Her desperation had played her into his hands.

Maybe she'd been better off tortured every night?

Tenele fished around on the bedside table for candles and flint, lighting one and using it to find her way to the lavatory. There wasn't a door.

She washed her face in a bowl of water and caught sight of the black bruising stretching over her wrist and hand. She flexed it, feeling the stiff, swollen tissue resist the movement, knowing he felt it too. Good. She doubted he'd feel remorse, but at least he'd feel discomfort.

"I'm going to get something to eat," she said, stepping out of the lavatory, giving him a wide berth as she went.

The tavern was far fuller than earlier, with most tables packed and the few stools at the bar taken. Tenele leaned against the counter and ordered a meal, keeping her hood low over her face. She wasn't worried about being recognized, but Grela were mostly extinct, and her silver hair tended to draw unwanted attention.

They delivered her food on a pewter tray—a bowl of stew and pint of mead. She ate quietly and, when finished, she drank.

And drank. And drank.

"You didn't pay," a female voice filtered over all the others. A woman with a mop of red curls stood before a seated brute, holding her small hand out to him. "You owe me four suls."

"I don't think it was worth four suls, to be honest," said a man, his voice slurring.

"I don't care what you think it's worth. I gave you a product, you give me money. That's business!"

He shrugged. "Nah."

"Give me my money, Tarly."

Tenele glanced over her shoulder, watching the angry red-haired woman half-haul the man out of his seat. The Maiden smirked behind her mug and went back to staring at the fire near the kitchen. A resounding smack echoed through the hall, quieting the room except for the sudden rumble of sobbing.

Tenele turned to find the red-haired woman on the floor, crying and cradling her pink cheek. The innkeeper lit into a tirade, screaming at the man about damaging goods. The man just laughed and waved him off, going back to his meal.

It was in Tenele's best interest to stay out of it, but the sobbing didn't fade and only served to drag her attention to the laughing man more. She sighed, sipping the dregs of her mead and sliding off the stool she'd commandeered when the last person left it. The Maiden wove her way through the tables, pausing at one and removing a bowl and mug from a pewter tray. She took the tray, snatched a full mug of ale from another man, and turned toward the table and crying woman on the floor. The prostitute dragged herself up, but the man called Tarly kicked his boot out and knocked her back down.

"That's not very nice," said Tenele as she approached.

"I don't care what you think is nice," he replied, tilting his head up to her. He smiled, showing a row of half-rotten teeth. He licked his lips, appraising her. "You work here?"

"No."

"Pity," he said, returning to his game of cards.

"Tarly, was it? Do you want to see a magic trick?"

He arched a brow, lowering the hand he held and twisting in his chair to see her better. "What kind?"

"I'll make a bet with you. You look like a betting sort of man," she said. "I bet—" She took a sip of ale from her stolen mug. "—I can turn this mug into two, maybe three. Want to bet?"

"Are you a mage?"

"No."

"Then, sure. I bet," he said, laughing. The group he sat with laughed too.

Tenele turned her gaze down to the woman on the floor. "Cherry—your name's Cherry, right?" The redhead nodded. "Would you be my lovely assistant?"

Tenele passed Cherry the mug when she was on her feet. "Hold it out so he can see it clearly." Cherry did, holding the mug on her flat, trembling palm. Tenele held the pewter tray in front of it like a curtain, waving the tray back and forth. Back and forth. Then, she lifted it.

"That's still only one mug."

Tenele scoffed. "Damn, sure is. Take a drink, and we'll try again."

Tarly took a swig of ale and Tenele waved the tray in front of the mug again. She drew it away. "How many do you see?"

"One!"

"Damn. Alright. Once more."

She held the tray with both hands, waving it back and forth in front of the ale.

Back and forth. Back and forth and back and—

WHACK!

She drove the tray into Tarly's face hard enough to dent it around his head. His nose shattered, blood spilling down the front of his shirt as he slumped in his chair.

Tenele reached forward, fisting a hand in his hair and regretting it as the greasy strands curled over her fingers. She lifted his face towards the mug.

"How many do you see now?" she asked Tarly. He groaned, wobbled, and slipped out of his chair to fall to his knees. "Never, ever hit a woman again. Understood? And always, always pay your debts." She reached down for the pouch at his waist, snatching it free. She released him, and he collapsed face-first into the floor. Tenele turned, taking the mug out of Cherry's hand and replacing it with the pouch of money she'd taken from Tarly's belt. "Take your cut. Then Tarly's buying a round for the room with the rest."

Tenele went for the stairs as Cherry took her cut and tossed the bag into the crowd. The Maiden had reached the second-floor landing when Cherry caught her by the hand and pulled her into an empty room. The woman wrapped her arms around Tenele's neck, hugging her tightly. "That was fucking amazing. No one's ever done anything like that for me before."

Tenele patted the woman's back gently, eyeing the door and inching towards it. "I don't like it when people get pushed a—"

Cherry's lips pressed firmly to hers. The shock of it sent her stumbling back into the wall. Cherry's hand fumbled out, slamming the door shut. Expert lips trailed to her neck as Tenele grasped the woman's shoulders. "Hey… ugh, you don't have to thank me… Not like this."

The red-haired woman smiled, the lamplight highlighting the freckles on her face. "It's okay, unless…"

"I just. I need to get back to—"

"Your husband?"

"He's not my husband."

"Your lover?"

"He's *not* my lover."

"Then he won't mind."

Tenele jumped when she felt Cherry's hand slip between her legs. She'd been so focused on the banter she hadn't paid attention to the woman's rather impressive ability to undo trousers with little notice.

The Maiden swallowed, distracted by her masterful touch. She braced her hand against the wall, clenching her eyes. "Okay, I really need to go now."

Cherry smiled against Tenele's neck. "Stay… I don't get to be with a woman very often…"

"I. Can't."

"Just a minute," Cherry mused, fingers working into a

heated rhythm against her skin.

Tenele bit her bottom lip, ignoring every voice in her head. Just a minute? What was wrong with a minute? Everyone she loved was dead… She'd been tortured every night for nearly a month, been in pain all day and night, and this was the first good thing she'd felt since… *Paelae.*

The forest came flooding back. Blood and screams and her sisters torn apart. The Shade with his golden eyes and burning touch…

Tenele caught Cherry's hand just as her body tipped toward bliss. Her cheeks darkened to crimson. "I'm sorry. Thank you. I can't. I'm so sorry." She pushed away from the woman, righting her clothing as she left the room. Once she reached her door, though, Tenele hesitated, leaning her forearm against the frame and taking a deep, calming breath. The ache of want burned in her center, begging for *more*.

Then, there was the matter of her connection to the Shade, but Tenele was almost certain it meant he only felt her pain. He had said he orchestrated it to hurt her—a weapon he could use.

She breezed into the room, finding Ranemir still sitting where she'd left him with his legs stretched out across the floor. His burgundy eyes glowed dully in the dark, and the candlelight accented his silver-gray skin with warm amber.

"I've been thinking this for a while now," his dark voice rumbled into the quiet. "but are you actually a Red Court Maiden?"

Tenele tripped on one of their bags as she went for the bed. She settled on the edge, dizzy with drink and buzzing from Cherry's precise touch. "Why do you ask? Am I not saying enough prayers?"

"Yeah," he chuckled, sounding more tired than malicious. "That's it."

Tenele ran a hand over her head, shoving the hood away so she could comb fingers through her tangled silver hair. "I'm old—older than I look. Maidens aren't as pure and holy as people think. You lock us up in a mountain fortress with nothing to do but kill monsters and watch the snow fall for years on end. People start growing old around you, and suddenly rules fade like weathered carvings." She stared at her hands. "You felt that?"

"Every touch," he said, his voice like rich chocolate. "Not going to finish?"

Tenele's gaze flicked to him. "Why don't you take a long walk off a cliff."

"Why not make it an order? See how you like the results."

"Fuck you."

"Perhaps tomorrow." He slipped down to lie on the floor, rolling so his back faced her. "Sleep well, Maiden."

The next morning, Tenele dragged herself out of bed and went to the lavatory. She stripped out of the large borrowed clothes that Rane had commandeered for her, chucking them in the corner. It didn't bother her that there wasn't a door because she was quite certain the Shade cared little about spying on her.

She washed with the bowl of water and rag available, running the coldness over her scarred arms and legs and shoulders, feeling drowsy and achy and longing to go back to sleep.

She donned the traveling clothes they'd purchased. Dark green pants, brown boots, a dingy cotton, long-sleeved blouse tied at the neck, and a brown leather belt with a clasp for a sword sheath. The boots were good. They stabilized her ankle enough that it didn't hurt as bad to walk. She was only slightly sad that it wouldn't be a nagging pain in Ranemir's mind for the day.

After dressing, she stepped back into the bedroom and pieced the leather armor on. She drew the bracers over her wrist and forearms, hissing as the leather buckled snug against the black bruise spreading from her wrist, out to her knuckles and mid-forearm.

The memory of his grip and the anger in his eyes sent a shiver down her spine. He liked her pain. Her fear.

Not so unlike the other Shade, after all.

Only Ranemir was *restrained*. Given half the chance, he'd pull her apart just like the other one, except he wouldn't do it in a dream to watch it happen over and over.

She glanced over her shoulder at him. What minimal budding trust might have been between them as servants of Sinead was gone. If given the chance at freedom, he'd turn on her. He didn't have her back, and he wasn't on her side.

The Shade sat up, facing the wall, and stretched his shoulders back. His horns were gone again, and his long hair was mussed from lying on the floor. The gesture made him almost human. Then, he stood as if an invisible set of puppeteer strings hauled him to his feet, breaking the illusion of normalcy. He turned enough to look at her, but didn't acknowledge her otherwise, opting instead to walk into the lavatory. He pulled his black shirt over his head and began using the water basin to rinse off his face, chest, and arms. The iridescent white tattoos creeping down the sides of his face and neck apparently… kept going.

Tenele tore her gaze away, angry that someone so cruel could be so beautiful. She began aggressively organizing the supplies they'd bought into her pack.

"Which way do we go to catch up with that Shade? The sooner we're finished, the faster I can get you back to your cell."

"Apartment," Rane corrected.

Tenele laughed. "Oh, yes. An apartment. At the bottom of a dungeon. One you needed a leash to leave."

14

Tenele Raider

Fading sunlight glinted against the canopy of leaves above them, the colors slowly shifting from green to yellow to red. She'd always liked fall. In the mountains, it was so hard to tell what time of year it was because it was always cold and always snowing. Everything was gray and black and white. Fall burst with color, a heatless flame spread across the earth.

Her gaze fell from the sky to the back of the Shade riding ahead. She couldn't remember the last thing they'd said to each other. It had been a week since they'd left The Muddy Hag, and their chatter had withered as surely as a flower in frost.

She wasn't used to traveling in silence. Maidens were loud—when not needing to be otherwise—and they laughed and sang as they traveled. A pang splintered through her chest. She missed the songs, the cheerful company and camaraderie. Sometimes she had felt alone among them. Her half-Grela age had set her apart, making her reluctant to form true bonds with anyone. But they were still her sisters. Now she had no one.

Not her order or her country. Not even her queen—the

only mother she'd ever known.

Tenele didn't warn him they were stopping for the night. He had an uncanny way of knowing what she was doing. She pulled her horse to a small clearing and dismounted, drawing her bags from its back and beginning to unsaddle the creature.

Sure enough, he circled around, riding back toward her. His mare took a nip at him as he dismounted. He reached out and casually messed up her forelock, which offended her more. The animal swung her neck into him and shoved him sideways. He stumbled before catching himself. *Interesting.* It was the first time she'd seen him do something that wasn't surreally graceful.

Ranemir left the mare untied and came to where Tenele sat. Without a word, he went to one of her saddlebags, presumably for the hunting knife. They'd each slid into their own unofficial duties when making camp. She wandered off in search of firewood, and he went in the opposite direction for food.

Tenele collected twigs and long, narrow limbs in the bend of her arm until she held a hefty stack. By then, the shadows had gathered so dark beneath the trees she could barely see the leafy ground. She dumped her hoard into the center of the clearing, stacking the items in a fashion that allowed for air flow and hotter burning. The brighter the fire, the less likely a Shadow was to venture near.

Ranemir arrived a short while later, a large raccoon in hand. It had not died well. He laid it out on a rock near Tenele's fire and started preparing it for cooking. As usual, he'd bled and skinned it out in the woods, but it was clear the head had been crushed in. Usually, Rane's kills were neat and efficient.

"It put up a fight?" she quipped, unrolling her bed across the leafy earth.

"Not a good one." His burgundy eyes flicked up at her and the staged wood. "I'll be ready to cook in—"

A low, mournful cry rose up from the forest, somewhere to the southeast. A few more voices rose to answer it. Some were close. None were human or animal. Rane stopped and listened closely.

Tenele eased to her feet, turning in the sound's direction. Her hand went to the hilt of her sword. "How many do you think there are?"

The Shade tilted his head. "I don't know." He rose to his feet, abandoning the raccoon, and waited. The cries went up again, deep and painfully inhuman. "Get your horse near the fire." He turned and started toward his.

Tenele drew hers close. The palomino snorted and stomped, ears rotating back and forth with the change and pitch of the howling. Its nerves grew worse when Rane and his demon mare approached them. She ran her hands over her creature's neck, whispering to him. "Shh… it's okay. They don't like the fire. Stay close to it."

Another sound echoed off the trees. A scream, a human one, but distorted and… wrong.

"Haven't heard this sound in a long time," Rane mused. He stood with his back to the fire, listening and watching the darkness. "They're circling."

Tenele's horse bucked and jerked, stomping to the point she had to use both hands to keep the creature from running away. A screech off to the side, so close it sounded in the clearing with them, startled the horse so badly it reared and snatched the reins from her hands.

"No!" Tenele reached vainly for them, but the palomino bolted into the forest. She was about to follow when the bone-chilling sound of the horse going down reverberated off the trees. She saw its body crumple, twist unnaturally, and swallowed by the brush. The Maiden froze at the clearing's edge, taking a careful step back.

A weighty silence settled in the air.

"Got anything gold?" asked Ranemir.

Tenele smiled, drawing her gold-threaded blade. "That's like asking a baker if they have any flour." The blade was steel, engraved and inset with thin gold filigree, a parade of holy script spiraling to the hilt. Rane squinted at it like he was looking directly into the sun.

"How many?" she asked.

"Eight. Maybe nine." His low voice carried just above the fire's crackling hiss. "Two to your left, one straight ahead. I'll take the others."

A branch cracked to her right, and then all hell broke loose. Indiscernible figures burst from the woods like blood from a severed artery. Holistically, they gave the impression of large hounds, but their bodies looked unstable. Their forms constantly split and reconverged, their only steady feature the familiar, glowing gold eyes. They launched towards her, chaotic cyclones of black blood, hair, and teeth.

Tenele's hands tightened around her sword. She slashed at the nearest one, through it, and then down on the next. Where her blade met flesh, it sizzled and popped like the arch of embers in fire.

She heard a crash of flesh against flesh behind her, something ripping and tearing. A creature screamed, and another roared. "I miscounted," Ranemir growled from outside her line of vision. More bodies emerged from the wood. Their unstable forms spread like writhing smoke. A tumult sounded behind her, and their fire scattered apart. Logs and embers flew across the ground. It scattered the light into near-useless patches around them. Yellow flickered through the darkness—some embers, most of them eyes.

A shadowy thing launched up from her side and slammed into her.

Her hands fumbled across the earth for her sword, clawing at dirt until her fingertips found it in the dark. Her hand wrapped around the hilt as a gaping maw bit into her cloak and tore it back, dragging her with it. The fabric tightened around her neck as it pulled her into the brush. She swiped her sword out at the snarling, writhing shapes, her other hand fumbling with the clasp at her neck.

Several Shadows moved at once, leaping at her as the brush swallowed her up. She drove her sword into one and kicked at the other. The howling screech of the dying hound deafened her to anything else.

"Maiden!" Rane's voice shouted behind her. A wave of power pulsed at her back, followed by screams. They were close, practically in her ears. She spun to see two sprawling bodies sliding away from her in the dirt. Beyond them, she made out the Shade's taller form tangling with several creatures. They were swarming on him like flies on meat.

That made no sense. Shadows didn't hunger for other Shadows, and especially not Shades. They rarely made enemies of each other at all, unless commanded by their summoners.

Through the frenzy of flesh, Rane's black-clawed hand reached out in her direction and clenched. The two Shadows recovering in front of her shrieked. Their skulls shuddered and then crushed in a splash of black ooze.

The hot liquid splattered across her face and she clenched her eyes, careful not to keep them closed for long. She was on her feet a moment later, rushing back toward Rane. She barely saw him now that the fire's embers were nothing more than smoldering ash. But she knew him by his burgundy eyes and the strange, unfamiliar feel in the air—a powerful current she'd never felt in a Shade.

Tenele whacked and sliced and stabbed at the beasts that swarmed him, careful not to hit him in the process.

Power swirled up, sucking away all light and sound, as if he'd plunged the clearing underwater. A force threw her backwards. Immense exhaustion beyond anything she'd ever known pounded through her body from her link with Rane. It was one thing to be tired, and another to feel all her veins somehow recoiling, feeding on themselves for strength. The sensation was maddening. She needed—she needed…what?

The sickening sensation washed out. She was on her back, staring up at stars. Turning her head, she saw black fluid strewn in sharp vectors across the dirt. Her gaze followed them to where they converged on Rane standing at the center of a gory starburst, his eyes alight with power.

The Maiden rose, slow and steady, drawing her sword across the leg of her pants to clean the blade. She didn't put it away. *Not yet.*

"Are there more?" she asked, stepping closer to him. Tenele wanted to know about the terrible feeling, the one she remembered like a sour aftertaste, but she didn't think he'd tell her.

"They fled." He walked out of the sludge, his boots making sucking sounds against the ground. The horns receded as he did so, his eyes dulling to a dim red-brown in the dark. He bent, picking up one of the displaced logs. It glowed orange and hot in his hand. He chucked it back into what was left of the coals with an aggravated jerk of his arm, and stalked to collect another one fizzling near Tenele.

His stomping made her nervous. The air shifted around him and his anger was like heat seeping into her. "Were you hurt?" she asked, shying away from him as he approached. "I… I know you heal fast. I might be able to help if you're having trouble."

"Ha." He dropped the second log on top of the other one. They caught together, slowly restoring some light to the clearing. He dropped to a seat against a tree near the fire. The movement was heavy, ungraceful. "If you're not hurt, help my horse."

Tenele had forgotten about the creature. She went to where it leaned against a tree, favoring one bloody leg. It snorted at her, nostrils flaring as she approached.

"I'm sorry," Tenele whispered to it. "It's alright. I'll help. Shh… Don't move."

Her hand smoothed down the horse's neck, over her shoulder, and down her leg. As Tenele's hand grew closer to the wound, her fingers glowed. Soft light hummed between her palm and the horse's wet fur, and when her hand passed over the blood, the wound closed. The creature relaxed, and Tenele went about healing other wounds she hadn't noticed before, now that the firelight was brighter. When finished, Tenele went back to the fire, sinking wearily down to the earth.

Tenele tugged off her belt, sitting it and the sword alongside her rumpled bedroll. She untucked her shirt and loosened her boots but didn't remove them.

"What was that?" he asked, staring at her from across the fire.

"What?"

"That, what you did with the horse…" There was a wariness to his voice. He seemed unsettled. Uneasy.

Tenele glanced back at the animal, at its blood-stained fur, but otherwise healthy stance. She was so tired… She'd forgotten about hiding it. Not that she would have been able to explain in the morning why their one remaining horse was perfectly fine.

"I… healed her."

He pursed his lips together before saying, "That's a divine gift, Maiden. A gods-given gift…"

"I'm not divine." She tossed a broken twig into the fire.

He doubled over with a groan, and she felt the wave of hunger and sickness wash between their link so fiercely her vision swam until she did the same.

"You don't eat," she muttered. "Not like I do. I haven't seen you feed on anything in, well, since we've been together. So how do you maintain that much power?" Her eyes fluttered up, boring into him from across the fire.

He frowned at the flames. It was hard to read him, even when his eyes weren't shining like some feral demon. Just when she thought he wouldn't answer, he said, "Sinead."

She frowned. Tenele had heard lots of stories about how

sorcerers maintained their Shades. Ritual sacrifices, blood offerings, power transference, and other… carnal means. She couldn't imagine Sinead doing any of those. Maybe she didn't know the queen as well as she thought?

"How often do you need to feed?"

He pressed a hand to his forehead and sighed. "Come here."

Tenele cocked her head at him. "Why?"

"I need to try and remove your Mark."

Tenele stood, edging around the fire, and knelt next to him. She didn't trust him. It didn't seem like something he would do, but there was a tiredness in his eyes. An exasperation. Perhaps he wanted to be rid of her. She curled her fingers in the hem of her shirt and lifted it until he could see the black spot staining her scar.

A foreign arousal tightened low in her belly. It blended with the same hunger from before, flickering through her nerves. Rane closed his eyes and reached for the Mark. Several deep gashes crisscrossed his forearm, painting his skin black.

She flinched when his fingers grazed her skin, shaking her head like it would shake away the feeling coiling inside her. "Why?" Her cheeks felt warm. "Don't need your weapon anymore?"

His lips twisted into a rueful smile. "You can feel it, right? My control is slipping." The words came out strained. "Sensations are getting through without my permission." He placed his hand lightly over her side, enclosing the Mark. "I can't reach Sinead. There's no point in us *both* going mad."

Tenele shied away from him. "You can't reach her? What does that mean?"

Rane's hand twitched, but didn't chase her. A dizzying excitement swept over her through the Mark, like something stroking her inside, demanding more. "Keep calm," he warned her, and the sensation squeezed out. He took a slow breath. "It could be the holy circle. Or she's gone somewhere else, where I can't feel her. Or…" He didn't spell out the last theory, but she was already thinking it.

Her gaze found the earth, tears brimming her eyes. "Gone…" She shook her head. *No.* That wasn't possible. The holy circle was the most likely reason. Sinead had lived through far worse. But that also meant Sinead wasn't free… that the army was still heading for the border, and the only way of stopping a war and freeing their queen was to finish what they'd started.

And she couldn't do that alone.

"Without her… you're going to…" Tenele swallowed. "She's your tether…"

"I have one, more or less." He touched his necklace and then glanced at her wrist. "I won't be able to hurt anyone. But the Mark is a dangerous loophole."

She shook her head, shifting away. "I'm not a sorcerer. I don't have any power… not any useful power." There that feeling was again, the hungry thrill of her retreat, the sweeping desire to chase. It begged her to run as much as it told her to be perfectly still, bouncing back and forth between the demands until Tenele grew dizzy.

If she didn't help Rane, he'd splinter apart. And if that happened, she would lose. Sinead would lose. Whoever started this would tear the world down with monsters.

"What do you need from me?"

Rane sneered. "What do you think you're offering?"

Tenele blinked at the question, looking away. She wasn't certain, but she laid out the facts as she saw them, trying to let reason decide instead of this aching, longing hunger in her belly. Her queen was missing, and the entire kingdom had turned against them. An army of monsters were ripping said kingdom to shreds without a single Red or Black Court member left to stop them—save her.

Tenele's mother had given her life to protect Sinead.

What was she willing to give?

"Anything," she answered, turning her green eyes back on him. "Everything."

He stared, eyes widening before erupting with a fake, startled laugh. "I could be tricking you. The only thing stupider than letting me Mark you would be letting me feed on you, too." As he said it, hunger closed over them both, turning them inside out. It felt like mice were chewing their way out of her. Air didn't taste like air, and she felt the world climbing through her, rejecting her, unmaking her. Rane leaned forward over himself, shuddering.

Tenele wrapped her arms around belly and winced. "Some trick…" She took a breath. "Stop being a prideful ass. This is a business transaction. I need you. Alive." Her hand slid across the earth and grasped hold of his arm. "Sinead needs you alive."

Something she'd said must have convinced him. He looked down at her hand on his arm, and placed his over it. "Do you even know what I live off of?"

"Sinead?"

"Sinead feeds me. She gives me what I need to live.

Offered freely."

"What?"

"I exist on pain and pleasure."

Tenele blinked. "You… with Sinead?"

"No. With men and women she sends to me."

"She gives you whores?"

He smirked. "More or less."

Tenele frowned. "So…"

"I can either torture you or fuck you. That's how you can feed me, Maiden."

Her cheeks burned, and she averted her gaze. He laughed, dark and pained. "Still interested?"

Tenele appraised him. His moon-gray skin had turned ashen, and the powerful glow had vanished from his eyes. His hunger was like knives along her nerves, and she knew he wouldn't last, and, if he didn't, she would fail.

Business transaction, she thought. *That's all this is.*

"Okay."

He laughed, and then stopped, as if the word finally filtered through his hunger-fogged brain.

"Maiden… do you understand what you're agreeing to?"

"Sex."

"Yes, sex."

"As you might have surmised, it won't be my first time."

He nodded slowly. "But with me. A Shade. Your mortal enemy?"

She shrugged, trying to throw up a facade of nonchalance, even if she was screaming inside. He could feel it. She knew he could feel her hesitation like a sick taste in his mouth.

"For it to work, you actually have to enjoy it, you know? I

feed on pleasure, not self-immolation. Well, technically I could feed on that too, but…" He grinned.

She scowled, and a second later kissed him, feeling his shock ripple through the Mark like a cold wave. She began to draw away, but he took her face in his hand, long fingers wrapping around her chin and jaw. He appraised her with dim eyes.

"You baffle me," he said.

"This is business," she told him. "I need you alive."

"Business…" His voice filled with the same husky need traveling through their link, and he flashed a wicked grin. "Are you certain?"

"Need me to sign a contract?"

"Technically, you already have." The words were a whisper against her lips. "It's here." His hand slipped under her blouse, warm fingers brushing along the Mark on her side, causing the muscles of her belly to jump at his touch.

Need bled through the link between them, a crashing wave of desire sending a soft gasp from her lips.

"Here?" she asked hesitantly. They'd nearly been killed in this clearing.

He nodded. "You're safe."

She doubted that. She was about to… with a Shade. A fucking Shade. She was going to *fuck* a Shade.

His lips found her neck, and she gasped at the feel. It was strange to sense the touch of his lips on her neck twofold, feeling her sensations and his tangled together. His need, his hunger, drove out every warning in her head telling her to flee. His desire was her desire. Her fear, his fear. Until the emotions spiraled together, turning delirious.

She pressed a hand to his chest as he shifted over her, putting some distance between them. There was a dull glow in the back of his red-brown eyes, a touch of burgundy burning in the distance.

"Second thoughts," he asked. His hand trailed up her inner thigh, dancing along smooth flesh. She shook her head. Where were her pants? Her back pressed along a spread cloak, and cool fall wind danced across her exposed legs. How had she gotten this way so soon?

"No," she said, dizzy. "I…"

He must have sensed her need—her intended command—because his smile shifted and he slipped away, lying on his back next to her. She hadn't wanted to be beneath him, at his whim and mercy.

A low purr rumbled through him as she rolled and straddled his waist. Large hands curled over her hips, dulled claws scraping against her flesh so lightly she shivered.

"No foreplay?" he asked with a laugh.

Her answer came with grabbing hold of his length, wrenching a choked sound from his throat. She hesitated because she hadn't been paying attention to him. In fact, everything had turned into a dizzying blur—as if she'd drank too much before this started—but now she had hold of him, felt the size of him, and began questioning her choices. It had been a long time since she was with a man…

Tenele guided him, felt him press against her slick opening, and her body resist. But she was determined to be done with this. She sheathed herself over him in a single, sharp drop of her hips. A breath lodged in her chest. She tilted her head back, exhaling it with a soft, ragged moan. It billowed out into the chilled air as a cloud of steam.

His hands tightened over her hips before one danced beneath her blouse and cupped his Mark. Any discomfort eased, melting as quickly as it began. Then both of his hands grabbed her hips, his firm grip lifting her, moving her, guiding her into a merciless rhythm.

"Ah…" She looked down and found his hooded gaze, saw the lust written on his face. The open, unabashed want of her was a beacon threatening to lure her in. She turned her gaze to the stars instead, imagining an old lover—a soldier who'd recovered in Lastower for a few weeks after an injury. She remembered his strong, calloused hands against her soft flesh. The feel of her back crushed to hard stone as he took her with a feverish, brutal need.

Tenele began to move of her own accord, no longer needing him to guide her. Her body relaxed, and she relished the feel of him, the sensation of his length striking the deepest parts of her and driving out a sharp moan each time.

He pulled her blouse away, baring her chest to the cool fall air. His dull eyes had warmed back to their rich burgundy color, and his gaze burned into her as he watched her enjoy him. He braced himself with one arm, pushing up to taste her skin. "That's it," he whispered against her breasts, taking a nipple in his mouth. He pinched it between his teeth and she arched over him with a gasp.

She felt his desire like molten fire in her veins, felt his want of her. He wanted control, to take her as he wished. She knew all the horridly wonderful things he wanted from her, all those depraved needs denied by her hatred of his kind. Suddenly, she wanted them to, but wouldn't dare ask. She wasn't certain if she actually *did* want them, or if it was his want of them that made her desire them too.

She allowed the Shade this much of her, and that was all he would have.

All he needed to have in order to live.

His tongue dragged across her flesh and his lips found her neck. He bit her and she cried out, grinding low over him.

Strong hands grabbed hold of her hips and she was lost to him. It didn't matter if she were atop him, he was a Shade. He was a monster. His strength was four times hers and he could control her, have her, take her any way he wished.

But he took her only as *she* wished to be taken, until pleasure shattered her world apart and she cried out into the night, like a wolf greeting the moon. She came down over him, felt the soft trail of his lips across her chest. Tiny kisses of tribute and thanks. She curled her hand against a horn on one side of his head and pulled, demanding to see his face. He tilted it up to her, his eyes blazing burgundy lights.

"You will feel tired," he whispered across her neck, his voice deep as a chasm. "Don't worry…"

She felt the exhaustion as he left her, as if he drew her soul from her body and left a heavy void behind. She wanted him back. Wanted the feel of him inside her again, driving her into oblivion.

Her limbs turned to lead weights, and the sudden sensation of being drained wracked her with fear. He laid her gently on his bedroll, drawing his blanket over her. He stood, a glorious half-clothed statue against the firelight. "You're safe," he said, knowing she needed reassurance.

Only it didn't reassure her at all.

And the world bled away… blurry, orange, dark, and deep.

RANEMIR STROUD

RANE ADJUSTED HIS trousers, buttoning them and buckling his belt while he watched the woman sleep. He drew away to the other side of the fire and sat on her bedroll, fighting every instinct he had to curl himself around her. Normally, he had no desire to tangle himself around a mate after devouring them. It was strange to look at her and want that, especially given how much she'd rather him dead.

Sinead supplied Rane's typical partners. They came to him often, so he memorized what they liked and didn't like in sex. Inevitably, they became attached and sometimes lingered afterwards, wanting him to hold them and be something he wasn't. He always sent them away.

It became almost painful sitting so far from the Maiden, but he did. He admired her. It was all he could do besides scan the dark, shadowed edges of their clearing and listen to the forest, stretching his senses out to detect anything awful stepping their way.

Nothing did.

What had attacked earlier—what remained of them—

had moved on to other prey.

For the best. She was in no shape to move. He'd been entirely depleted—too hungry—and had taken more than he usually did from one person. Not by choice, either. He'd tried to hold back, but at the end she'd tasted too sweet and given too freely. Of course, she didn't understand how it worked, how to keep herself… herself.

Firelight glowed against her skin, shining in her silver hair. Rane hated how much he thought she was beautiful. Mostly, though, he felt unsettled.

She tasted familiar. It was as if he'd had her a million times before. She tasted like moonlight and madness and… divinity. Like holy water without the agonizing burn, and he wanted more.

TENELE RAIDER

TENELE WOKE AT morning with what felt like the worst hangover of her life. She groaned against the pale light filtering in through the trees, dragging the blanket over her head. It took a second to understand why she was cold, even with the blankets. Her hands skimmed beneath the wool, along naked flesh. The night rushed back in a dizzying, blurry rendition of carnal hunger and bitter climax.

She covered her face with her hands, trying to get rid of the image of his lips on her breast, his hands on her hips, the feeling of him inside… She exhaled an exasperated groan.

"Good morning," Ranemir's voice sounded just above her.

She peeked her head out from beneath the blanket and found him standing over her with a tin mug of piping hot liquid. It steamed into the air as he set it next to her.

"Your body?" he asked, and she hated the question. In fact, she'd never hated a question more in her entire life.

"Fine," she said as she snatched the blouse folded neatly next to her, tugging it over her head. She drew her trousers beneath the blanket and wormed her way into them with minimal grace.

When she stood, she swayed, stumbling dizzily on her feet until he caught her by the elbow. The mug floated up from the earth and into her hand. "Drink," he said. "Have a seat. Breakfast is almost ready."

"Does the next morning always feel like getting run over by a carriage?" She settled back down on his bedroll, drawing the wool blanket into her lap and sipping at the coffee.

"I took a bit too much," he admitted. "I was… starving. It won't happen again."

"You're right," she said. Because she wouldn't be doing that again. Unless… "How… often do you need to feed?"

He smiled as he took the squirrel from the fire and placed it on a tin plate. "Depends on how much energy I burn. Once a week, if I'm not exerting myself."

Tenele frowned at him as he passed her the squirrel. He grinned, showing sharpened teeth. She felt along her neck where he'd bit last night, and hissed at the bruise.

"And how long can you go between meals if you're exerting yourself and are short on food?"

"Depends on how much you like that hit-by-a-carriage feeling…"

"I'm sure we can find you a whore in town."

His smile turned devilish. "Was it so unpleasant, Maiden?"

Tenele pursed her lips together, glowering at him before she took a bite of his peace offering. She tamped down the budding desire to have him again. She eyed the horns on his head, his gray skin and the iridescent tattoos dancing along his cheeks and brow. *Monster,* she told herself. *Enemy.*

"Unless severely injured, I can contain my hunger for a while," he said. "So don't worry. I won't be asking for your help again."

She tried to ignore the disappointment washing through the link, trying even more not to share her own. Tenele chewed and finally said, "Good."

RANEMIR STROUD

WHITEHALL'S CHURCH WAS a pale, gothic specter towering over the moonlit town. Rane observed it without pleasure as they rode through the gates and into the empty streets. He'd expected a set of guards to welcome them, but there were none. Perhaps Shadow activity had driven everyone in after dark.

He searched along his connection with Tenele, pulling up the imprint of the other Shade's magic. Even weeks later it lingered in her, a faint whisper of dark power clinging to her soul. The creature had been here. The question was, was it *still* here?

His gaze drew back to the church. Normally, no Shade in its right mind would stay in a town with such a relic. Its presence alone should have been enough to keep most Shadows well at bay. But there was something *wrong* with the church. Rane couldn't put his finger on it, but he had the nagging urge to draw closer to the temple instead of fleeing it.

The nearer they got, the more every muscle in his body drew taut, waiting to fight.

He shifted his attention to the warm pressure along his back. With only one horse, they'd abandoned the saddle and rode double. He had walked whenever practical to spare the mare's back, but even still, he and the Maiden had spent *a lot* of time in close physical contact over the last two weeks.

Right now, her pressure appeared heavier than usual along his spine. He wondered if she'd actually fallen asleep. The Shade glanced over his shoulder without twisting too much. All he made out was her hair glinting silver in the moonlight. She usually wore her hood. It must have fallen off while she dozed. Amusement prickled through him. He gave the mare a signal to turn sharply to the left. She obeyed with an annoyed flick of her ears, pivoting with a harsh stomp of her hoof.

The Maiden began to slip off the mare's back, and she jerked awake. Her hands fisted the fabric at his sides, dragging herself upright. She held tight to him as she appraised the town with a half-lidded gaze. "We're here…" Her breath fanned warmly into his hair. He resisted the shiver of pleasure threatening to ripple through him.

The Maiden slid to the ground, walking slightly ahead before stopping short. She was more awake now. He recognized her emotions keenly through the link, and he didn't miss the bud of fear as her tired mind realized what their arrival meant.

"Do you sense him?" she asked.

"This is where he was when I encountered him in your dream."

Now that she'd dismounted, he had a better view of her. The high moon glowed against her hair, setting tiny strands of silver shimmering like diamonds. She must have sensed his admiration, his… fondness of it, because she reached back and drew her hood over her head.

Rane sighed. "I don't know if he's still here. I can't imagine Shades are a welcome sight in a town with a church like that… We're not going to find him walking down the street."

She frowned, studying the dark places between buildings and trees. "Is it foolish to hunt for him tonight?" Her head turned up to the moon. "It's bright enough."

His gaze settled on the glow of her face and the cold line of her throat in the night. He wanted to run his lips across her skin. Rane shoved the thoughts away before they strayed through the Mark and swung down to stand next to her. "Looks quiet. Could be worth looking around before the whole town knows we're here. But it would be good to find a place to put up the horse. She looks half dead. If only you weren't so heavy."

The Maiden smiled. "If only." Then, pointing to the church, she said, "There's a clearing and a well behind there. We can let her graze and tether her to the well. Father Drowsky won't mind."

Rane stiffened, angling his face towards her. "Father…" He hesitated, following her finger back to the church. "You've been here before?"

Tenele nodded. "This is where…" She paused, looking down the main street of town. "Not far down that road, we were attacked. That's where he Marked me." It may have been the moonlight, but her face paled ever so slightly more. "Father Drowsky heard the screaming and gathered people to find us. I was the only one left alive… Thanks to the Shade and the Mark."

"This road?" he asked, focusing where she'd pointed. "I want to see it. The place where you were Marked."

"Poor Athena," said Tenele as she walked back to the horse and brushed a hand down her neck. "She'll have to wait a little longer for dinner."

Rane scoffed at the name. He didn't understand naming a creature likely to be Shadow food. "You said the priest heard your screams. The church isn't within earshot?"

She looked down the road. "I suppose it is. I'm not certain. I didn't make the journey into town conscious, and I didn't head back once I woke. It has to be, though. If he heard it."

Tenele guided Athena out of town and down the road. "I remember seeing the glimmer of lights in the distance, a faint amber glow through the trees… It can't be too far."

They came to a place where the road had been burned. It wasn't necessarily within earshot—not from the church at least. The earth had blackened, and the trees charred, and just off to the side, out of the path, was a large, dusty pile of ash.

The sight, for Rane, should have felt relatively routine. Of course the queen's little task force had been slain fighting Shadows. That was what they were trained to do. Soldiers died. He hadn't thought much more about it than that. But this wreckage wasn't a battlefield. It was a fucking massacre.

"It would have been impossible to bury them. They were… torn apart." The Maiden stared at the charred remnants of her sisters, her eyes watering. "There were hundreds of Shadows stacked on top of each other. A wall of teeth and eyes. I should have made camp. I was supposed to make camp… But I could see the town's lights and thought we could make it." She stepped toward the pile and sank to her knees, touching a bone too mangled by fire and brutality to be recognizable as human. "I should be dead. I should be in this pile of bones with them."

It took a minute for her words to register. *Shit*. The Maiden was so single-minded about her duty, Rane had assumed that was all there was to her—mindless devotion to the cause. He hadn't thought about her having *friends*. He shouldn't have asked her to show him this.

He approached, a hand flexing to touch her shoulder. "Maiden. We should head back." The words didn't feel helpful as they left his lips.

She stared at the poor excuse for a grave another minute, then swallowed and said, as if nothing were the matter, "So, are we camping or am I going to sneak you into an inn through the window like some lovesick girl?"

The last thing he wanted was to sleep in the shadow of that blasted church. "Find an inn. A place with a tavern should still be open at this hour. We'll do as you said. You can wave me up when you're ready."

The inn was on the opposite end of town from the church, but its glaring presence loomed over the modest stone structures. The Maiden took her things and drew them over her shoulder, groaning wearily as she headed into the warmly lit building. Several long minutes later, a window opened at the side of the structure, overlooking a narrow alley. Tenele's pale hand stretched out and waved him up.

Rane climbed lazily up the cobblestone wall. It felt good to use his claws, like he needed something he could shred. He swung into the room, observing the cozy space. There was one double-wide bed, a fireplace with a single wingback chair tucked into the corner. A makeshift bathing area with a copper tub and privacy screen sat in the opposite corner.

He shrugged off the pack he'd been carrying and started settling into their usual, wordless routine for making camp. Rane removed the meat he'd smoked for her two nights ago and some wild pears from the sack, and then dug out a bedroll. Not that he was in any mood to sleep. "Leftovers," he announced. "Unless you want to build me a cooking fire."

"It's a cold night," she said. "Why not have a fire." She knelt at the small fireplace and used flint to light a stack of wood already waiting in the hearth. "Besides, I could warm water for a bath."

"Hm," he grunted, sitting against the wall and watching her fuss with the fire. She was back to business. Rane could almost believe he'd imagined her show of emotion in the woods… "You don't sit still much, do you?"

She paused her work on the fire, staring into the growing flames. "If I sit still, I think, and I tend to think too much." She leaned the fire poker against the bricks and glanced over her shoulder, a hint of a smile tugging at her lips. "Am I making you restless?"

Rane blinked. He hadn't seen a smile like that, not from her. He smirked back. "All the time, Maiden." He watched her work, pumping water into a pot to heat over the fire. "You said there was a wall of Shadows that night?"

"Too many to count, and they were stacked on top of each other. Just… surrounding us. Then it collapsed into chaos and blood. I got cut across the back and then struck in the side, nearly impaled. I was bleeding out, and they were about to finish me, but the moon came out and they… stopped. That's when *he* showed up and Marked me." She placed a hand over Rane's Mark, over the white webbed scar. His gaze followed the gesture, but looking at the Mark lately had the wrong effect on him. He snared in the sudden shot of possessiveness and hunger before it escaped into his expression. *Not his. Mine.*

Like hell she was his, either. He shook out his thoughts and tried to get back to what she was saying. "Well, I suppose you *are* something else in the moonlight," he scoffed without thinking it through.

She grinned. "I see… You're not so bad in the moonlight yourself. I'm actually growing quite fond of your horns. Don't tell anyone, though."

He stopped cold. *What?* Somehow, he ground enough brain cells together to say, "Like they'd believe me, anyway."

She gave that rare, warm smile again. "True."

Tenele made several trips to fill the tub, stopping when the water was near the rim and steam wafted into the air. Then, she tugged the paper-thin screen around it and slipped behind the covering.

"So, what did you do to pass the time in that cell of yours, other than play that board game?" The sound of fabric dropping and buckles clattering against the floor followed her voice. He watched her shadow shift against the rice paper panel, entranced by the graceful curve of her form sinking into the tub.

She had to know, by the firelight's placement, he could see her through the screen. Was she trying to provoke him? What a bizarre woman. He could provoke right back, if he wished. "Well," he murmured, "My 'cell,' as you put it, was very, *very* private."

She chuckled and slipped under the water. He knew because of the amount that splashed out onto the floor. A few seconds later, she surfaced with a content sigh that tightened things low in his body. He was careful not to focus on the sensation, lest it bleed over into her.

After several minutes of quiet, and the consistent trickle of water as she dragged a cloth over herself, she said, "Maybe we should split up tomorrow. We could cover more ground. I might be able to lure the Shade out, if he's still here." She paused, a heaviness settling in the air. "You'll know when I've found him, of course."

She didn't say why, but it wasn't hard to guess. If the Shade found her, Rane would feel the pain through the Mark.

"So I'll get some sightseeing done while waiting for you to experience excruciating pain, and just pop over after you've engaged an enemy alone. One who handedly beat you last time, I might add. Should work out fine."

"He only beat me because I was distracted," she replied, anger in her voice. "And I thought you could do more than sightseeing. But, if you need me to hold your hand…" Her shadow smoothed hands along her head and dropped low into the tub. He wondered if she'd submerged herself again to scream beneath the water.

The gentle crackle of fire became a roar in his ears. Rane watched the screen as she reappeared. "He didn't beat you because you were distracted. He beat you because he was stronger than you." He took a breath and let it out. "There were too many, and they were too strong. It isn't your fault. It's not your fault you survived and they didn't."

"They were my responsibility." Pain marred her voice,

hitching it higher. "I have to be stronger than him—than all of them."

"Alright." He quieted the protective rage boiling up in him. Ever since he'd fed from her, his instincts had been going haywire. "Alright, Maiden. If you want to keep your weapon hidden tomorrow, so be it."

There was a rush of water as she rose. He watched her through the hazy, mostly opaque screen as she reached for a towel and pulled it around herself. A minute later, she stepped out from behind the screen, hair stringy wet over her shoulders, and a towel the size of a sheet clinging to her. Perhaps it was a sheet, he thought, because it appeared near-translucent in the places it clung.

An ache of longing burned through him as he admired the way water dripped down her legs. He forced himself to meet her eyes. They burned bright with anger.

"I know you think I'm some helpless human. I'm not afraid of you or them or death."

How stupid. How fascinating.

She stepped closer until she towered over where he sat on the floor, and his gaze locked on the way the fabric clung to her hips and the soft curve of her breasts. The sight tore the same hungry need and urgent arousal he'd felt when feeding on her over a week ago. He wanted to consume her—wanted her pleasure and pain, to drink it like wine. He could tear her apart, if he desired, and it would fill him with bliss. Rane was used to that sort of hunger, having mastered it centuries ago. Not afraid? She knew nothing about him.

Angrily, he let the temptation to tear her flesh from her bones, to hear her screams like music, pass through their link.

"You should be afraid, Maiden."

She flinched. Her foot shifted as if to take a step back but, instead, she took a step forward. Slowly, she knelt until they were eye-level. "I should be a lot of things that I'm not, Shade."

He stared at her, his chest rising and falling in deep breaths. Apparently, there was no scaring her. He closed the link off and smiled. "That makes us a pair."

"Who knew we'd have so much in common." She let the towel sway low over her breasts. He wanted to drag his tongue over the drops of water still lingering on her skin. "It's been a week since you fed." She arched a brow at him. "Are you grumpy because you're hungry?"

Rane's disbelief culminated in a helpless laugh. "Which of us is acting hungry?"

A lovely shade of rose stained her cheeks as she hitched the towel up to her neck. She stood and ducked back behind the screen. "As if I would try to seduce you."

His teasing grin widened. "What was that you said about my horns and moonlight?"

"Let's not forget who started the moonlight talk, Lord Stroud!"

"Well, it was true," he snorted, letting the words drift off. He stretched out on the bedroll and let some of his muscles relax. He lay quiet a few minutes, thinking about her question. It was honestly a surprise that she'd offered to act as his meal a second time. Not that she knew any better. He scowled. When Sinead learned what he'd done with her Maiden, she would make him wish he were dead.

"About the hunger," he said quietly. "I'm grateful you're willing, but I'm not like I was that day." He raked a hand through his hair, around the familiar curve of one horn. "The teleport I used at the castle, and tearing up the other Shade's Mark, those spells were large investments. That's why I ran low so quickly."

She emerged from behind the screen wearing a clean blouse and no trousers. She stepped past him and climbed into the bed. His gaze followed her, eyes locking on the muscled legs disappearing beneath dingy cotton. They were marred with crisscrossing scars and burns.

"Can't heal yourself?" he asked.

"If I could, I wouldn't have needed the Shade's Mark Mr. Nightmare gave me. I can only heal others, unfortunately."

"Inherited? Your mother perhaps?"

"I suppose. I'm not certain… I never knew my mother. She died in the war as one of the first Red Court Maidens."

Ranemir frowned. Everything in him told him to bite his tongue, and he didn't. "What mother leaves her infant behind to go off and die in a war?"

"Fathers do it with ease. Why not mothers? She was Grela. Her people were burned away in the war, and I think hate consumed her."

"And your father?"

"I never knew him either… I suppose one of them had it as a gift. The queen and the High Maidens told me to keep it hidden and to use it sparingly so as not to draw attention."

"What sort of attention were they concerned about?"

"You called me divine when you saw it."

"I did," he said, and kept the rest of his thoughts silent. It *was* divine—a blessing from Attara, the Goddess of First Breaths and Healing. Only Attara was dead and had been for a very long time. He shifted uncomfortably on his bed. How did a goddess bless a child born hundreds of years after her death?

18

TENELE RAIDER

TENELE WOKE WITH a clearer head. The pile of ash and bones had filled her with a need for vengeance, to destroy the monster who killed her sisters at her own expense. Anger and grief made her irrational, but there was more at stake than vengeance could settle.

They needed to find who'd lured the monsters over the wall, who had called the dream-walking Shade, and what the brands on the bodies left behind meant.

They decided Rane would search the town's outskirts. The townsfolk would not take kindly to a Shade stalking their streets, and he wished to be as far from the church as possible. So Tenele went to speak to Father Drowsky.

As Tenele approached the Church's front doors, she heard Father Drowsky's voice echoing off the walls. His sermon floated out in a cadence of highs and lows, a hypnotic melody.

"Have the gods abandoned us?" he asked as she slipped in. He stood behind a stone altar, hands smoothing over the rough granite.

Briefly, the world eroded, and she knelt on that same altar

beneath a shower of moonlight. A gold-eyed Shade stood on an aisle of pale petals sprinkled between weathered pews. His mouth opened into a frightening, wide smile.

Tenele shook her head, and the world righted itself.

Father Drowsky leaned heavily over the altar. "I have asked myself that same question. Even faithful followers of Thar doubt. It is human to doubt. I mean, why wouldn't we? Our village—our kingdom—is threatened by monsters we could scarcely imagine."

Murmurs fluttered up from the packed crowd. The pews were full, the overflow of attendees standing along the walls. With her hood pulled low, she blended unnoticed into the crowd.

"We pray. We beg. We make offerings and sacrifices and still no one hears us. Are we forgotten?" The priest sighed. "Perhaps… or maybe it is more complicated than that. Maybe we haven't given enough. Maybe Thar wants a greater tribute than simple prayers."

"What?" someone asked. "What can we give Him to save us?"

"I don't know," replied Father Casimir Drowsky. "I'll pray that Thar speaks to me again."

Again?

"Is it true that some of the Shadows aren't evil?" someone else asked.

The priest flinched, righting himself. "That's a peculiar question…"

"I heard it from a woman down the road."

Casimir seemed to mull the question over before smiling. "What is good or evil but actions? Do we not see examples of this every day? Just because someone is human doesn't make them good. Perhaps the same could be said for Shadows. Though I haven't met one that didn't yearn for blood."

More questions floated up, but Casimir lifted a hand. "We must break for today. May Thar's Light be with you."

Tenele lingered in the narthex's corner as the townspeople filed out. They were slow in doing so, conversing in the aisle and endlessly shaking hands with their neighbors. She'd forgotten what community could be like, and how some would offer twenty-three goodbyes before leaving.

When the church was mostly empty, Casimir disappeared through a door in the back. Then, a minute later, she was alone in the cathedral. When the priest didn't reemerge, she edged to the door he'd left through. A steady, rhythmic clanking echoed faintly behind the thick mahogany. She followed the sounds of a hammer and chisel through the doors, finding Casimir on the floor, breaking the mortar between stone tiles.

"Father Drowsky?"

The priest jumped. His hammer came down hard and wrong on the chisel, sending its sharp edge into his knee.

"Ahh!" Casimir tossed the hammer away, wrapping his hands over the steel lodged in his flesh. Angry, dark eyes lifted towards her, but the fury quickly melted when he saw her. "Maiden…"

"Raider," she finished for him, assuming he didn't remember the name of the strange woman he'd plucked from the forest and patched up over a month before. "I'm sorry I startled you." She knelt next to him, appraising the wound. "You don't take breaks, do you? Right to work on the next thing. A priest one second, a mason the next. Here, let me see that."

She pried his shaking fingers from the wound. For a second, he resisted her touch before grunting and slumping back along the wall.

"What are you doing here?" he asked, his voice weighted and hard-edged.

"Apparently, scaring you half to death." She wrapped her hand around the chisel. "Take a deep breath."

He did.

Tenele pulled it free. Casimir's growl eased into a painful roar as a river of blood poured from the hole in his trousers. She placed her hands over it, pressing hard to stifle the bleeding. "Look at me." His gaze flicked from her bloodied hands to her face. "Deep breaths."

She kept his gaze, though he didn't follow her instructions to manage his breathing. It rushed out of him in angry puffs of air. A soft white light bloomed under her hands, filling the dark hall just enough to capture Casimir's attention. The tension in him eased as the wound mended and the pain fizzled away. She lifted her hands, admiring the red on her skin before she wiped the blood away on the hem of her cloak.

Casimir drew his knee towards him, admiring the hole in his pant leg and the patched flesh beneath. He reached out and caught her hand as she cleaned it on the dark green cloth, turning her palm up to the candlelight and tracing a finger lightly across her skin.

"You're divine…"

Again, that word. *Divine.* She was starting to hate it.

Tenele shook her head, trying to draw her hand away. "I'm not, really."

His brow furrowed. "That's why…"

"Why?"

He appraised her, hesitating before releasing her hand. "Why Thar spared you."

"That's not why—"

"Why are you here?" he asked. "The last I saw you, you'd left to tell the queen what happened. The border has fallen since. Are you not supposed to be on the front?"

Tenele frowned. "A lot has happened…" None of which she could tell the priest. She stood slowly, looking down the hall of broken stones and slabs. "Seems you've been busy too."

"Repairs," said Father Casimir. "This place… is wrong."

She didn't like the way he said it or how he looked about as if expecting the walls to come to life and devour him.

"I have someone you should meet. He's the reason I'm here. We tracked the Shade who Marked me to this town. He's still here, Father."

Casimir stiffened. "Are you certain? You tracked him?"

"Yes. He's still here, somewhere. The queen sent us to find out about the brands left on the bodies slain at the border—to find their source and, hopefully, whoever called the Shadows over. Do you recall if my Sisters' bodies were branded before you burned them?"

He frowned. "There wasn't much of them left to brand…" He tilted his head and stood, testing his healed knee. "Do you know what it looks like?"

"Some Shade language… My partner wasn't able to decipher it." Tenele went into the room next to them, to Father Drowsky's desk and the parchment and quill laden in ink waiting atop. She sketched the rune from memory, handing the paper to him when she finished.

He took it, frowning deeply. "How did you track him, the Shade who Marked you? Who's your partner?"

A few minutes later, Casimir and Tenele stepped out the back door to the grassy clearing bordering the wood. He went to the well and drew up a bucket of water, splashing his face. "He's near here?"

"Should be here soon, if he isn't already," said Tenele, casting a gaze into the forest for Rane. She was vaguely aware of a shadow crossing over them before a large form dropped to her side.

"Father…" Rane greeted. He looked back at the roof he'd jumped from. "Your church is broken."

Rane was the second person in minutes to announce something was wrong with the church. She eyed it as Father Drowsky dried his hands on his black robes and turned towards them. He stopped when he saw Rane, his face paling, but Tenele couldn't tell if it was fear or not. He seemed… lost. Sick. Shaken. Then, he blinked it all away.

"It's, uh, undergoing repairs. Hopefully, it will be less broken in the future," said Casimir. "Ranemir Stroud, I take it?" The young priest took a few cautious steps forward, eyeing Rane thoughtfully before holding out a hand to him. "Father Casimir Drowsky. I promise, it won't burn if you shake my hand."

Rane eyed Casimir with a sour frown. "The priest is broken, too," he told Tenele flatly, making no move to touch the holy man.

Casimir smiled, flexing his fingers before withdrawing his hand. "Not too broken, I hope. Maiden Raider's already patched me up once."

Tenele chuckled nervously, avoiding the predatory, possessive flick of Rane's gaze.

"Maiden Raider says you tracked a Shade here?" Casimir motioned to his church. "I'm curious how one could do that."

Rane gave Casimir an appraising look. "You've heard of a Shade's Mark?"

"Unfortunately," Casimir replied, casting Tenele a knowing look.

"I ate one," Rane said.

Casimir faltered. "I didn't know such a thing was possible." The priest looked to Tenele. "I hope it wasn't too painful."

Rane sneered. "I didn't chew on her, if that's what you're imagining. I consumed it and threw the other guy out." He looked up at the church. "I thought he couldn't possibly be here, but I just sat on your church and didn't feel a blessed thing."

"Father Peeble, the priest that was here before me, wasn't very holy, if you understand what I'm saying." Casimir stared at the church. "His creatures turned on him, I guess. They found the man torn apart at the edge of town. I'm trying to understand what he did to the church."

"Which is why you're chiseling up the floor?" Tenele asked.

"Precisely. But don't tell any of the townspeople. Chaos would break out if they knew the church had been desecrated."

"How does one desecrate a church?" Tenele asked, looking at Rane.

"Not easily," the Shade muttered. "Not even a horde of shadows should be capable of it. A human would have to use it against its purpose. If the old priest was summoning Shadows from inside, that would probably do it."

"At any rate, I haven't seen any Shades or Shadows. Maybe I've scared them away. You're welcome to look around or stay to see if he comes back. I'm curious though, if you could track him, could he track you in turn?"

"Depends how good he is. If he did get a good read of me, it was days ago. The Mark was our point of contact, and I destroyed it." Rane frowned at the priest. "Your church is barely better than a scarecrow. The Shadows will notice eventually. Have any approached the town?"

"Whitehall has always had Shadows lurking around it. There is a curfew for a reason. It isn't unusual to see one or two, but with the surge over the border things have gotten worse. I'm trying to keep people calm, but it is difficult without a holy site for safety. I've heard a sorcerer lives south of town, and they've been stirring things up."

"Maybe they're also the source of the brands on the bodies?"

"Likely," Casimir muttered. "Maybe they're looking for someone? Though, I'm frightened by the idea of what they want this person for."

Tenele tapped her chin. "Maybe they're the one telling your townsfolk Shadows aren't all evil? Fishing for sympathetic accomplices?"

"And what are your thoughts on that matter?" Rane asked the priest. "I've never heard of a priest trying to shake a Shade's hand."

Tenele eyed Casimir as he smiled unflinchingly at Rane. "I'm a black stain on the church, according to the Archbishop.

Who better to send to a town full of monsters than a priest fascinated by them? I've seen a lot of the world, and I've yet to see anything that tells me humans are any better than Shadows. The only thing that separates us is prayer and power."

Irritation glowed in Rane's eyes. "You're a fool if you believe that. After what happened to the border, this town doesn't need someone who wants to empathize with monsters. It needs an order of priests to reconsecrate the damned church." He spat and looked at Tenele. "I don't believe I just said that."

Tenele patted Rane on the arm, grinning. "I get it. Deep down, you care about people. It's endearing." She turned her attention to Casimir. "He isn't wrong, though. The church needs to be reconsecrated."

Casimir bristled. "I know. I'm not receiving any help. I'll get it worked out on my own. The Church feels their priorities are better focused on more important tasks. There's an invasion happening. They don't care about this dying town or its crumbling relic of a church."

"Invading? Who do people think is invading?" Rane asked.

"Alykith, of course. The town received a raven just the other day. Sinead's been poisoned. She's raving mad from a Shade's influence, and the High Council has given orders to march the army north."

Tenele turned a wary eye on Rane, and his burgundy gaze met hers.

CASIMIR DROWSKY

CASIMIR WAITED UNTIL he couldn't see the Maiden and her monstrous partner before he went back inside the church. He locked the front doors, bolting them with a heavy wooden beam. Then he went to the altar and smoothed his hands along the stone, fingers curling into claws over it.

"Jyn," he called, his voice low and even.

The shadows in the church shifted, their heaviness falling to the floor and fluttering to the center aisle before rising and taking form. The form solidified, growing seven feet tall, golden horns glinting in the oil-flame light.

"Casimir…"

"I told you I didn't want anything drawing that woman here!" Casimir's fist clenched. "Your very presence has brought a Red Court Maiden to my door, which is bad enough, but she brings a *Shade* in the employment of Sinead! You didn't mention him or the fact he purged your Mark from her."

Jyn lowered his gaze.

"Kill them," Casimir said.

"He's quite powerful…"

"More powerful than you? That's not surprising," Casimir seethed. "I conjured you on my first try. You came with such ease, too. As if you'd been waiting for my voice." He paused, digging into his pocket. "What is this?" He opened the parchment and laid it flat on the altar, jabbing a finger against it. "Why are you branding bodies? What does this mean?"

"You'll speak our tongue soon enough," said Jyn. "When you find the door, you'll have all your answers and all the power. Verin will reward you beyond measure."

"Verin isn't here now, and I want to know what this means. What are you looking for that I haven't asked you to?"

Jyn pursed his black lips together. "It is just a brand. Like the tallying of a kill."

Casimir frowned, tracing the lines on the paper. Jyn was not supposed to lie to him, but he could cleverly omit the truth if he wanted, and Jyn seemed to do that quite often. "Kill them or risk everything we've worked for. I need more time to find the door. I'm so close, I can feel it. The voice grows louder and the air…" Casimir looked around, tears in his eyes. "The air hurts."

Jyn tilted his head, confusion wiping his face clean of emotion. "Hurts?"

"Take as many Shadows as you need. A hundred if necessary. Kill them."

"They were ordered to never harm a silver-haired woman, they won't kill he—"

"I want her dead!" Casimir slammed his fist into the stone. He didn't like the way she made him feel. He didn't like her smile or how it cooled the angry fire in his heart. How the air felt less painful when she touched him. She had haunted his dreams every night since Jyn dropped her bleeding, shredded form into his arms.

He thought about her hand over his knee and the warmth of her power flowing through him as she mended his wound. Such an impossibility, this divinity wrapped in flesh. Healing belonged to the gods alone.

He shook his head violently. She was like a memory he'd forgotten. An important piece to a puzzle he'd never finish.

And now she'd brought that Shade here, and the creature fit. Another piece to the same puzzle. He felt familiar. So familiar that when Casimir closed his eyes he saw the Shade as vividly as if he'd known the beast his whole life. A nagging in his soul begged him to pursue and find out why he felt those sensations at all. Instead…

"I want them both dead."

"I *can't* kill her," said Jyn.

"Then compel some small-brained, vicious human to do it for you," said Casimir. "You whisper and men obey. Find someone to follow your silver tongue."

"You don't want—"

No. No. No!

"I do." He had to cut it out. This feeling. This irrational *compassion*. A need, not for flesh, but soul.

Jyn stiffened before bowing low. "As you wish." He seeped back into the shadows, inky lines following the cracks in the floor.

"And Jyn," Casimir sighed, resting against the altar. "If they make it back to this town, I will shred your tether like parchment. I will leave you to wander, mad and alone, until you crumble apart."

"Yes, Master," was Jyn's reply, hollow and fading as he left.

20

TENELE RAIDER

"HER MIND WAS poisoned by a Shade," said Tenele, frowning as they walked. "So that's what the High Council is telling people to cover their treachery."

Ranemir shook his head. "I don't understand the point. What is their motive for overthrowing her? Because she wanted to send me to the border? Who's the leader in this, the High Council or the Church of Thar?"

Of course a Shade would point blame towards the Church.

He stopped short. "We're running out of time. In a week or more, the army will reach the closest border with Alykith and almost two hundred years of peace will end."

"Maybe that's what they want? Easier to line their pockets with gold when the treasury is open for war," said Tenele. Still, nothing felt right. "Sinead killed a fucking god, Rane. How did they overtake her? How are they keeping her down? Do you think…"

"She's dead?" He pursed his lips together and began pacing. "I would know."

"Would you?"

He nodded. "She's my master. She's my tether, whether you're wearing that pretty bracelet or not. It is just an extension of her power. I think, if she were dead, then it wouldn't keep me in line anymore."

Tenele shivered. Was that all keeping Rane from a murderous rampage, from being as twisted and broken as the first Shade to Mark her? A little gold chain and a ruby?

He seemed to notice her response and eased towards her, a predatory look in his eye. "Does that worry you?"

"What would you do if you were free? Join your brethren in destroying us?"

He stood over her, a shadow blocking the sun. Wind tossed his black hair around his beautiful silver-gray face. "I haven't known freedom for as long as I can remember. My memories of anything beyond this servitude were burned away. I can't answer your question truthfully." His hand slid over her side, curling around his Mark. There was something possessive in the way he did it. "Freedom or not, this—you—are mine. You're protected."

Mine. Her pulse jumped at the word.

"Until you become bloodthirsty? Will I be protected then? The other Shade had no issues torturing me, and he Marked me."

"I am not the other Shade," Rane seethed, moving past her to the path.

Tenele watched him walk away. "We need to find our proof. Maybe we can head the army off and stop the war before it begins."

Rane looked over his shoulder. "Or maybe we need to face

Alykith. They broke the truce. The monsters coming over the border are of their doing, and we are hindering the inevitable."

She shook her head, unwilling to think that her mother had died for a temporary pause in slaughter. "We should follow up with the lead Casimir gave us. Visit the sorcerer or whoever that's south of the village. Maybe we'll find our answers and be rid of this mess."

"Fine," said Rane with a shrug. "That's all we have."

Athena was still recovering from their recent abuse of her back, and requesting two horses was too suspicious to risk for a single woman. They made their way on foot southward. The wooded area rarely opened for a clearing, but there was a path of sorts worn into the ground. Even hermits needed supplies.

They followed the trail, and sure enough, they came upon a hut. "I'm a little surprised," muttered Rane as they approached. "The priest didn't seem like the sharpest fork in the drawer, so I had my doubts."

Tenele smirked, heading for the door. "He's kind… Though a bit strange, I suppose."

The hut was small with moss-covered wood shingles covering the roof. A little garden sat off to the left, brown and weed-riddled in the brisk air. Knotty wood posts held up the front porch while homemade chimes and wards dangled from the rafters. The steps groaned beneath Tenele's feet.

She ducked under a doll made of straw and string and… human hair, grimacing as she avoided it. Glancing once more to Rane, her knuckles rapped against the old door. The Shade pulled his hood up over his head, down low over his face. Best to keep the element of surprise until they knew who they were dealing with.

The door slammed open. "Who the hell is it at this hour of the morning?" snarled a rusty voice. The woman standing in the doorway was perhaps in her late forties with long, tousled apricot hair. She wore nothing but a towel wrapped around a body that was toned, but not slim. Looming in her doorway, she squinted out at them like the mid-day sun was a terrible offense.

"Good morning," said Tenele, glancing inside. "We heard a rumor, so we're following up. I'm Maiden Tenele Raider. This is…" Tenele glanced back to Rane. "This is General Ranemir Stroud. We're hunting Shadows and heard someone in the forest was conjuring them. Would that be you?"

"A Maiden? Are you announcing your virginity or are you one of those Red Court lot?" Loud seemed to be the woman's standard volume. The look in her eyes transformed from irritation to intrigue as she took them both in. "And a general, is it? How felicitous. The spirits believed you might arrive today."

"Did they?" asked Tenele, arching a slender brow. "Well, how fortunate." She called to Rane. "The spirits have foretold our arrival!"

Her green eyes settled again on the woman. "I'm sorry, I didn't catch your name."

"Reagan." She smiled and offered a graceful bow. "Reagan of the Wood."

Reagan's eyes fell to Tenele's wrist, and she leaned down to inspect the golden bangle around it. "I see. Yes. You were right to come here when you did." She turned into the house and beckoned them brusquely. "Come in. Oh, but leave that sword out front. My darlings won't like it." Her gaze dropped to the weapon belted at Tenele's waist.

Tenele hesitated, disliking the idea of leaving the sword outside. But, if it came to it, Ranemir was more than capable of holding off any assailants. She obliged, unbuckling the belt and leaning the sword against the porch railing before slipping into the house. Rane considered the sword for a moment before lagging behind her.

The interior was more or less what one would expect from looking at the outside. Books crowded unmatched shelves, and tables were strewn with all manner of strange objects. A music box, several broken milk pails gathered in a ring, feathers, puppet dolls, chests crowded with dozens of tiny drawers. Next to the doorway, a large cage housed two black, skittering creatures. They were vaguely rabbit-like in build, but their legs were too long and their muzzles too broad. Their angry chittering sounded anything but herbivorous.

"Oh, don't worry about the babies. They get nervous around clients."

In the center of the room, an area stood out a bit from the rest. On a large oval carpet sat an old oak desk. Reagan swung into a black chair behind it with practiced ease and gestured to the two chairs in front. Her earnest green eyes met Tenele's expectantly. "Sit. Ask your questions."

Tenele sat. "Have you heard the border fell? That Shadows and Shades are invading?"

Reagan closed her eyes and gave a sage nod. "The spirits have indeed been restless." She stroked her chin. "More and more have come to me, seeking protection. We do what we can, but even my babies and I must ration our power during such times." The woman turned her gaze to Rane, who had strayed toward a bookshelf and begun examining it. "But you two are not looking for protection."

"We seek who is drawing the monsters here," said Tenele. "We heard it was you. If it is…" Tenele drew a dagger from her boot and set it on the desk.

Reagan stared down at the dagger for a moment before a hand shot into her drawer, rummaging for something. Rane's muscles drew taut, waiting. The woman's hand re-emerged with a jeweler's magnifier. She leaned over the dagger and studied it with zeal. "Hm. It's nothing special," she said. "But you two seem like good, honest folks. This won't cover the cost of a dark summoning, but there must be something I can do for you." She glanced between them and grinned. "A talisman for love, perhaps?"

"Oh, no amount of power will make him love me," said Tenele mournfully. She held a hand to her cheek to block Rane's view of her lips. "I'm not his type."

The Shade pretended not to hear, rolling his eyes.

"Perhaps I could interest you in one of my lesser Shadows, for protection in these dangerous times," Reagan gestured to the cage by the door. The creatures flailed like a pair of bottled wasps. She leaned forward solicitously. "If your pockets aren't that deep, I also perform fortune readings and a demon-warding massage."

"Demon-warding massages?" asked Tenele.

"Yes. I use sacred Ongorian salt and lavender oil. It's strong against unwanted spirits, and also excellent for posture."

"Uh-huh," said Tenele, nodding. "What if I could pay you to conjure a Shadow? The sword you made me leave outside is over two hundred years old. It was forged by Phillip Krump, the most famous blacksmith to the Church of Thar. It is blessed, tenfold. Would that buy me a Shadow of some note? Maybe even a Shade?"

Reagan cupped her chin between her thumb and forefinger, humming. "A sword like that would indeed be worthy of my work. But a summoning of equal value would be against my code. My babies are one thing. They're perfectly safe, and affectionate toward me, as you can see." Reagan gestured to them, and the creatures chittered angrily in their cage. "But what you're asking would require twenty… no, at least twenty-five percent of my actual power. It could raise something terrible. I would lose all face in the professional community."

Tenele stared across the desk at the woman, whose green eyes bored into her with a placid expression. "Twenty-five percent, huh?" Tenele reached for the dagger on the desk. "So much power." She curled her hand over the hilt, lifting it and leaning against the desktop with her elbow, twirling the dagger point in the air so it came dangerously close to Reagan. "How unfortunate. You aren't who we're looking for."

"Ah, a skeptic," she sighed. "It is so hard for the normal to perceive the divine, especially when they're in such a hurry all the time. But you won't kill me." Reagan smiled, touching the tip of the knife with a lazy finger and pushing it away. "For one, I could read you the moment you arrived. You're searching, struggling. No mother to guide you, no allies you can trust. You left your weapon outside and sat down in my home. You've already decided not to kill me. Besides, I've seen the face of the one who will end me, and it's not yours."

Tenele's jaw tightened. "And how is it you saw this?" Her hand was still on the dagger, tight around the hilt.

"One of many tools of my trade." Reagan leaned over

slowly, conscious of the blade pointed at her, and scooped a palm-sized item from the shelf behind her. She turned and showed them a clamshell compact. "This mystic mirror will show the holder the true face of their death. If they won't die violently, of course, it will simply show their own face."

"Your own face? How convenient," muttered Rane.

Reagan shook her head. "Not at all. If anything, it makes suicides especially confusing."

Tenele took the compact from the woman, slipping the dagger back into her boot. "Well, let's see if you really are a sorceress," she murmured, popping the golden mirror open.

Rane leaned over her shoulder curiously, seeing Tenele's thoughtful expression reflected in the mirror. "Looks like a normal compact to me," he scoffed, taking a step back. "We've wasted enough time here."

Tenele stared at the mirror as Rane slipped away. She tilted it up and down, side to side, and all she saw was her own reflection. She'd almost tossed it back to Reagan when the image changed.

The mirror's surface shifted, rippling before her eyes like a disturbed puddle of water. Her reflection shifted into a familiar charcoal-skinned Shade with gold eyes and gold horns. He smiled. Suddenly, the mirror was a lot larger in her hand, growing until it swallowed the room. The Shade towered over her. Panic became a vise around her chest. But then he rippled, as the mirror had done before, shifting into a new monster— one more beautiful than a night sky.

His skin was midnight blue, speckled with starlight, his hair a fine black mist. His eyes were a multicolor array, two dying stars in blackened orbs. Wrath marred his gaze, but just as he reached for her, he became something else. He turned white gold and lovely—too perfect and precise. His skin was a mine of wealth, his teeth opalescent stones. His eyes were a clear sky, his smile a vat of burning acid. A hand thrust into her chest, wrapped around her heart. She glanced at the wound, then back to the god with his hand in her chest.

Now, instead, she saw Rane.

Tenele jerked, feeling as if she'd fallen asleep on her feet, and snapped the mirror shut. She tossed it onto the table. "Parlor tricks," she spat, but gave Rane a wide berth as she passed.

"Maiden?" He glanced at the mirror she'd thrown down, then headed after her.

"Didn't like what you saw, eh?" Reagan chuckled as they left. "And not even a donation in payment?"

RANEMIR STROUD

THE SHADOWS IN the cage leapt and chittered at Rane as he passed through the door. He snarled, and they flattened back against the corner of the cage, suddenly silent. "Noisy brats," he muttered, following Tenele back into the midday light. She'd grabbed her sword and was heading stiffly back toward the trail by which they'd arrived. He sighed, lengthening his stride to keep up with her. "What was that about?"

"Nothing," she said, shifting away from him as he approached. She stopped short in the road, cutting her gaze to the cabin. "She's batty. It was a parlor trick. It got under my skin. Worst of all, we came all the way out here for nothing."

He glanced over his shoulder while they walked. "There's no way she conjured those two shadows. If she had used her own power, they'd be servile to her. She must have caught them somewhere and caged them to show off to those who wouldn't know any better." He slowed to a stop. "If I had my hands on them, I might be able to track them to their true master. It may not be the mage we want, but if she caught them nearby, it's possible."

"Alright," said the Maiden, nodding. "Two Shadows, coming up." Tenele marched back to the hut, up the steps, and through the door. "We'll be taking this." Her hand curled over the cage and lifted the small creatures.

"Not so fast," said Reagan from her perch behind the desk. She held a loaded crossbow aimed steadily at Tenele. "Thought you might come back. Set my babies down. I'd hate to shoot a Red Court Maiden."

Rane slid in front of Tenele, eyes glowing purple beneath his hood. "Just a loan, Reagan of the Wood." He took an ominous step toward her. "Or would you prefer to ask your loving pets who summoned them?"

The woman flinched and shot. Rane snarled and summoned up a writhing shield the color of old blood. The arrow crushed against it and fell to the floor. The impact of magic crashing against matter rattled the bookshelves around them and blew back his clothes, exposing part of his face from beneath the hood. He dropped the shield and stalked to Reagan.

"Shade," she breathed, dropping the crossbow from her trembling grip. "Shade!"

"Some great sorceress," muttered Tenele, turning with the caged, tiny Shadows and heading out. Rane chuckled, following her. The Maiden dropped the cage in the dirt outside.

Rane circled around it, unclasping the lid before scruffing one of its frightening inhabitants like a kitten to coddle. The tiny beast hissed and writhed under his grip, its long nails seeking purchase on his arms. He curled his lips back and made a fierce, inhuman sound directly in its face. The Shadow went stiff and still.

Tenele reached up and stroked a finger at the back of the creature's head. "It's sort of cute," she said. "Cuter than you."

"Words hurt, Maiden." His eyes closed, and he held the Shadow firmly between both hands. He sent his senses out along his nerves, through the creature, and back into himself. Power tightened, spiritually sewing the two of them together. He focused his awareness down to the feeble hum of the creature's magic and allowed it to fall into a resonant pattern with his own.

The creature's link to its master was like a shining strand amidst the duller thrum of its mind. Rane closed off the rest of his senses and tried to bring one thread into focus. The link turned brighter, clearer. He slowly, slowly wove up the string of energy. If he tracked his way through without getting lost, he'd be able to sense the creature's master on the other end.

"Do you feel that?" asked Tenele, faint and distant. Rane was vaguely aware of the shudder beneath his feet but was too intently focused on following the thread.

Even behind his eyelids, the world darkened around him, like a shadow passing over his soul. Blinding pain ripped through the side of his chest. Something was wrong, and it had nothing to do with the Shadow he held. He choked out something unintelligible and scrambled to untangle himself from his own spell. When he finally tore free, he found himself midair and crashing through the front wall of Reagan's hut.

What in Verin's name?

Rane dragged himself from the ruins of Reagan's study, shoving a bookshelf off like a worn blanket.

Reagan was on her feet, backing away, and no longer

holding the crossbow. Rane wiped blood from his eyes, blinking to bring things back into focus. As the dullness cleared, a discordant barrage of warning bells in his head replaced it. Power. The air was full of power, and it wasn't his.

Rane took stock. He was injured—he wasn't sure how badly yet. And Tenele—

He lurched to the hole he'd made in the wall. "Maiden!"

She stood amid Shadows, hacking at the largest one. The beast stood as tall as the house and almost as broad. A writhing mass of tissue, eyes, and teeth made up its body, giving the appearance of jumbled carnage crammed into one hulking monster. Worst of all, each individual gaping mouth littering its form had its very own terrible, pitched cry. It had no discernible face, only a gaping maw of multi-layered teeth.

The creature screeched at her, dragging its heavy arm across the earth and knocking her legs out from under her. She hit the ground hard but rolled to her feet almost as quickly. Behind her, the trees shifted. Wood popped and groaned ominously before limbs crashed to the ground. A horde of monsters dragged themselves into the midday light.

He had never seen this many Shadows—at least, not that he could remember—and there were far too many for a human to handle, no matter how well trained.

The massive Shadow Tenele faced off with drew its arm back for another swing.

Adrenaline jolted him forward. Rane charged out for her, his feet scrambling for purchase over the splintered wood around him. He launched up behind the attacking beast and tore a long claw across its throat, nearly severing its head. It gargled out a scream, treelike arms falling limp at its sides.

Rane shoved the body out of the way and maneuvered to Tenele's side. By the time he put his back to hers, they were nearly surrounded.

Blood kept getting in his eyes. He threw the hood back in disgust and scrubbed a hand over his face. "Are you hurt?" he demanded, trying to get a good count of the creatures approaching them.

"No," said Tenele, pressing her back to him. "But the odds of staying that way look slim." She stiffened. Fear rippled through the link between them so strong he could taste it like wine on his tongue. Her hand grasped hold of his. "He's here… The Shade."

Rane's hand tightened over hers, feeling an irrational need to hold on to her, to protect her. The Mark was a potent thing, and feeling the Maiden's fear of the other Shade made him territorial of her.

Then, confusion replaced her wave of terror. "He's gone."

Rane turned and followed her line of sight. The Shadows surrounding them seemed to be gathering, rallying after seeing their ally slain. A few were bipedal creatures with warped, black bodies, but most were animalistic. Their slick, dark forms shone like tar in the sun. Rane scanned the pulsing crowd of monsters but saw only lesser Shadows. There were no Shades among them, least of all the one they sought, and all were waiting for some kind of signal.

"He's still here somewhere…" Rane trailed off.

The horde went still, frozen eerily like a painting. Seconds ticked on. Then, the painting shattered in a burst of motion. Beasts squeezed in and separated him from Tenele. One second she was next to him, the next she was some ten feet away, her holy sword gleaming with each desperate strike. The sea of monsters swallowed Rane up in teeth and claws.

Fangs latched onto him like hooks, mouths sucking hungrily at his flesh. The pain didn't impress him. Very little could, these days. Rane growled and drove foot-long claws like knives into the closest Shadow, cutting through it like paper and drawing out a watery scream. He grabbed it by the muzzle and hurled it into the group behind it. They tumbled and scattered, chittering and screeching.

He kept moving, slashing his way through the throng of bodies. The violence was intoxicating, but the strangeness of the attack made it harder to enjoy. And he wasn't usually worried about an ally.

Where was Tenele? Was she their target? He doubted this many Shadows caught the scent of his power and showed up for dinner. If they were as interested in the Maiden's flesh as they were his, she was dead already.

Rane spared enough focus to reach through his Mark and assess her condition. It was difficult to separate which sensations were his and which were hers amidst the chaos. *Maiden*, he called into her mind.

Here, her voice rang through the link. Even the thought sounded winded. Her sword's glint, like a light in the dark, shifted and disappeared into another body. If he couldn't find her, he could find it—even if only for a second.

Agony that wasn't his own spread up his arm like a bolt of lightning. More pain arced through his shoulder, near his throat. Panic traveled through the link, along with the distinct fear of being swallowed. Drowned.

Then, it stopped. The pain settled into a burning

aftertaste, followed by the strange sensation of being airborne and landing hard on her back. Something had just rejected her like spoiled food.

Rane shook his head to clear the sympathetic connection.

An enormous pair of jaws crunched heavily on the back of his neck. Rane's anger rose up, hot and vicious. He reached back with both hands, took hold of the Shadow's maw, and ripped it in half. More teeth tore at him, burrowing into his guts.

Impertinent whelps. He needed more room. His clawed fists tore the hungry creatures away from his flesh and flung them so that they crashed through the others.

Rane called power to his fingertips. It pulsed and coiled, demanding an outlet. He smiled wickedly and dropped to a knee, slamming his palms into the ground. He hurled the energy downward and out, pounding into everything around him hard enough to damage organs. He might have done more, but Tenele was nearby, so he kept the attack tight. The yard went shock-silent as everything within a few yards of him lost the air from its lungs, including himself.

There wasn't time to recover. They were dazed, but it wasn't a killing blow for most of them. The air was full of blood, and it excited him. As his adrenaline surged, he threw himself at his enemies, fast as a nightmare, claws hungry.

A second later, Tenele was back at his side, cutting down stunned Shadows with her teeth bared. None of the creatures went at her nearly as viciously as they did him. Was it her Mark? Were they fearful of it? They didn't seem to fear Rane, so the Mark should have been useless.

They could have torn her apart like a paper doll—she

should have been dead by now—but most snapped and clawed at her like puppies playing with a bird. Even when she drove that menacing, burning, holy light into them.

Though not all were so hesitant to rend flesh. The smaller shadows swarmed her body like frenzied piranhas. Rane moved so fast it was hard to get a look at how Tenele was faring. Every time he stole a glance, her damned sword was so bright it cost him several precious seconds of eyesight. He didn't stop moving, but they needed a different plan. The sword was better than her bare hands, but it was a poor tool for fighting small enemies up close.

He hesitated as a gritty substance sprinkled over him like sand, itching faintly at his wounds. All around him, the Shadows screamed like something was ripping them apart. The smaller creatures attacking Tenele fell to the ground entirely, spitting and tearing at themselves.

What?

"What's the matter? Don't like salt on your food?" a female voice shouted triumphantly. Rane turned to see Reagan standing on her ruined front porch, holding a basket full of what looked to be salt balls. Her victorious expression faltered when she saw him staring back.

"How are you… I salted you! Even if you're a Shade, you should…" she trailed off in horror.

Rane raised his left wrist to his lips and licked his skin curiously. "Oh, I'm a new model." He smirked at her darkly. He wouldn't waste the advantage she had given them.

The Shadows wailed with a different brand of pain as Rane took full advantage of their frenzied state. He lunged into a bear-sized shape near him, tearing into its already burning skin. The enraged beast twisted and clawed at him with a giant arm, throwing him to the ground like a rag doll. Darkness ate at the corners of Rane's vision, his body telling him he'd had enough. He needed to cut his losses, get the Maiden and escape.

No. He wasn't some weak, pathetic, second-rate Shade. He wasn't losing. Not against a bunch of half-formed *weaklings*. He just needed to be faster. Fiercer.

"Go stand by Reagan," he snarled to Tenele, his world narrowing to just his anger and his enemies.

TENELE RAIDER

TENELE'S LIPS CURLED, but Rane was gone before she could argue with him, disappearing into the mass of black ooze, scales, and power. They needed to leave. *He* needed to leave. She felt his hunger through the Mark like insects scurrying beneath her skin. He was bleeding power and blood, and he wouldn't last if he kept going as he was. But stopping him would be impossible…

Wait.

No, it wouldn't.

Tenele thought of how angry he'd gotten when she used the tether to command him last, when she'd made him kneel before the patrons of that inn. He'd nearly crushed her wrist and threatened to torture her to see which one of them broke first. He'd terrified her to the point where she'd forgotten all about her power over him. She could stop him from killing himself.

He'd hate her. But at least he'd be alive to finish this.

Tenele charged back to Reagan, and not because he'd *ordered her* to. "How much salt do you have?" she asked.

"Whatever's left, get it. Now!"

Reagan looked more than a little pale. She was nearly green, and so transfixed by what was happening in her front garden she barely looked away to answer. "I do a lot of baking," she muttered. "What do you have in mind?"

"Just get the salt!"

Reagan passed the basket of rolled salt to Tenele and stumbled toward a cabinet in the corner. Tenele tossed the rest of the salt pouches at the screaming Shadows while Reagan dragged out a large glass jar. "What else do you need?" she asked as she took it back to Tenele.

"Hold this," said Tenele, hesitating before handing Reagan her sword. She pressed it into the woman's empty hand as she took the jar under her arm. "Now, listen. Grab hold of the back of my shirt. Stay close no matter where I lead you, and don't drop that sword. Do you understand me? If you lose that sword, the Shadows will be the least of your worries."

Reagan answered by grabbing the hem of Tenele's shirt and steadying the sword at her side. It was a heavy weapon, and Reagan needed to cradle part of the hilt against her upper arm to hold it one-handed. "Please tell me you're not planning to go into *that*," she said, eyeing the writhing mass of Shadows destroying her front lawn.

Tenele smiled. "Close your eyes if you don't want to know where we're going." She popped the lid off the jaw and pressed forward, slinging handfuls of salt at the creatures and carving a line towards Rane. When one Shadow got too close, she doused them with a fist of salt and kicked them away. She moved fast and prayed Reagan could keep up.

When they reached Rane, Tenele hurried around him,

emptying the jar on the earth in a messy circle and shaking what remained out on the creatures left inside. "Ranemir Stroud! Get us out of here. Now."

The Shade's opponent collapsed into a shrieking heap. Rane froze mid-attack, a bloody arm still raised to strike. He jerked his attention to Tenele, towering over her. There was nothing human in his fire-lit eyes. "Maiden—" he tried to growl. "No."

"None of us are dying for your pride!" she shouted over the screeching and snarling. "Back to the inn. Now!"

His long fingers closed hard over her shoulder, squeezing until it hurt. It wasn't hard to inflict pain; a Shadow's teeth had torn into her, shredding skin like paper. Blood soaked her blouse and rushed over his grip. Reagan yelped as his other hand clenched around her upper arm. For the second time since meeting Rane, black power sucked Tenele momentarily out of existence. A freezing cold ate through her, darkness spotting her vision.

When they came out on the other side, they were in the room at the inn, and all her wounds felt worse than before. Her shoulder throbbed angrily within his grasp, and her arm was on fire. Rane's hand left her shoulder the second they were solid again. He dropped to his knees and lurched forward onto his hands, wheezing for air that didn't seem to make it to his lungs.

"Rane!" she sank down next to him, shaking hands grasping his shoulders. "Shit. You pushed too far." Her mind raced, coming to the only definitive solution to his problem. "Reagan... step outside."

"Look, I don't know who you are, but I'm not leaving a human alone with *that*," Reagan panted, pointing Tenele's sword at the Shade.

"Both of you… get out," Rane rasped.

Tenele growled and pulled her shirt loose from her trousers, unbuttoning the top. "You need to feed, you stupid creature. That's the only thing going to make this better." She opened the crimson stained shirt, hissing as she pulled it from the shredded flesh at her shoulder. She curled her finger beneath his chin, trying to lift his head to look at her. "Come on… let's go."

When he raised his face to look at her, his eyes were black. It was the darkest she'd ever seen them.

The wall separating them through their carefully controlled link was crumbling away, baring more and more of his sensations to her. Starving, mind-splitting agony shot through her body. Her heart convulsed, searching for power that wasn't there.

He looked like he wanted to curse her, but the glare was all he managed. "I'll… kill you," he choked out. She couldn't tell if he was trying to threaten her or warn her.

Tenele doubled over, nails dragging against the wood as his pain became her agony. She'd nearly fallen onto her side now, leaning heavily onto her arms. "Don't make me order you."

His expression darkened, and he collapsed next to her, wrapping his hand around her neck, dragging her to him.

"Stop!" Reagan shouted, aiming Tenele's sword within inches of his eyes.

The Shade winced, and the hunger buzzed up into a roar. His hand shook around Tenele's throat. "Shit," he hissed miserably.

"Woman, whatever you're doing, it's a bad idea," warned Reagan.

"Step outside, Reagan," said Tenele, feeling strangled by his grip. "This is none of your concern."

"No," said Rane. "Stay there." He pressed his forehead to Tenele's, taking a steadying breath. "I'm not safe. This isn't safe. I don't want your pleasure, Maiden. I want your agony. I want to taste it in your screams."

Tenele shuddered.

I won't. I won't. I won't hurt you… his mind gasped into hers. A mantra. A prayer. A hope. She wasn't certain if he was saying it to prove it to himself or to her.

He pressed his lips to her collarbone, dragged his tongue along the rough edges of her wounds. She hissed, and his hand tightened over her, locking her to the floor.

She couldn't move. Couldn't escape. If this went sideways, she was doomed, and he was too hungry to pull back or tame his monster… She could use the tether around her wrist, command him to stop, if it came to that. She hoped it didn't.

His grip on her continued to shake as he squeezed his other hand over her waist, enclosing her Mark. *His Mark.* Power flared up inside her, a heavy wave of relief and need. It was everything and not nearly enough. The Mark grew warm beneath his hand, unbearably hot all the way to her center. Bliss washed away the pain in her body, as if he'd smoothed a healing hand on every tear and scrape and ripped hole. Desire bled through the link between them, lust and territorial need.

She groaned, hands curling in his filthy shirt. *This* was why she wanted Reagan out of the room. She didn't want an audience to this sin—her sin with this monster.

"Go," hissed Tenele.

"Not on your life. I'm not letting him kill you!"

Rane's fingers dug harder into her side and his mouth sucked at her chest in long, deep draughts. Power flowed between them in a rapid, sensuous rush. It was dizzying. It became a relentless storm building too fast, and he hadn't even slid inside her yet.

"Reagan," said Tenele, barely able to speak. "Turn around."

It was hard to tell if the woman obeyed, but the sword drew away from Rane's face, and Tenele was vaguely aware of footsteps moving to the corner of the room.

Rane didn't bother sparing what was left of her ruined shirt. He dragged a claw across the front of it, shredding the fabric and dragging it open. His hand loosened from around her neck, fingers tracing lines along her ribs, down to her trousers and belt. He tore them like paper, hard hands grasping her legs and parting them.

"What the fuck?!" cried Reagan.

"GET OUT!" screamed Tenele.

Rane snarled, "Turn around or get out!" He lifted his head, dull eyes locking on the woman in the corner. She turned, pressing her forehead to the plaster.

Rane's gaze slid back to Tenele, dark irises boring into her. He reached a shaking hand to her face, trembling fingers brushing along her cheek and down over her lips. She shivered, and a predatory growl rumbled out of his chest. He kissed her, fingers curling in her silver hair, his body flattening out against hers.

His kiss was hungry. Devouring. His hands stretched over her body, running over cuts and scrapes and bites and she felt the sting of pain only for a second before it became ecstasy. Sharp nails trailed the inside of her thigh, dulling the closer they got to the warmth between her legs.

His hand trembled as his fingers slipped into the wetness at her center. She moaned, legs falling open in invitation.

A spark of color lit in his eyes, and the edge of a smile curled his lips. He lowered them to her chest, his tongue gliding over her skin, tasting flesh and blood. Teeth grazed her, and she arched against his probing hand.

"Stay turned around," Rane warned Reagan with a purr.

Ready? His voice echoed into her mind.

Tenele nodded.

His hand slipped away, and she whimpered at the retreat, only to feel his length press against her, promising.

I'll be gentle…

There was something oddly comforting in the promise, even if it came from a monster. He slipped into her. Filled her. She clutched onto him, holding for dear life as he drove in with a brutal hunger. Each barely restrained thrust slid her against the wood floor, along the blood pooling beneath them. Was it hers? His? It was slick and warm along her back.

She didn't think much more of it. She couldn't. All she knew was the feel of him inside her, cold fire burning in her belly, bliss and delirium breaking her mind open like a drug.

Maiden…

Her fingers knotted in his shredded clothes, grasping on as he drove her into the floor and into heaven all at once. "Rane…"

Yes…

Her voice rang out, each strike deep within driving a

sharp moan from her lips as she treaded towards paradise. Tenele curled a leg over him, dragged him into her and held him fast as a wave of pleasure burned through her, leaving her shaking beneath him. Ranemir's hips bucked against hers, and he grasped hold of her waist, rising to a rhythm that became maddening, incomprehensible rapture. A low, monstrous growl rumbled out of him as he buried into her a final time, and he sank over her, heaving air against the heat of her neck.

His lips trailed tenderly across her skin, over her jaw and cheek and up to her temple. He nuzzled his face into her hair before drawing back to look at her, eyes burning burgundy— though not as bright as their first encounter. He had taken enough to gain his sanity, but not enough to sate his hunger.

Ranemir slipped out of her body and mind, and she felt the ache of her beaten form anew.

"You okay, Maiden?" Reagan demanded, her voice sounding miles away. "Hey! Say something."

Tenele's lips parted, her mouth dry. "I'm… fine," she murmured. She was just tired. Like the last time.

"You've got a screw loose, girl." Footsteps pounded back toward her from somewhere in the room. A flash of metal crossed her peripheral vision, and then a scream of pain along the side of her face. No… it wasn't *her* face. The pungent smell of burnt flesh filled the air, along with an inhuman howl of agony from the man above her.

"Stop!" Tenele shouted, slinging her arm out blindly toward the blade. "Don't hurt him." She felt his burn on her face. The pain mingled with bites on her arm and shoulder, tiny scratches littering her skin. She didn't have the strength to move or slip out from under him to rid them of the intruding woman.

Even if she had the strength, she didn't want to move. She wanted to stay close to him… Why?

"Maiden," breathed Rane. She felt him rise onto an elbow. Testing fingertips moved from her shoulder to her chest and stopped just beside her throat. The link between their minds slammed shut. "Maiden, can you see me?" he demanded.

Tenele blinked, gaze darting around the room. She saw his shape against the warm, evening light falling through the window. She saw his glowing eyes in the shadow of his face… But she couldn't really see him anymore. Her hand reached out, fingers brushing along his face and into his hair, over one of his horns. "Yes," she lied, voice heavy in the air.

"Okay. Okay, don't try to move." He was quieter than she was used to. She felt him shift next to her, moving away from her hand. An arm slipped under her shoulder, lifting her up so he could support her back. His other wove beneath her knees, and then she was in the air.

The room's crude straw mattress felt like a cloud once she was lowered into it. "Get water," Rane murmured, off in another direction as he dragged the blankets over her.

"*You* get it."

He didn't argue. A second later, she heard the door open and click shut.

Tenele didn't want him to go. But he was gone before she found the energy to protest. Her hands fumbled down her arm and touched the stinging ache before trailing back to her chest and shoulder. It couldn't be too bad.

She closed her eyes. She was just tired. Like the last time.

"Red Court Maiden," crooned Reagan as she came to

stand by the bed. "What the hell just happened?" She reached down and touched Tenele's injured arm, tilting it enough to inspect.

"He's fine…" Tenele jerked, inhaling a sharp breath of air and trying to pull her arm free. "Stop."

Reagan released her slowly and sighed. "Stop acting like that was normal." She peered at Tenele sideways. "Or *is* that normal?"

"He's my responsibility," Tenele muttered. "I have to keep him alive."

The door opened again. Rane let himself in without knocking, carrying some rags, a spare bedsheet, and a pitcher of water in his hands. He and Reagan exchanged a sour look before he walked past her to Tenele's bedside.

The Shade pulled up a stool next to her and sat. He dipped a rag in the pitcher and held it near his lap. "Some of these can't wait," he said meaningfully.

Tenele frowned, closing her eyes tight. "Fine."

She wanted whiskey. At least that would dull the pain. Her brain felt fuzzy from helping Rane, but her nerves were raw now that his power had slinked back into him.

He leaned over her, but then paused. "Reagan of the Wood, I forgot to get a drinking glass."

The witch crossed her arms at him.

"By the bar downstairs—"

"Yeah, yeah," the woman scowled, throwing up a hand. "Try not to kill that poor girl while I'm gone."

Rane waited for the door to click shut, then reached for Tenele's arm. He lifted it lightly over the edge of the bed with one hand and squeezed water from the rag over it. His movements were slow, surreally gentle. A sharp contrast to the cold glint in his eyes.

Tenele hissed and almost drew her arm away. After a minute, she adjusted to the stinging sensation and relaxed against the bed. "How are you feeling?"

"The wounds will close quickly now, other than the face." He didn't meet her eyes as he spoke, and his words came out mechanical and withdrawn.

Tenele snorted. "Should have sent her out."

"I didn't want to risk… If I had lost control, if I had gone towards pain rather than pleasure, you would be dead." Rane set her wrist carefully back on the sheet and stood to get salve from their pack. He returned, coating his fingers in the waxy goop. With a steady touch, he eased the ointment over her broken skin. Then, his claws slit the borrowed sheet into strips that he used to wrap the wound on her arm.

"I should be dead. With that many Shadows… I should be a lot worse than this." She thought of her sisters, all torn apart in seconds while she was left alive. "Is there something…" *Wrong? Poisonous?*

Rane looked down at himself. His clothes had been torn half off, and the flesh underneath had received the same treatment. "They were favoring you for some reason. You should be dead," agreed Rane. "The shoulder next." He lifted her, guiding her up right against the headboard.

She mulled over a hundred questions, none of which she was ready to ask. "Must be the hair."

He leaned forward to inspect the wound on her shoulder. "Maybe in the moonlight," Rane muttered, his breath fanning against her skin. The frost in his expression didn't match the humor in the words.

He placed a towel against her side and squeezed cold water over her shoulder with the rag. The water washed away pink. "I'll investigate the reason tomorrow."

She tilted her head back, appraising him. "They were there to kill you. How did they know where to find us?"

"The only people who knew we were there are the priest and the witch." He glanced at the door. Reagan was taking a while to come back.

"Maybe someone followed us?"

"Perhaps you got your wish. You said you wanted to lure them out." Cool fingers carefully circled around the deep valleys of her bite. "This needs stitches."

She clenched her eyes. "Of course it does," she said, lifting her hand to their pack. "Side pocket. How good is your sewing?"

"Adequate. Don't expect any embroidered flowers." He rose and rummaged for her kit.

A tap came on the door, and Reagan poked her head back in like a curious squirrel. "Oh, good. No one's dead," she muttered, coming in backwards with a huge tray filled with a fresh pitcher, a cup, a loaf of bread, and some cheeses. She set it down on the table next to Tenele, grimacing at the blood-tinted water and stained rags. "Gods. Your shoulder is a disaster."

Rane glowered at the woman. "Is there a reason you're still here?"

"Is there a reason, he asks!" She threw up her hands. "Says the one who put a hole in my wall. I have an evil-cleansing massage client coming tonight. Tell me, how am I supposed to

cleanse evil with a Shade-sized hole in my cottage? It's deface-
ment of property. How do you intend to compensate me?"

The Shade pinched the bridge of his nose between his
thumb and forefinger. "At least go get a different room."

"Oh, now you want a different room? After doing that
while I was in here? Well… Who's paying?"

"Us," he sighed.

"And room service?"

"Get out!"

Reagan's mood grew chipper instantly. "I suppose it'll do
for now." She clapped her hands on her thighs and stood, going
to the table and ripping off a hunk of bread for herself before
heading to the door.

Rane rubbed at his temples and sat beside Tenele. He
opened her kit and began threading the stitching hook without
a word. His eyes stayed carefully away from her neck as he
leaned in to make the first stitch.

Tenele stiffened, fingers knotting in the covers. She'd been
stitched back together on countless occasions, but the pain
never lessened. She once imagined it as something one might
grow used to, if experienced enough, and yet she never did.

The Red Court Maiden tilted her face away and set her
teeth tight together. As the needle went in, she made a tight
sound in the back of her throat. She hated the feeling of thread
passing through flesh, a painful tickling sensation she couldn't
snatch away.

"How many of those do you think I need?" she asked,
exhaling.

His hand paused. "It's a complicated wound…"

She grimaced and pressed into the headboard. "Alright,

on with it."

The needle pressed against her, sending an instant throb down her arm. It started to pierce forward, then stopped.

"After what you just allowed, we might as well," Rane said, almost under his breath. He set the needle down and lowered his face to her shoulder, gaze rising to hers. He hovered there, as if watching for a sign of protest.

"Might as well?" She didn't shy away, but weary curiosity kept her focused on his eyes and the way he hovered over her wound.

He reached for her good wrist and drew it up, closing her hand around one of his horns, just above his hair. "Push me away if you want me to stop," he said to her. He lowered his lips to her wound and slid his tongue over it in a slow, wet line of pressure. He was *licking* her. Pain throbbed down her arm, chased by a sense of lightheadedness.

For a second, she thought it would make her sick. Then, a fuzzy sensation claimed her skin where he'd touched her. The pain gave way to a slow pulse of pleasure. This time, there was no draw of power. He wasn't feeding on her, but there was a seductive way in which he ran his tongue over the wound again.

She should have shoved him away. There were a hundred things Tenele Raider should have done. Instead, she let him take away her pain.

A relieved breath escaped her lips and the tension in her body subsided. She relaxed beneath his touch, so very thankful that Reagan of the Wood was not there. A soft, sad laugh fluttered out of her. "I'm the worst Red Court Maiden alive."

Then Tenele laughed a little harder. A little sadder. She

was the only one left alive. Her eyes burned.

Rane paused, drawing back enough to meet her eyes. "Now, now. We don't know that." A thread of his usual teasing humor reached his expression for the first time since they'd gotten back. "Maybe you're an excellent Red Court Maiden, and I'm just the worst Shade."

She smiled. "That does make more sense."

"Don't rush to defend me or anything," he said, pulling a stitch tight. She hadn't even felt it go in. He closed the stitch with a surgeon's knot and passed the hook through the next point, falling into a precise rhythm. He'd definitely done some sort of sewing before. She imagined him needlepointing in the dark of his endless solitude between lovers and Sinead's company. "I could have finished those Shadows," he said. His burgundy gaze didn't rise from his work. "They were weak. They're just going to come back, and we still don't know who summoned them."

Tenele thought about how weak he'd been after porting them away—how shredded he was from the fight. He really thought he could have won? "We'll be better prepared for them next time." She tried to look at his handiwork, but tilting her face to see brought it closer to his. "That's an interesting trick you've got... changing pain to... something else."

He gave a rueful smile.

Her fingers uncoiled from around his horn, brushing against the texture curiously before her hand returned to her lap. "How long does it last?"

"Maybe another minute or two," he said. "I'll work quickly."

Tenele nodded and grew quiet, letting him finish. She had

a host of prying questions to ask, but she'd rather him finish before the pleasant feeling wore away. He was nearly done when the sharpness of pain began to bleed back through. She stiffened and pursed her lips. She'd been through worse for longer and, to be honest, she wasn't certain what she would do if he licked her again.

Fortunately, he was through the worst of it. He tied off the long run he'd been working on and moved on to some of the smaller punctures at the edge of the bite, placing single sutures on the deepest of them. As he cut the last thread, he leaned back and surveyed her calmly. She couldn't make heads or tails of what was going on behind those strange eyes of his. Finally, as if there had been no intermission at all, he turned and lifted the salve jar. "And the rest? Would you rather do them yourself?"

Tenele swallowed. "You're gentle," she said, green eyes meeting his. "For a Shade."

He reached out and touched the edge of a small bite over her breast. "This should not have happened. I should have ported you away and finished the fight..."

"And when you finished, when there was nothing left to give, who would see to the end of this? Me? Alone?" She laughed. "Of the two of us, I'm the most expendable. Sinead..." She faded off. They still didn't know Sinead's fate. The country was in the hands of war-hungry nobles who wanted them dead or religious zealots eager for another holy war with Verin's worshipers. What were they fighting so hard for if Sinead were gone? What was a Red Court Maiden without a queen, or a Shade without a master? "You're the best chance Ighten has against whatever has brought those creatures here. Don't let pride and recklessness doom us all."

"That should be my line," he said. He dunked the rag in the water and smoothed it over the skin of her chest, washing away the blood. "I'm a science experiment in her basement. What would happen to that woman if she lost you? You're her daughter."

"A broken heart is easier to mend than a destroyed kingdom. If Sinead wasn't prepared to lose me, she would've given me an easier job." Tenele looked away from him, out the window to the darkened sky.

REAGAN OF THE WOOD

IT WAS NOT hard to forget about the Shade and his warden once Reagan settled into the comforts of the inn's bed. How long had it been since she last enjoyed the luxury of bedding other than straw-filled pillows?

Then there was the food. A few minutes ago, she'd pulled a cord on the wall, and a moment later a waitress appeared to take her order. She'd never imagined a place so upstanding lurking in Whitehall, but then again, she rarely made the venture into town.

The room was small but cozy, adorned with richly carved furniture, a roaring fire, and a copper tub. Instead of bathing, she nestled herself into the covers of her bed and stared at the fluttering glow of firelight along the plaster ceiling.

It almost lulled her to sleep, but the shadow of a large male figure with spiraling horns stepped up to block the light.

Reagan opened her mouth to snap at the Shade, but the one standing on the side of her bed was nothing like the other.

The witch decided, very promptly, that she was dreaming. She had to be. Because why else would there be a Shade in *her* rooms?

This one had charcoal skin and eyes like liquid gold. His horns were gold too, and she was half-tempted to tap them to see if they were *real*, something she might be able to cut off and pawn. After all, this was a dream, and she was very good at changing her dreams into what she wanted them to be.

"Reagan of the Wood," the Shade said, his voice a velvet caress that sent a shiver of pleasure through her.

"Y-yes?"

"Would you do me a favor?" he asked, slipping closer to the bed. He knelt on it, and she swallowed hard as he came to straddle her hips. He took her chin in his fingers and bent so low his hair fanned like a cage around their heads.

"Depends on the favor," she admitted, and he chuckled.

"You know what you saw between those two was wrong," he said. "It is an affront to your god, Thar."

Reagan scoffed. "Not my god."

"He is now," whispered the Shade, and, suddenly, Thar was. Yes, of course. Her god.

"An affront to Thar," agreed Reagan.

The Shade leaned forward, his lips brushing her ear as he spoke. "A regiment of soldiers will enter this town in two days. They will bring inquisitors with them, seeking the Shade and his jailer. Turn them in. Expose them. Expose *her*…"

Reagan shivered and nodded. "Of course…"

"Thank you, Reagan," the Shade said, pressing a kiss to her lips.

Then, she was staring at the projected glow of fire on the ceiling, the strangest tickle on her lips and a distaste for the Red Court Maiden in her mouth.

How dare she do *that* with a Shade?! It went against all the Holy Laws she knew... None of them she could name specifically. But she knew it was wrong. She knew it down to the fiber of her bones, and she would make sure the inquisitors knew too.

TENELE RAIDER

NIGHT BLURRED INTO day. Tenele slept restlessly with Rane feeding her medicated tea to keep the pain down. By mid-afternoon the next day, the pain had ebbed to a slight ache, and by nightfall it was gone completely.

Tenele dragged herself from beneath the blankets and gingerly stepped behind the paneled changing screen, stripping the tattered remains of her clothes and unwinding the bandages from her arm and chest. The wounds, at least every wound Rane had licked, were mostly healed. She replaced the bandaging around her arm, where he hadn't applied his apparently magical saliva, and stretched. A dull soreness clung to her muscles, and weakness turned her joints hollow. She still needed to recoup some of the blood spilled, but otherwise she felt… better than she should.

"Can you bring me my bag?" she called over the privacy screen.

Rane gave no response, so Tenele peeked out and found him hunched in the wingback chair near the fire, black hair sweeping over ash-gray skin. He looked exhausted, likely still weakened by the magic he'd spent fending off the hoard and spiriting them away to safety. He'd taken enough from her to stabilize his sanity and bloodlust, and not much more.

Well...

She touched her nearly healed shoulder. He'd also done that.

Tenele gave herself a sponge bath, removing the remaining dried blood and dirt from her skin, then tiptoed to her bag and drew out her last remaining blouse, pulling it on over her head. She sat on the edge of the bed, watching the firelight dance along Rane's skin.

The day before flashed into her mind, a searing vision of blood and pleasure. It should have revolted her, and instead she felt herself responding to it. She rubbed her palms over her thighs, as if she could rub away the feeling, but that only reminded her of his fingers trailing along her inner thigh. Parting her legs and...

She growled, low and irritated.

Tenele bit her lip and stood, stepping towards him and looking him over. His wounds were mostly healed from what she could see of them, but his skin was dull gray instead of the luminous moon-dust color he usually sported.

This wouldn't do. Especially if someone was out to kill them.

The thought of bedding him again should have repulsed her. He was a monster—a beautiful monster, but a monster nonetheless. And his kind was the reason her entire order was gone.

She exhaled a tight breath from her nose. She could tell herself all the rationalizations she wanted. That she needed him alive. Healthy. That of the two of them, he was most likely to survive and finish what Sinead asked of them. But the truth was, Tenele wanted to feel him inside her again. She wanted his hands on her, that overwhelming bliss burning her inside and out.

What did that make of her?

What would it mean for her when this was over? When they'd found their sorcerer and stopped a war and freed a queen? What would be left of a Red Court Maiden who fucked a Shade of her own free will?

Well, she thought, that was for Future Tenele to decide.

She reached out and took his chin gently in her fingers, lifting his head ever so slightly. It startled him awake. His dull eyes flashed open, and a hard hand grabbed her wrist. The grip was nearly bone-breaking, but a second later he realized who stood before him and it relaxed—strong… but not painful.

"Maiden," he said, gaze drifting down to her feet and back. "You look rested."

"And you look like shit," she replied, taking a step forward and pressing her knee into the chair's seat, next to his hip. His brow arched as she did the same with her other leg, coming to rest in his lap.

He pursed his lips and sighed. "Perhaps you were right," he said. "Maybe you are the worst Maiden to ever live."

"You aren't healthy enough for another go at whoever attacked us," she pointed out.

"And you aren't lively enough to feed me," he said. "You're light. I can barely smell you."

"Do I smell good?" she asked, smiling. "What of me that you can smell?"

His jaw tightened, and he released her wrist. "You're suicidal."

"Yes, and I'm not wearing any pants."

He made a low sound, lifting his head to stare at the ceiling. She hated how much she liked the look of his throat, the flutter of dark lashes as he stared down his nose at her. Tenele nipped at his jaw, reaching up to curl a hand around one of his horns and pin his head back. She leaned over him, staring down into his dully glowing eyes before she pressed her lips to his and kissed him with all the longing she felt blooming between her legs.

He responded, his lips melding with hers, his tongue dancing along her lips and teeth. Hard hands slid up her thighs to her hips, beneath the blouse and to her waist. She felt his fingers dance around his Mark, the others trailed featherlight circles across a breast.

She didn't want this to be fast—a quick meal to make him whole. She wanted the slow, torturous languor of lovemaking. To feel all he had to offer her, and to show, in turn, her appreciation of it.

His hands drifted over her until they reached beneath her, cupping her bottom and thighs. Then he came up out of the chair with an unnerving grace and crossed the room, depositing her onto the bed with ethereal ease. He was over her, lips pressing against hers, dancing along her jaw and down her throat.

The Shade kissed his way over her blouse, nudging the collar open as he went, and then further down, pushing the fabric above her navel with his nose. His tongue dragged along her ribs and down over the Mark on her side just beneath them.

Her breath hitched at the sensation, his mind opening to her until she felt his desire like molten fire in her veins.

She wanted his mouth between her legs, his tongue dragging over her clit.

"Be careful what you ask for, Maiden," he whispered against the divot of her hip, reading her mind like she'd shouted the thoughts out loud.

She sat up on her elbows, locking eyes with him as he nipped at her skin, sharp canines pinching the flesh enough to entice but not hurt. His hand slid between her legs, fingertips running through her warm, wet folds, brushing against the sensitive bud of flesh within. She gasped, and he grinned, tsking her. "Maiden… So ready to sin, are you?"

His thumb brushed along the bud between her legs. She bucked against the touch, focusing on that, rather than his question. Then, his fingers slipped inside, and she forgot the question altogether.

His breath fanned over her belly as he rested his cheek on her hip, his gaze focusing on the fingers thrusting into her until her back arched and she dug her nails into the sheets. But just as she was set to cross the threshold into bliss, he drew his hands away.

Tenele flattened against the sheets, a disappointed growl rumbling in her chest. Again, she propped herself on her elbows, watching him sit up and slip those fingers into his mouth. She lost her breath.

"Ask it," he said, nudging her legs apart with that same hand.

"Ask?"

"Ask me for what you're thinking, Maiden." He grinned so dark she trembled.

Tenele clenched her teeth, feeling her cheeks burn at the thought. She wasn't normally a shy one, but he wasn't her normal bed partner either. There was something submissive and wrong in this, in asking a *Shade* for what she wanted.

"Taste me," she said, and he chuckled. Not exactly a request, but he seemed all too happy to oblige.

His hand slid up her leg, over her hip and to the Mark on her waist as he lowered himself between her legs. The moment his hand touched the Mark, his tongue ran over her sex. A soft, startled cry escaped her as pleasure—far more than was justifiable for the action—arched through her. She flattened out along the bed again, moaning at the feel of his mouth on her.

His hand tightened around her waist, over the Mark, and a protective, territorial sensation accosted her.

Mine, it said, and she should have hated it. She should have told him to stop, that she belonged to no one, least of all a Shade, but the thought of being *his* sent a shiver through her.

Mine, she thought as she ran a hand over her belly and tangled it around the curve of his horn. A possessive snarl rumbled out of Rane and his teeth grazed her sex. She shook, arching and clutching the horn as a wave of pleasure sent her crying his name.

His tongue lapped at her, a ceaseless, merciless claiming until she quivered and begged him to bury himself inside her.

"Ask," he growled against her flesh.

She huffed, clenching her eyes and dragging her hand across her brow. *What was she doing? What was she doing? What.*

Was. She. Doing? "Please... fuck me." His tongue slid from between her legs to her belly. She covered her head with her arms as he glided up her body until his lips were on her neck. His hands curled around her wrists, and he gently pried her arms from her face, pressing them to the covers at either side of her head. She hissed at the pain in her injured arm, but he didn't relent. In fact, the hiss sparked a flare of light in his already glowing eyes.

"Don't be ashamed of asking for what you want, Maiden," he said, pressing a kiss to the burning scarlet on her cheek. "Especially if what you want is me."

He guided her hands together above her head, pinning them to the bed with one of his own. She tugged against his grip, a moment of terror racking through her at the strength behind his seemingly effortless touch. Again, she was trapped. If this went sideways...

"It won't," he said.

Then, he opened his connection to her, and she knew she was safe. Pinned. Captured... but safe. His want caressed her soul, and she sighed at the swell of him pressing against her opening, the tightening promise of it.

He slid in, burying deep with a single fluid motion that drove a low groan from her lips. She met his eyes, those blazing purple-red orbs of power. His skin had regained most of his luminosity, which meant the foreplay had been enough pleasure for him to be mostly sated. This... this was for fun.

This was for her.

He rocked against her, driving out and in until the bed cracked against the wall in a steady, sharp rhythm. He kept her hands above her head, and she loved it—being unable to escape the predator above her, the beast she should fear instead of inviting inside her. She tangled her legs around his hips and he growled, thrusting brutally until the line between pleasure and pain tangled together in blissful union, until she thought it would splinter her apart.

That's it, Maiden, he demanded into her mind. ***Scream for me.***

Her hands fisted, knuckles whitening, toes curling. His pleasure burst into her mind, washing over her like the scalding lick of flame, and then it was both of them—both of their sensations traveling through the link, until pleasure compounded on top of pleasure and she was shattering. Breaking. Screaming.

She came and he with her, and the world whited out.

RANEMIR STROUD

"I HAVE A name, you know," murmured Tenele. They laid on their sides, finally naked after a second round of "feeding." Her bare, warm back pressed against his chest, the tickle of her silver hair along his cheek. His fingertips trailed her side, over the curve of her hip and along her thigh. He grabbed the sheet and drew it over them, using it to hide her from himself as much as to keep her warm.

She sounded half-asleep, and the fact she was still conscious baffled him. He'd taken all he needed in their first round, and she'd almost dozed off then. But his mind had buzzed, as it always did after sex because sex for him was not a draining act. Their connection had been so strong, his whirling thoughts had passed between them like wordless love letters, stirring her awake and fueling her desire for another go.

He'd been only too happy to oblige, and bent her over the pillows, clawed hands clutching her hips, driving them both into oblivion. He had not fed on her then. That had been for the pleasure of it.

He clamped the connection between them shut and did

his best to quell the craving to have her a third time. She needed rest—all the rest she could get.

"I said, I have a name, you know," she repeated, her voice faint and dreamy.

"Hmph," he grunted into her hair. "Perhaps I will use it one day."

She nodded off a short time afterwards, leaving him to the ever-darkening room. The fire was going out, the last bit of embers burning and begging for fuel. He glanced over at it, and a log near the hearth lifted of its own accord and placed itself over the coals. A gust of unfeeling wind blew over it, sending the coals piping red and angry enough to light.

He settled back down with her, resting though he didn't require it. His arm slid around her, his hand wedging between the mattress and her side to cup the Mark on her waist. Rane felt… compelled to be near her. To hold her.

He didn't like it.

And, then again, he liked it very much.

He held his Mark.

His.

She belonged to him, his mind said, and he knew it was lunacy. For fuck's sake, she was a Red Court Maiden. Tenele Raider had sworn an oath to kill his kind, and, if that was not enough to dissuade him, she was divine—gifted the healing arts by a dead goddess.

He'd lived a long time, and much of his memory—all right, all of his memories—were mush. He couldn't recall what it meant to be blessed by the gods, but he knew he was in trouble. Fucking her might as well be like fucking holy water. Though it didn't burn in the least to be with her. And, he thought, even if it burned a little, he might still enjoy it. Rane groaned, both aroused and irritated at the thought.

He'd had every manner of flesh—male, female, and some between—but he had never been with anyone who made him feel…found. It had to be the Shade's Mark, he told himself. That was the only difference in all the other meals he'd ever had.

The Shade sat up, looking at her peaceful, sleeping face. She was… beautiful. He had seen many beautiful women before, and yet, right now, she seemed the most beautiful creature he'd ever laid eyes on.

Must be the hair, he thought with a soft smile, shifting a lock of silver from her cheek. She stirred a little at the touch, and he held his breath, feeling her warm bum brush along his need. It swelled, aching to have her again.

There lay another difference compared to all his other meals. He didn't linger with his food afterwards, didn't ache for them, didn't long for them. He'd never had the temptation to drag them back into bed, almost immediately, for another round—especially not for the sheer enjoyment of it.

And he wanted her.

Craved her.

His cock pressed against her, hard and ready. Gods, he was a mess. Rane kissed the Maiden's shoulder, reluctantly drawing his hand away from the Shade's Mark, and slipped out from beneath the sheets, going to his bag tucked near the wingback chair. He dragged out a pair of pants that didn't have a thousand tiny cuts in them.

He fell into the overstuffed chair, watching her sleep until it made him too restless to sit still. His gaze kept drifting to the bandaged arm, and the faint, remnant traces of wounds he'd licked clean and sewed shut over a day ago.

She should be dead—dead as dead could be.

He donned a shirt and grabbed his tattered coat from the floor, leaving the room through the window. He could work off some of his pent-up energy by figuring out why the monsters wanted the last Red Court Maiden alive.

Rane snarled at the church. Even though he knew it was broken, the idea of stepping inside it made his insides twist into knots. However, it was their only clue to what was bringing the monsters over the wall. He had tracked the Shade here, after all. He needed to look inside.

He entered through the back door, the one the priest had used to visit him by the well two days before. The inside lay in shambles. The floor was ripped up, stones chipped and broken. A layer of dust coated the wood molding along the walls. Rane only made it a few feet inside before his instincts screamed at him to throw himself out the window, as if he were on fire.

He wasn't, though. He felt no discomfort, no pain, nothing he should have felt as a Shade inside a church. It was as desecrated inside as it was outside, which should have been comforting, but it only unsettled Rane more.

Something terrible had happened here.

He followed the hall towards the double doors leading into the main cathedral. Dull, early morning light poured in through the stained-glass windows, coating the pews and flooring in a twinkling carpet of color. Rane walked along the outer wall, taking in each window as he passed until he stood before the large mahogany doors marking the entrance. Then, he headed down the center aisle, towards the altar.

Halfway to it, he stopped short, overcome with a blood-curdling sense of familiarity. His gaze swept the space before locking on the stone altar and traveling to the statue of a multi-winged, opalescent, faceless Glory perched behind it, tandem wings curving protectively over the shrine.

Rane had never seen a real Glory. He wasn't certain they actually existed. Likely, they were the Church's way of dealing with the fear of Shadows and Shades.

Don't worry, little flock. Thar will send a Glory to save you from the nightmares in the dark.

The faceless creature looked down towards the altar, drawing Rane's gaze to it as he approached. The faintest scent of blood filled the air—so faint, so minuscule, only someone like himself would be able to pick up on it. The scent lingered in the stones at his feet, in the veining of the altar—new blood, old blood, and very, very, very old blood.

This church had been desecrated long before Father Peeble or Father Drowsky tended it. Rane felt a little disap-pointed, because he'd begun to suspect the young, strange priest as the mage they were looking for. But from what he could tell, the Church had been a problem for hundreds of years. It was shocking, really, that it had gone so long without being reconsecrated.

"You shouldn't be in here," a voice called to Rane. The Shade tore his gaze from the altar to Father Drowsky standing in the back doorway. The priest stood half in the room and half out, as if he wanted to run the other way.

"Why? Are you hiding something?" asked Rane,

smirking.

Casimir shook his head, frustration glittering in his dark eyes. "No, I mean, you *shouldn't* be in here. I thought I'd managed to reconsecrate it…"

"You didn't use enough holy water," said Rane, casually leaning against the altar as Father Drowsky found the courage to step into the room. "Truth be told, *Father,* I don't think there's any saving your church. Whatever severed it from Thar happened hundreds of years ago."

Father Drowsky came to stand at the altar, leaning on it as Rane did, meeting the Shade's eyes. Desecration or not, something was off about this fucking priest.

"So, it has nothing to do with the Shade or the monsters you're looking for? The ones leaving those brands on the bodies at the border? A coincidence?"

Rane flashed a dangerous, toothy smile. "I didn't say that."

"Where's Maiden Raider?" he asked, but his gaze didn't leave Rane.

"Resting. We were attacked and she…" Rane didn't want to admit she was injured. That she was weak. He was aware, then, of how he shouldn't have left her alone when she was too exhausted to hear anyone come into the room… He opened his connection with her, feeling along their link to the peaceful rhythm of her heart in slumber. He kept it open so he could watch over her.

"Was she hurt?" asked the priest quietly, an edge of concern in his voice.

"No, but it was exhausting."

"Who attacked you?"

"A horde of monsters and our little friend we tracked."

Rane thought about the golden-eyed Shade, and then he understood why the cathedral felt so familiar. He turned his gaze on the pews, on the carvings they bore along their backs and arms. Then he looked down at the altar he leaned against.

Tenele's dream—the nightmare the other Shade trapped her in had used the stone altar and pews like props. Rane smoothed his hand over the rough granite where the Shade had bled her in the dream. Why would he use this place?

"Something wrong?" asked Father Drowsky, reaching out and brushing his fingertips over the back of Rane's hand. The Shade flinched away, as if burned. He wasn't uncomfortable with a man's touch. He enjoyed the company of men as much as women, but he didn't want a priest touching him. The last time a priest had touched him, he'd been chained to a slab while Sinead's little minions poured blessed metals into wounds and studied his reactions to them—or a lack of them, if the day was going well.

"There's something wrong with your church, Father," said Rane. "More wrong than either of us realize, I think…" Rane paused as he felt a blast of fear burn through his link with Tenele. Then he felt the crack of pain along his jaw, and another along his ribs—hard enough to snap bone. He doubled over at the sudden bite of sensation, taking a ragged breath he didn't need. After all, *he* wasn't the one hurt.

"She's in trouble," said Rane, eyes going wide. *Fuck.* He'd left her alone…

"The Maiden? Where?"

"The inn," said Rane, and he was gone.

He reappeared inside their room, finding four Ighten soldiers lurking in the space with her. One stood by the partially closed door behind him; one by the fireplace, admiring Tenele's sword; and two by the bed. One of them was draped across it, his hand tangled in Tenele's silver hair so that her face was forced to look at him. The other held her face-down, his armored forearm braced against the back of her neck. His pants were slouched around his knees, thighs bare to the air, hips bowing towards her.

Rane was through him in a second, ripping him off Tenele, and plowing him through the oak mantle and chimney until he was wedged within. Fire ate up the soldier's lowered trousers and bare legs. A shrill, pitched scream filled the air. Rane held him there a second longer, watching hungrily.

The guard closest to the fire swung Tenele's sword at him, but Rane ported out of its reach and behind him, slashing across his throat with footlong claws.

The one still on the bed released Tenele's hair and charged Rane just as Father Drowsky barged in. The priest froze at the door—at the sight of the shrill, screaming soldier trapped in the fire, the partially decapitated one on the floor, and then the naked woman dragging herself off the bed. Tenele stumbled to her feet. In an instant, Father Drowsky removed his robe and wrapped it around her, helping her steady her balance.

Rane might have been concerned by the way the priest held her—how he took her face in his hands and admired the blood on her lips. How his fingers stroked her hair to soothe her... How rage bloomed like a quaking furnace in his black eyes. However, the site of Tenele's blood burned the feral need to punish those who had harmed her into Rane, and it was all he knew after that.

His.

She was his, and they had hurt her.

It didn't take but a minute to dispatch what was left of the useless mortal soldiers in the room.

"There are more downstairs," said the priest. "Inquisitors and…Gold Clerics."

Tenele's eyes widened, turning on Rane. "You have to go."

Rane snarled, stalking towards them and reaching for her. "Then, let's go."

The door broke open, a surge of power blasted into the room so strongly it sent them all to the floor. The air felt like shattered glass against Rane's skin, and he sat up just as a Gold Cleric swooped in. The hooded, robed man had a coil of holy magic writhing around his hand. It wasn't enough to kill Rane, but it sure as hell would hurt.

Then, just behind the first Cleric, another one appeared, carrying a gold-laced staff humming with magic.

Fuck.

"Go!" screamed Tenele. He met her wild green eyes, felt the fear for him punch through their link at the same time her order took hold. "Go and don't return. I'll find you."

Rane roared at her in the same instance his brain obeyed, porting him away to a place he didn't even know he was going. It was wherever the Maiden wanted him to be, an unspoken command laced within spoken words. Then he was in the forest, standing in the shattered ruins of Reagan of the Wood's home.

26

TENELE RAIDER

TENELE'S HEAD COCKED back, a blast of pain cutting across her cheek. Her skull throbbed, white light exploding behind her vision. She let her head stay where it was, resting over the back of the chair, as she took in a ragged breath and tasted blood.

"Where is he?" the soldier snarled, grabbing a handful of hair and forcing her head up right, forcing her to look at him.

"I don't know," she murmured, barely meeting his eyes. "He doesn't tell me where he goes. I'm not his keeper."

"You quite literally are," said the Gold Cleric tucked into the cell's corner. He nodded to the chain and ruby bauble around her wrist. "Did you send him away? Where to?"

Tenele spat. "I told him to go, and he did. I didn't order him. He saw you lot coming after him and buggered off."

"It's your funeral," snarled the Cleric as he slipped out of the cell. "Come, Vastar, Father Drowsky seems to think he might talk some sense into her."

Vastar, one of Ighten's famed guardsmen, released the mass of hair he held and backed away from her. She nodded to him, mouthing "fuck you" as he departed. Even before getting pummeled in the face, she had never liked him.

Tenele slipped out of the chair as if she were melting away from it and crawled to the corner, to the straw bed waiting for her, and curled into it, tugging the cotton gown they'd given her over her freezing feet.

A few minutes later, Casimir appeared at the cell door, and the guards keeping watch let him in. She lifted her face towards him and he froze, his dark gaze taking in her battered appearance.

"Just tell them what they want. Is he worth dying over?" He came closer, kneeling on the stone near the pallet of straw. "Tell them."

She shook her head. "They're lying. He didn't poison the queen's mind. She sent us here, and they—the High Council, the Church, someone—betrayed us. Betrayed Sinead. Rane is the only one who has a chance of stopping this. Of stopping those things…"

"They're just monsters, Tenele," said Casimir. "Something brought them here, yes, but I doubt it was a conspiracy against Queen Sinead."

She shook her head. "I don't know how it all fits together, but it has to. It has to fit."

"It doesn't," whispered Casimir, resting a hand on her shoulder. "War with Alykith is unavoidable, whether they sent the monsters here or not. It is the nature of these two kingdoms. They will always be at war because their ideals are too different. Turning the Shade in will not make you a failure. It will save your life."

She laughed, smearing the blood from beneath her nose

with her sleeve. "Haven't you heard?" Her voice cracked. Tears burned her eyes. "I'm a harlot. I broke my oath as a Maiden of the Red Court, and it's worse because I broke it with a Shade. I've committed a great sin, Father Drowsky, and will pay the price of it if I give up Rane or not." How they'd found out was beyond her.

"And what is that price?" Casimir asked, concern creasing his brow.

"Lashed until death," she said, her throat hoarse. "Tomorrow morning. Still trying to imagine how many lashes, exactly, it takes to kill someone."

His hand tightened on her shoulder. "Tenele…"

"You see, Father? I'm dead either way."

Casimir's hand withdrew. "Did you?"

Tenele's gaze rolled up to him. "Did I what?"

"Fuck a Shade?"

The use of the word from his lips sent a jolt through her. Such a frank way for a priest to speak. Her cheeks burned at the pleasant memory of Rane's body draped across hers.

Casimir didn't wait for her to respond. There was no judgment in his eyes. No anger or disgust. Only placid, contemplative stillness. "Do you love him?"

Tenele laughed. "I barely know him." She hated the tears in her eyes, the feel of them on her cheeks. She reached up and wiped them fiercely away. "I kept him alive. He was—is—my responsibility."

"Then tell me," said Casimir. "Tell me where the Shade is and I will tell him of your situation. Maybe we can get you out of this… together."

She laughed, dragging her shoulder out of his grasp. "Very

good," she said, cramming herself into the corner and away from him. "You're the good patrolman in this situation, I take it? Come to soften me with your sympathy? Be my ally and cater to my fears of death? Well, fuck you. I'll take the lashing now if you'd offer it."

He arched his brow. "I'm not here to snitch on you."

"Then what are you here for?" asked Tenele, hard gaze locking on him.

He appraised her, dark eyes roaming her bruised face. His jaw tightened, and he stood. "A hundred lashes," he said, stepping towards the door. "That's how many it usually takes to kill someone."

CASIMIR DROWSKY

CASIMIR SLAMMED THE heavy church door behind him, turning to drag the wooden beam into place to lock it tight. He could already sense Jyn's presence above the crossing, in the rafters' shifting shadows. As he set the beam in place and turned towards the apse, Jyn dropped down from the ceiling, landing in a sitting position across the altar top.

"You failed me, Jyn," said Casimir as he approached the Shade.

"Not entirely," replied Jyn. "The woman will die tomorrow. I will find the other soon. I have done as you asked, just not in the time in which you wished. Soon, it will all be over."

Casimir frowned. "You say that as if it foils our ability to find the door."

Jyn's gold eyes flicked from one of the stained-glass windows to him, but he said nothing. A murderous growl rumbled out of Casimir. "I hate your riddles! Who are they? Really? Why do I feel as if I know them? Both of them."

At first, it had been the woman. Casimir thought his interest in her had been because she was beautiful and he enjoyed beauty, when he had the time to appreciate it. Then, she left, and it was as if she'd carved her name on his bones. He couldn't rid himself of her, and he wanted to. He wanted to be rid of the feeling she sparked in him—the cut of loss and ache of longing.

Then the Shade appeared, and Casimir had felt this painful clawing at the back of his mind. Ranemir Stroud's face was a beautiful sorrow, a nagging visage screaming to be remembered, and Casimir had felt as if his heart had been ripped from his chest.

He didn't understand. All of it had to be a trick of his mind. He didn't like not remembering and, judging by the pain he felt, he didn't want to. Especially when it seemed neither one of them remembered him either.

Jyn sighed. "I can't tell you, Casimir. You must find the answers on your own. It is a test."

"A game!"

He nodded. "Yes, a game."

Casimir shook. "I don't want to play it anymore. Tell your god to get out of my head!"

Jyn tsked him like he was a child. "Verin has led you here, to this moment, so you might fulfill your destiny, Casimir. I can't tell you why you feel as you do, or what purpose it has. It's against the rules, remember? In the end, their place in this will determine if you fail. Heed the voice in your head."

Casimir sneered. "The voice inside my head? The one that talked non-stop until we arrived here? Not even the dreams will tell me what to do. I only dream of her!"

Jyn's lip curled with a snarl. "Perhaps tonight you will dream of the other and have your answers."

Casimir lifted his hand, twisting the gold ring on his middle finger with his thumb. "Kneel."

Jyn slipped off the altar and cracked his knees against the church floor. Casimir stepped forward, his boots clunking against the stone until he came to stand before the Shade. "Why can't you tell me?"

"I can't. Just as I can't kill the silver-haired woman. It is beyond the powers of my tongue. Open the door, and you will have your answers."

"If I were to order you to tell me?" asked Casimir.

"I would go mad before I answered," whispered Jyn, gold eyes flashing.

A harsh knock sounded on the church door and Casimir turned his gaze towards it. "Get out of sight," he ordered the Shade, and Jyn returned to the rafters.

The knock sounded again a second later, followed by a fierce beating that didn't let up until Casimir threw the heavy beam from the latch and dragged the mahogany doors open.

A Gold Cleric stood on the church steps, his white hood pulled tight over his head, the veil concealing most of his face. Casimir stiffened as the Cleric's sky-blue eyes settled on him. They were as chilling as the air blowing into the narthex.

"Father Drowsky," greeted the man, his gaze flicking to the interior church at Casimir's back. "Might I come in?"

Casimir buried his irritation behind a cool mask of pleasantness. "Of course, Cleric," he replied, bowing and shifting out of the way. "Might I have your name?"

"Cleric Holden," the man replied as he slipped in, running his fingers over the pews as he went.

Casimir glanced down the path outside the church,

looking left and right before he closed the door and barred it shut again. The Cleric looked over his shoulder, brow creasing.

"Can't be too careful," said Casimir. "Not with all those creatures out there, and now that a Red Court Maiden has fallen prey to their seduction…"

The Cleric nodded. "It is a sad thing to lose the last to such a sin," he said. "I know you answered their questions, but I thought I'd ask a few more."

"Of course. I'm happy to help."

"Why were you at the inn?"

Casimir paused. "I came across the Shade outside my church. He seemed in pain. Then he said, 'the inn.' He disappeared, so I went to the inn."

The cleric nodded. "Why go up to the room?"

"I thought he was harming the Maiden," he said. "Look, she came to me and told me the queen had sent her and the Shade here. I didn't have any reason to believe they were traitors or that there was more to their relationship than… allies. She's a Maiden of the Red Court, for Thar's sake…" Casimir almost winced at his vainful mistake.

The Cleric paused his swaying step. "Where did you complete your seminary, Father Drowsky? When I checked the rosters for Whitehall before leaving Loight, Father Peeble was said to be in charge of this flock."

"Father Peeble was ripped apart at the edge of town, and I took over soon after. I studied at Pietist Julla's Cathedral in Hepian. I was not a very good student, and I think they were happy to be rid of me and send me here," said Casimir. "We can send a raven, if you like. I can have my transcripts…"

The Gold Cleric pressed a hand to his hood and shoved it

from his head, revealing platinum blond hair braided down his back. He tucked the veil beneath his chin. He was handsome, with a face so sharp-edged it cut the air like a knife. "Pietist Julla ended its seminary program twenty years ago."

Casimir's jaw twitched. "I'm not as young as I—"

Jyn dropped down from the ceiling, landing behind the Cleric without a sound. His gold eyes burned like two suns as he bent forward until his chin nearly rested on the Cleric's shoulder.

"Tav Holden, Gold Cleric of the Church of Thar, be still…" Jyn said, his voice a deepening chasm. Casimir knew the power Shades wielded, but he still didn't understand how they knew the names of people without ever knowing them personally. The Cleric stiffened, but he didn't turn or flee. Instead, Casimir saw a bud of gold light spark in the depths of his pupils.

Jyn turned to Casimir. "Shall I kill him?"

Casimir shook his head. "It will lead more of them here. I need more time to find the door."

Jyn nodded, tilting his head until his charcoal lips brushed the Cleric's ear. "Go back to your jail. See to your prisoner. There is no mystery to solve here." No sooner had the words left his mouth, Jyn had slipped back into the rafters' shadows.

The Cleric shook his head, running a hand over his face. "Traveling has exhausted me," he said. "I'm sorry to trouble you. Your story sounds good enough to me."

"It's no trouble at all," said Casimir, walking with the Cleric to the front door. He lifted the beam as the Cleric donned his hood and veil once more. "When will you begin the execution tomorrow?"

"Likely right after morning bells."

Then he was gone, off down the road towards the jail-house. Once again, Casimir pulled the door closed and latched it shut, then he turned towards the front of the cathedral and began his search for a door he might never be able to open.

RANEMIR STROUD

RANE PACED THE edge of the path leading away from Reagan's destroyed home and back towards Whitehall. Every time he attempted to go down it, his feet turned back of their own accord. His mind and body were not in sync, and it was maddening because he felt her. He felt every strike. They were beating her, and he had to stand here and… take it.

The hits eventually stopped, and he was left with a persistent dull ache down to his bones. Well, not *his* bones.

The sun set, and the sky blackened, and eventually Reagan of the Wood stumbled into the moonlight. "You," she said, eyes widening. "What are you doing here?"

Rane glowered. "Come home now that your free ride at the inn is over?"

The woman blinked at him. "I came home because this is my *home*. And you didn't answer my question."

He stalked away, tugging on the gold necklace around his neck. "Did you hear anything? They took her prisoner and you didn't hear anything?"

"Who took who prisoner?" barked Reagan as she stepped

onto her porch.

He frowned. "The Maiden…" What if the person hurting her wasn't a Gold Cleric or an Ighten soldier? What if it was the Shade?

"Oh," said Reagan, as if something dawned on her. "Oh, yes. The Maiden." She stood on the porch, staring out at Rane with the faintest gold glow in her eyes. "I told them about her. I told them what she did. An affront to Thar, it was."

Rane knew it wasn't her speaking. He knew by the dull glow of Shade's power in her eyes, but he still wanted to slit her throat. "What, exactly, did you tell them, Reagan of the Wood?"

"What she did with you," she said, her voice a hollow drone. "What I saw."

Then, Reagan blinked, and the dull gold faded from her pupils. "Look at the state of this place. An absolute mess. I'll be sending that queen of ours an invoice, I will."

Rane turned his gaze on the dark path ahead, feeling a heavy weight in his gut. He knew the punishment for the crime Reagan had accused Tenele of. It would have been the fate of anyone sent by Sinead to feed him, if she didn't do it in secret. The Church did not understand what he lived off of. Sinead had told them he drank the blood of mortals, and they had allowed people to come to him and bleed.

Now, Tenele would truly bleed for him.

And she would die.

CASIMIR DROWSKY

CASIMIR BROUGHT HIS hammer down on the chisel, watching the stone behind the altar crack. It broke open, revealing nothing but an external wall of granite. He smeared the sweat from his brow and moved to the next one.

The room was cool, but he had spent all night looking for the door. His nerves were lit with tension, and every time he'd thought about resting, his mind drifted back to Tenele and the harsh words he'd left her with.

He knew how many lashes it took to kill. Not only had he witnessed someone being lashed to death before, he himself had nearly died of that punishment. He might have died too, if not for the fact he couldn't. No, that wasn't right. Sometimes he did die, briefly, and then woke, his body wounded but unrelenting.

The morning bells tolled, and Casimir stopped his attack on the floor to lift his gaze to the pale light spilling in through the stained-glass windows. Just after the bells stopped, the screaming began. He couldn't hear the lashes, but he knew when one fell because a shrill cry echoed faintly through the stone walls.

At first, it was like any other cry he'd ever heard. He'd been the source of many, and so he was mostly desensitized to the pain of others. He began working again, chiseling at the stone until the fifth scream. His hand slipped and he almost stabbed himself in the knee again, the same way he had when Tenele had healed him. His gaze fell on his mended knee, his hand tightening around the hammer's handle before he set the chisel down.

At the sixth scream, he lifted his head, feeling as if the sound had grabbed him by the chin and turned his face toward her pain.

It sounded far away, but it drove into him like a knife.

A strange bud of rage flickered to life inside his chest. At once, he was overcome with the desire to tear the arms from the person driving the whip against her skin. Her pain bloomed into a beacon, and he found himself on his feet, then on the church steps outside, where the sound was keener in his ears—a grating painful scratch against his soul.

Casimir walked to the center of town without his priest's robes, wearing a dirty tunic and an equally dirty pair of trousers. His skin was smeared with granite dust and soot. So when the townspeople noticed him, they did a double take to make sure they were, in fact, seeing their priest.

In the center of town there was a stone square. It was where punishments were dealt and announcements made, and they'd tied her between two wooden posts. She was on her knees, hanging forward against the ropes binding her to the posts, her head bent and a wash of silver hair covering her face like a curtain. The cotton chemise she wore had been stripped down to her hips. It hung loose, tied there by the sleeves. Her chest and back were bare to the world and brisk fall air.

Ighten soldiers waited on the four corners of the platform, and a Gold Cleric stood behind her, his hand tight around the whip. He lifted it and brought it down with a sharp crack against her skin.

Tenele screamed, flinging herself forward, trying to escape the searing tear of leather against her flesh. Casimir felt the strike like a lash against his soul. Her pain was a terrible taste in the air, and the sight of her tears… She met his eyes.

The Gold Cleric reared back, the whip high in the air. Casimir's gaze followed it, and her eyes widened because she could sense it. Every muscle in her arms and legs coiled taut. She clenched her eyes. His heart clenched with her. The whip came down.

CRACK.

He flinched at the sound, at the sobbing scream cutting through him. As the Gold Cleric lifted the whip to bring it down again, Casimir yelled, "Stop!"

The word tumbled out of him before he even realized he was speaking. The crowd around him was as silent as any grave, their eyes turning on him as the Gold Cleric hesitated in dealing out his punishment.

Tenele's drooped head lifted, her teary eyes meeting his.

He was lost.

Shit.

"What's the meaning of this interruption, Father Drowsky?" asked Tav Holden. He stood at the front of the crowd, just before the bound Maiden. He'd been quietly observing her punishment, so still that Casimir hadn't even noticed him. The Gold Cleric's gaze narrowed suspiciously.

"I…" His mind raced. He took a step forward, the crowd parting for him. "Thar sent me a vision." A flurry of murmurs fluttered through the crowd. It was not the first time he had claimed such a thing to the citizens of Whitehall, but, to the Clerics, it was a revelation… or blasphemy. "This is a mistake, Cleric Holden."

Holden scoffed. "A mistake? Dealing out Thar's punishment for her sin?" The tone was oil to Casimir's fiery rage.

"I had a vision!" cried Casimir so the whole square heard. "If you do this, you will bring down the wrath of Thar. She is touched by gods, blessed with the gift of healing. She is meant for more than this, and, if you kill her, you will doom us all."

The whispers in the square grew into deafening murmurs.

Tav Holden sneered. "She's touched alright. Touched by a Shade! Look at the Mark on her!" He ascended the stairs and grabbed a fistful of Tenele's silver hair, pulling her head up and her back straight so that the town could see her body, see the black, inky stain of the Shade's Mark on her side. "Tell me, why would any god bless this creature?"

"I can prove she's blessed. I can prove my vision is true." Casimir stepped up to the platform, hands clenched at his side to keep from clocking the bastard in the jaw.

Tav Holden smiled. He was hooded and veiled, but Casimir could see the glint of pleasure in his eyes. "Fine," he said. "Prove you have had your vision. If you can't, then you will join her and bleed your blasphemy before your flock."

"As you wish, but give us space," said Casimir, his voice cold and even. Tav Holden went to the Cleric standing behind Tenele and folded his arms, waiting.

Casimir knelt before Tenele, tilting his head to meet her eyes. She gazed at him through strands of silver hair, her entire form trembling.

"Heal yourself," he whispered.

She shook her head. "I can't."

He leaned in, taking her face in his hands. "You healed me once," he said so only she could hear. "Heal yourself. Show them what you can do. Spare yourself this."

"I. Can't." Tears fell from her eyes, and she melted into the touch of his hands. "I can't heal myself. It doesn't work like that."

Casimir stilled. His thumbs brushed the tears from her cheeks, and he nodded solemnly. Then, he stood and held his hand out to the Gold Clerics behind her. "I need a knife for my demonstration."

Tav Holden pulled a dagger from his belt and passed it to Casimir, placing the handle in his palm. Casimir grabbed the rope binding one of Tenele's wrists and cut. The Ighten guards brandished their weapons, but Casimir put his hands in the air and knelt before Tenele.

"I believe," he said, loud enough for the square to hear, and took the dagger in both his hands. He raised it above his head. "I believe in the divine, that this Maiden has been blessed with a dead god's gift. I believe she will save my life."

Casimir met Tenele's eyes and drove the dagger into his belly. The crowd gasped. Some screamed. He heard nothing but the burning rush of pain across his nerves, blocking everything but the vivid green gaze of the woman kneeling with him.

Casimir dragged the dagger from his belly and watched the blood rush from the wound, felt it soak hot across his tunic and trousers. He'd bled before—he'd died before—several times over his one-hundred-and-fifty years. He had no fear of it. But he made a show for the crowd.

He collapsed forward, and dragged himself closer to Tenele, laying before her as an offering. He tasted the metal of death on his tongue, felt the warmth of blood pool on the stone around them, and then the cold pressure of her hand over his wound.

He saw the light beneath her palm reflected in the wild wideness of her eyes, felt the flood of pleasing, painlessness replace the searing, screaming agony of what he'd done.

The crowd hushed.

Casimir jerked, gasping as if coming back to life, and sat up. He was closer to her now, so close his lips nearly brushed her tear-stained cheek. The crowd erupted in a triumphant roar, and the Ighten guards fell upon him, dragging him away from her. Then, Tav Holden came and tore open his tunic, inspecting the place where he'd plunged the dagger in. The Cleric ran a gloved hand over the still wet blood smeared across his abdomen.

"Would you like me to do it again?" asked Casimir. "Shall I tear a hole in you, and have her heal it? Who do you know with the gift of healing, other than the dead goddess Attara?"

"And your vision…" asked Holden. "What if we kill her, as our law demands?"

"For snuffing out the last spark of His dead wife's light, Thar will take everything from you," said Casimir. "I have seen it. He will abandon us to the monsters, and hand us over to Alykith."

The crowd's murmuring became a roar.

"Release her!" someone cried.

"Free her now!"

"Blessed Thar, forgive us!"

Tav Holden's bright blue gaze burned into Casimir, hard and unyielding. *He doesn't believe,* Casimir thought. He'd taken the Gold Cleric as a simple-minded fool with how easily Jyn had turned his mind, but here he seemed an impenetrable force. But then, Holden nodded, and the guards released him.

They cut Tenele's other wrist loose, and she collapsed forward onto the podium, into the pool of blood he'd left behind.

"Take her then," Tav Holden said. "Give her the sanctuary you offered. We must pray and thank Thar for the merciful gift of your vision, Father Drowsky."

"Yes," said the crowd.

"Thar's mercy be praised!"

Tav Holden clutched Casimir's shoulder tightly. "And we must also pray your sanctuary redeems the sin of her acts, no?"

Casimir hesitated, his gaze flicking to the hand on his shoulder. He had the strangest urge to sink his teeth into the man's flesh. Instead, he stooped and grabbed Tenele, pulling her light form into his arms, and stood. He'd lost blood, so the movement sent a momentary rush of dizziness through him. She wrapped her arms around his neck, turned her torn back so his arm didn't press against the wound, and rested her head along his shoulder. The dizziness faded.

Casimir carried her to the church with a procession of worshipers following in his wake. They murmured prayers. Some tried to touch her, to touch a bit of divinity wrapped in flesh, but protective rage tugged at Casimir. He flashed a glare black enough to send them away.

When he reached the church steps, he turned to the townsfolk who followed him—at least half the village, he realized—and said, "Be gone. She needs rest and healing."

They did not leave, but Casimir put distance between them, entering the church and kicking the door closed behind him. He set Tenele on her feet, helping her lean against a pew while he dropped the heavy beam to lock the door.

When he turned back for Tenele, she was drawing the knotted sleeves of her chemise loose, tugging the stained fabric over her breasts and back, slipping her arms through the sleeves—shielding herself from him.

Casimir went to her and grabbed her face with his hands, as he'd done when he found her in the inn. He remembered the territorial anger he'd felt at seeing her injured and naked and afraid, and it burned in him now—a spark of hate for what they'd done. What he'd allowed to be done.

He stared into her eyes, into the wide green sea, and wanted to kiss her—to fall with her on the floor of the cathedral and devour her.

"You're safe here," he said, but that was a hollow promise. Few things were safe with him. "I'm sorry I didn't stop it sooner."

She glanced away, eyes brimming with tears. "You stopped it. That's all that matters."

"Let's clean your wounds. Bandage you up," he whispered, thumbs brushing the tears from her cheek. "Then we can figure out what to do about your Shade."

TENELE RAIDER

TENELE MIGHT HAVE felt ashamed of pressing her bare chest to Thar's holy altar, but the church had not been a House of Thar for many years. And after what his Gold Clerics had done, she felt little desire to please the God of Light and Life.

She rested her head on folded arms, feeling the cool stone beneath her as she bent over the altar and allowed Casimir to run a wet rag along the tears in her back. She hissed at the sting, flinching away until his hand retreated to give her a minute to catch her breath.

He dipped the rag in the bowl of water next to her, dipping and squeezing, dipping and squeezing, as if he needed something to do with his hands while she resettled against the cool stone.

"I used to have nightmares about this altar," Tenele murmured, clenching her eyes shut. "The Shade that Marked me first would make me gut myself on it. Over and over."

Casimir's hand stilled against her back. "That sounds… horrible."

"It was pleasant compared to what else he did. What he

made me do."

A heavy silence settled between them, and Tenele regretted saying such a thing.

"The lashes aren't deep, but you'll scar," he said, his voice low. His fingers traced a wide berth around the lashes, up her spine and across her shoulder blade until he found an old scar to admire. His touch was light enough to send a shiver through her. "Seems you aren't new to scars, though."

Tenele picked at the bandage around her arm, the one Rane had wrapped for her. That would scar too, she thought, and add to the hundreds of small white lines littering her body.

"It comes with the job," she said.

He chuckled. "And your relationship with the Shade? Is that part of your job?"

She stiffened as he pressed the rag to her back. She owed him no explanation. "You're not a great priest yourself, you know? Perhaps we're just both very bad at our jobs."

"And what about me is so unpriestly, Maiden?" There was amusement in his voice, a light touch to his hand. She pushed up, biting back the pain at rising. He backed off, only enough for her to stand straight and turn slightly to him. His dark eyes locked on her face, his jaw tightening. She matched his stare until his gaze broke, dipping for a second to the bare skin of her breasts and belly.

Restrained hunger lurked in his eyes, and she thought, if the situation were different—if she wasn't injured and he wasn't a priest—he would have her against the altar. But then the hunger in his eyes shifted, became a little less restrained. Perhaps he would have her anyway, injured or not, priest or not.

Would she mind either way?

"That," she said, her voice low. "The way you look at me."

His lips quirked and he bent his face closer to hers. "And how is it that I look at you?" The words were a whisper against her skin.

"Like you want to devour me."

He grinned. "That's because I do."

She stiffened at his honesty. "Priests don't desire—"

"Oh," he laughed. "They do. Most are just better at hiding it. I don't care to hide it from you."

"Why?"

It was his turn to stiffen. His gaze dipped once more to her breasts, her belly, and hips. His hand stretched out, fingers brushing around the black Shade's Mark marring her side. "I wish I knew," he said, heaviness in his voice. His gaze flicked back up to her. "Since the moment you fell into my life, I have not been able to rid my mind of you."

Her mouth went dry.

"You feel it too, don't you?" he asked, taking a step closer. He loomed over her, dark eyes locked on her lips.

She shook her head, even as longing knotted low in her belly.

"I want you," he said, and she stepped back, pressing her hands into the rough texture of stone behind her. "I want to take you against this altar. I want to hear your voice echo off the vaults. The only thing holding me back is that I do not want to hurt you. Which is odd, because I care little for anyone else's comfort." He bent forward, his lips close enough to brush against hers. "But I care for you, Maiden."

Her breath caught in her throat, and she stared into the endless black of his eyes.

She did feel the draw towards him, the tug of familiarity and warmth. The same strange sensation she got from Rane, but she had been certain it was caused by the spell that bound them together. Now, she wasn't.

He reached down and grabbed the tangle of fabric at her hips. She thought he would push it away, bare her entirely to the cold air in the church. Instead, he pulled it up, taking the wrist of her uninjured arm and guiding it into the sleeve. He touched the gold chain at her wrist, thumped the ruby with his fingers.

"Is this it? How you control him?"

"I don't control him."

"You sent him away, and he's not back."

"I did that for his own good. The Gold Clerics would have killed him, and I need him alive. We still don't know who called the monsters over the border, why the Shade is lingering in Whitehall, or what any of this has to do with Alykith. If an entire army of monsters is here or coming, he's the only one strong enough to fight them."

"And you?"

"I'm tough, but I'm not fight-an-army-of-monsters-alone tough." She waved a hand up and down her form, as if to put on display how fragile she was. She hated being weak—admitting her weakness—but she was also a very practical person.

"And you just... fell for him? I mean, he's lovely, but..."

"He feeds on pleasure," she said, and Casimir let out a barking laugh.

"I'm serious," she continued "He feeds on pleasure and pain. Guess which one seemed more appealing to serve him?"

Casimir's smile shifted. "Shades and Shadows feed on lots

of things, Maiden. Blood, pain, fear, hate—darkness and flesh. Never pleasure."

Tenele felt suddenly defensive. "He didn't trick me…"

The priest pressed a hand to her side, over Rane's Mark. "Are you sure?"

She hesitated, and a flicker of sympathy washed across his face. He gave her side a gentle squeeze and withdrew his hand. "If he didn't trick you, maybe he's not a Shade at all."

"Of course he's a Shade, what else would he be?"

Casimir glanced behind her at the opalescent statue of the Glory, then shifted his gaze back to her. "I've got to dig through Father Peeble's things for some bandages. Wait here." He reached for the bowl of bloody water, fingers grasping for its edge. "Perhaps you should call your Shade back while I'm gone." He dragged the bowl towards him, but miscalculated how much room he had before the altar disappeared beneath it. The bowl tipped unnaturally fast, the contents sloshing out across the altar and floor.

"Shit," he cursed, and Tenele stooped to help mop up the mess. She took a spare rag from him and blotted the stone, but the rag was soaked and the pink water spread into the cracks between tiles.

A flash of blue light caught Tenele's eye. It glittered in the cracks, becoming a steady hum.

"You… found it." Casimir's voice was hollow. Angry. She followed his gaze to the altar. The stone edging had a rim of runes carved so faint she might never have noticed them if not for the pale blue glow where bloodied water had touched. "You found the door."

"The door?" Tenele frowned.

He jumped to his feet, looping around the altar, his eyes wild. Manic.

Wrongness burned in the air, unease settling in her stomach.

He stopped where he'd started, dropping to his knees next to her and feeling his hands along the stone where the cracks glowed. "Your blood…" His dark gaze met hers, his head shaking as a wash of disbelief radiated from him. "Who the fuck are you?"

CASIMIR DROWSKY

CASIMIR STARED AT the Red Court Maiden. He'd known she was unusual, and not just because she drew him like moth to flame. She was half-Grela—a race that had died out almost two hundred years before Tenele's birth—and blessed by a dead goddess with divine healing. Everything about her made him want to run as much as it held him still. He never imagined her to be the key to the door the voice in his head sent him to find. Now, it all made sense—as did Jyn's reluctance to kill her.

Jyn *knew*.

He thought of the countless dead Maidens and soldiers along the border, and the brands Tenele had mentioned. Verin's monsters were hunting for *her*, and they'd found her— lured her here for this.

"Who. Are. You?" he asked again, enunciating each word.

She stared at the glowing runes on the altar, a wave of uncertainty and disbelief passing across her eyes. "You know who I am..."

"Then your mother. Who was your mother?"

She flinched as if he'd struck her. "I... Why is it glowing?"

"Because of you."

She frowned. "But what does it mean?"

Casimir, a voice whispered in the back of his mind, and he stiffened as if a cold, clawed hand had dragged over his soul. It had been... weeks since he'd heard it—since it told him to summon Jyn, to call the Shadows and Shades from the dark crevices of the world, and to come to Whitehall to find a door in a ruined church.

Open the door, Casimir.

Free me.

Casimir felt a strange pull towards the altar. He touched one of the glowing runes, and it sparked against the tips of his fingers. Then he bent and grabbed the blood-soaked rags from the floor, smearing them along the outer edge of the altar.

Her dreams were a clue. Jyn had gutted her on this altar. It needed blood. Her blood.

"What are you doing?" asked Tenele.

"Don't you want to know why?" asked Casimir hastily, rubbing the pink-tinged cloth against the stone. "Why your blood is doing this?"

"Anyone's blood might do it."

"No," he said. "Not anyone's. Yours."

She took a step back, drawing the sleeve of her chemise up to her shoulder, clutching it around her neck. She took in the altar, her face growing pale—likely understanding the reason for Jyn's nightly tortures.

"I don't want to know," she said, turning to leave.

Jyn dropped from the shadows above them, landing with a stone-shattering thud in her path. His hand curled tightly around her arms and drove her back into the altar. She screamed as torn flesh bit into the stone, and he dragged her along the altar's edge, grinding red into the granite.

The sound of her pain became a dagger in his heart and Casimir stopped his frantic bathing of the altar to grab hold of Jyn's arm. "Let her go."

"Run," Tenele told him, her face twisted with agony. "Go. Before he—"

Jyn laughed so cold and cruel even Casimir felt a twinge of fear at the Shade's malice. Jyn dragged her a foot more until the blood on her back connected the line Casimir had started with the rag. Blue runes glowed along the altar's edge, and a terrible crack echoed into the air. The floor beneath them dropped an inch. Then, a foot. Then, gone.

Casimir tumbled with Tenele into the space beneath it, sliding through a narrow funnel into a black void. When the dust settled, the broken altar remnants lay in chunks around them, granite veins shimmering blue and bright enough to give the black space a pale glow.

Tenele coughed the dust from her lungs, dragging herself to her knees. Casimir lumbered to his feet, helping her stand and holding her close as they turned to get their bearings.

The space was small. Made of solid stone, the roofline was low enough to brush his head. It was cold, but dry. The air smelled of dust and old blood. Thick, stringy vines wove their way through the room, stretching from the outer walls across the space, towards the center, where their strangling grip held a figure to their knees.

The dull blue light illuminated the figure's face. It was hard to tell the color of their skin with all the centuries of dust and vines tangled over them. It was not a corpse, though. The form was not shriveled or mummified or made of bones, though they held bones in their arms.

The skeleton draped across the figures lap was wrapped in tattered cloth, plated armor, and chainmail. The kneeling figure looked down on the bones, their face contorted in permanent, frozen anguish.

"What is this place?" whispered Tenele, moving closer to the tangled forms.

"A tomb," replied Casimir as he followed her, and not because he had a fierce grip on her arms. Some force pulled him towards the dead.

"Why would—" She didn't finish her thought. Tenele reached out and touched the bones, going suddenly grotesquely rigid, as if frozen in the first burst of agony when struck by lightning. Casimir tried to pull her away. Her eyes had glazed over with a milky film, and he reached to pry her hand from the clavicle. His fingers brushed the skeleton, and electric energy bolted through him, blinding and painful and then... gone. *He* was gone. The *world* was gone.

A dark void swallowed Casimir, and he was alone. Then, he waved his hand across the air, tearing a hole in space, and there was light...

And he was Verin, God of Night and Shadow—God of Monsters.

VERIN

VERIN FROWNED AT Thar as he exited the shimmering purple-black veil separating his realm from Thar's. His brother stood at the very edge of a cliff, his toes hanging out over the air, his hands hiding in the pockets of his pale robes. Thar stood as a shadowy silhouette before a blinding bright sun, and Verin shielded his eyes until they adjusted.

His brother was a glimmering, pale gold—like the sun of his world—with platinum hair and eyes the color of a cloudless sky. By contrast, Verin was a depth of dark blue—the color of midnight, speckled with silver freckles like glinting stars, and hair of living shadow. His eyes were a cascade of colors, the brilliant array of a dying star.

"Why did you call me?" asked Verin, coming to stand on the cliff's edge with his brother, looking out over Thar's world.

"I wanted to play a game," replied Thar, smiling. His voice was a brutal, beautifully deep chime. "It's been so long since we played one."

Verin scowled. "Because you're a sore loser. I don't want to deal with the fallout of you not getting your way. A million years is not enough time to purge your reaction to your last ruinous failure from my mind."

Thar grinned and grabbed Verin's shoulder. "Come now, brother. I'm bored. Play with me."

The God of Night and Shadow sighed, turning his attention to the green expanse of land before him. All that he could see and all that he could not belonged to his brother.

"What sort of game?" he finally asked.

Thar clapped his hands together. "A challenge. Nay, a bet. .. We will each show our gifts to a single village of my choosing and ask them to pick one of us as their patron god. Whoever is chosen will rule this world."

Verin arched an eyebrow. "Already trying to get out of your responsibilities? Immortality doesn't suit you, brother, if you cannot handle four million years of the same world..."

Verin had been born in the dark void of space, and as such, his magic reflected the eldritch darkness of existence. They did not call him the God of Monsters for nothing.

His brother, on the other hand, had been born in the light of a star. For the joy of his birth, their mother had given Thar a planet in the light of that star to tend and care and love as she loved him. But Thar had not been kind to his gift, and after three million years of neglect, their mother had punished him for it. Now, he was bound to the world, and its people, until the end of time.

Thar waved his hand. "This is just for fun. I'm bored."

"My gifts are not received well by your mortals," Verin reminded him. "I'm guaranteed to lose."

"Not so! These are different, I assure you. You may win, and if you do, you get a planet!" Thar wrapped his arm around

Verin's shoulder and led him away from the edge. "You'll need to oversee the world in my name, of course. Our mother, in her infinite cruelty, has chained me to these creatures. I must keep them happy in order to live prosperously. My vitality is directly linked to their worship. Their temples are my body. Their prayers, my breath. Should you win, you will need to carry out the tasks of their god in my name."

Verin laughed. It rumbled out of him, black and hot. "You want me to play a game in which I will be forced to do your chores if I win?"

"Well, when you say it like that..."

"Goodbye, Thar," said Verin, waving his hand. A portion of Thar's world tore in two, revealing the black expanse of space.

"What if..."

Verin paused.

Thar tapped his chin. "What if the game were different, then? What if we pick a mortal, and we compete for their love?"

He scoffed. "Love?"

"Come on, brother. I know you enjoy your solitude, but aren't you lonely?"

"I have Ren. I am not lonely."

Thar frowned. "My old chew toy doesn't count."

A burst of rage tore through Verin at the mention of Ren being nothing more than Thar's plaything, though it had been true. Their mother had made Ren for Thar so he would not get lonely on his gifted planet. Yet Thar had been crueler to Ren than to his beautiful world. So their mother, when she bound Thar to this world, took Ren away and gave him to Verin instead.

Verin was always given Thar's scraps. Though he would not dare think of Ren as one.

Thar draped his arm over his brother's shoulder again. "Have you ever had a mortal?"

"I care not what it is like," said Verin, glowering.

"It is like nothing you've ever tasted, Verin. They are fragile, delicate creatures. Their life is shorter than a blink, and so their potency is... unimaginable."

"Are we talking about eating them or loving them?" asked Verin with the curious raise of a brow.

Thar grinned. "Both. Come on… Play with me."

Verin pulled his hand down, and the tear in Thar's realm closed. "The terms?"

"I will choose a mortal. What do you prefer?"

Verin arched an eyebrow.

"Let's go with female…"

"Does it matter?"

"Well, you've had Ren, so why not try the opposite anatomy?"

Verin sighed. "The terms, Thar, before your precious planet's sun dies."

"I will choose a woman, and you and I shall woo her. We announce our strategies and each stick to them until she chooses one of us. Neither one of us will check on the other's progress. Agreed?"

"And how will we know who she chooses?"

"She will tell us."

"What's the prize?"

Thar walked a slow circle around his brother, his white

robes shifting like morning mist around his legs. "Whoever wins gets to keep her."

Verin frowned. "Keep her?"

"Yes."

The God of Night and Shadow sighed. "These mortals have no autonomy to you, do they?"

Thar seemed to bristle at the words. "We are gods and they are insects, and you haven't spent enough time with them to know that. But you will…"

"Fine, Thar… what will be your strategy in winning her?"

"I will visit her twice a month for a year with a gift, and in exchange for that gift, she will love me. What about you?"

Verin brushed his jaw, stepping away from his brother to look out over the world. "I will visit her twice a week and give her nothing."

"Nothing?"

"I have a condition," said Verin. "Ren must be included. He must come with me, and she must love him too."

Thar shook his head. "Out of the question, you can't use Ren's gifts to win."

"I won't allow him to use them." Verin glanced over his shoulder at his brother.

Thar laughed. "You won't… Do you even want to win, Verin?"

"If I'm to keep her, she must love both of us. I love Ren, and he loves me, and he must know her too—either to love her or to let her love me."

"In that case, what if we make the stakes higher? There must be a drawback to losing, right?"

"I've already walked the House of the Gods naked, Thar.

There is little you can do to embarrass me."

"Should you lose, I think you should give Ren back to me."

The fiercest rage bloomed in Verin's eyes, and he turned to leave. "Out of the question."

"Fine. Should you lose, you will give me a monster of my choosing."

Verin tapped his chin thoughtfully. "You may take anything from me but Ren."

Thar clapped his hands together. "We'll begin tomorrow."

"And what if you lose?"

Thar thought for a moment, then smiled. "I will give you a temple on my world and allow you to be worshiped as I am."

Competition, Verin thought, was Thar's worst fear.

Verin met Thar in a Grela village the next day. The air was full of smoke from night fires. It blanketed muddy streets running between wood huts. Chickens clucked and ran wild, pecking at bugs in the dew-wet grass. He followed his brother through town, and as the Grela emerged from their tiny homes, they paid them no mind. They couldn't see them unless Thar or Verin wished it.

"Are these considered mortals?" Verin asked, touching the silver hair of a man as they passed. The man turned, grasping at the back of his head and looking for the source of the touch.

"They live longer than humans, but they are not immortal. A human's life is so brief, their decisions so rash. A Grela must live with the consequences of their choices longer, and thus don't make decisions lightly. Speaking of the consequences of our decisions, isn't Ren supposed to be with you?"

"Ren preferred not to see you," said Verin, trying to keep the ice out of his voice. Even though he'd had a few million years to compartmentalize what Thar had done to Ren, he still felt angry when he thought of it. "He'll arrive when it's our turn."

"I'll go first, then, and leave you to it."

Thar led him to the only stone structure in the village—a one-story building with no doors or windows, only a stone porch held up by granite pillars. Within the structure was an altar, offerings laid all around it. A woman swept the steps, her long silver hair woven into a spiraling braid like a crown around her head. Her skin was sun-kissed, warm sand, and her eyes the color of sage. She wore a simple tan dress, tied around her center with a roughly woven rope, and no shoes.

"A priestess? *Your* priestess? Isn't that cheating, Thar?" Verin sneered.

"If you don't want to play…"

Verin scoffed. "I don't, really. I'm humoring you."

"Only a woman of pure heart and body can tend my altar…"

The God of Night and Shadow snorted.

"…so she will be a challenge to us both," finished Thar.

Verin closed his eyes, pinching the bridge of his nose and wondering, not for the first or tenth time, why he was doing this. "Her name?"

Thar sighed, settling a lustful gaze on the woman. "Attara."

ATTARA SARRA

WHEN ATTARA WAS young, her father had told her that when she got her first blood and became a woman, she would marry their chieftain's son—Yur Mataha—so her father's station would rise among their people. She was his only daughter, and the only one who could unite their family with their father's ambitions. But Attara had no desire to marry a boy who was cruel to his sisters and mother and the animals they kept.

So one day, while they were at temple and giving their prayers, she prayed to be spared from marrying Yur. She promised anything Thar wished in return. The next day, the young priestess who had served their temple for three hundred and ten years was robbed and murdered on its steps. The day after that, the village held a lottery where every eligible, unmarried, and untouched girl was required to submit their name to become their village's new priestess.

Two days after she prayed for Thar's aid, Attara Sarra wore shoes for the last time.

Every morning, Attara rose from her bed in the small hut

nestled within a cluster of overgrown brush behind the temple, then went to the altar for her morning prayers. Next, she swept the temple and steps, preparing for those who would come to the temple to pray. She would pray with them, and then she would clean again.

This had been Attara's day for one hundred years, and if she were to live for a very long time, it would be her day for seven hundred more.

Like every morning, Attara woke and said her devotion to Thar, then went to sweep the steps. The village came alive next, its sounds fluttering into the air as she busied herself. But, no sooner had the sounds begun, then the village silenced. A gold light appeared before her. At first, so blindingly bright she cowered and shielded her eyes.

Then the light spoke.

"Attara," called a voice like heavy chimes, and she parted her hands to peer out at the man standing shrouded in a thousand suns.

She had only ever heard descriptions of Thar, had never seen him—even though he had answered her prayers by making her a priestess of his temple.

They said he had the sky for eyes, the sun for skin, and the golden sand of Ongoreth's shores as the color of his hair. And he had all those things, standing seven feet in height, with fabric shifting around his hips and feet—layers of fine mist tearing in the breeze. Hard muscle covered his bones. He was the most beautiful thing she had ever seen in all her short Grela years.

In his hands he held a shawl of fine, soft spider silk. Attara almost touched it, longing to feel something other than the harsh scrape of poorly woven cotton against her skin.

"Would you accept this gift in exchange for your love?" he asked, and she drew her hand away from the cloth before touching it. Attara looked out at her village, at all the Grela coming and going and not paying any mind to the god on the steps of his own temple. They could not see him.

Attara was young for a Grela, but she was a woman with enough years of experience to know this was a test of some sort. "No," she said, and fisted her hands at her sides. She wanted very much to take the cloth, to wrap it around her skin and feel the softness on her flesh. But she didn't trust what would happen if she did.

Thar smiled, and the spider silk shawl disappeared. "What gift would you want in exchange for your love?"

Attara frowned, glancing back at the temple. *Freedom,* she thought. Freedom to leave the temple and to take a man and to feel the pleasures now denied to her because of her station. But Attara could not go back on her word. She could not deny the answered prayer that had been her salvation against Yur Mataha. So if this was a test, or a game, Attara decided to answer truthfully.

"Time," she finally said, and Thar tilted his head, an amused smile revealing teeth like opals.

Then, he was gone, and with him the light. The sound of her village came back to her, and Attara continued her sweeping.

34

VERIN

VERIN WATCHED THAR offer his gift of white spider silk and watched her refuse it. He knew Thar well enough to know that this first gift was a test, and Verin was still deciding whether she'd passed. When the test was over, Thar gave him a wave and was gone. He waited a few more minutes to make sure his brother would not return before he tore a hole in Thar's world for Ren to step through.

If Verin was the color of an endless night, Ren was the pale silvery-gray of a full moon. White tattoos in a language too old for even Verin to know swirled along his skin, up his neck and across his brow and into the silken, shadowy hair sweeping around his matte-black horns. He wore nothing but a shroud of fine black fabric low upon his waist, stretching down to shift and writhe around his legs as a living black fog.

Verin touched his husband's face, placing a kiss on his lips as he directed his attention to the priestess.

"That's her?" Ren asked, voice dripping desire. He could not help it. It was his nature, and if Verin were something other than a god, he would have been swept away by it. "She is…"

"Plain," admitted Verin, tapping his chin. "Are you ready?"

"Will we not frighten her?"

"She will not see us as we are," said Verin, and walked Ren to a trough of cool water. They peered into the stillness, admiring their reflections against its surface. Ren's gray skin bled to pale ivory, hair turning inky black, common mortal garb clinging to his shoulders and legs. His handsomeness lingered in the rise of his cheeks and the sharpness of his jaw.

Verin turned the color of deep umber, his long misting hair curled short and tufted against his head, and his clothes became as simple and unassuming as Ren's. "Now we are ready."

Ren sighed. "I still don't understand why we're playing this game with him. You know he will cheat."

"That may be true, but if we win, it will be good to rub it in his face."

"If we win, we're taking home a mortal pet…"

"She isn't a toy," chided Verin. He pressed his hands to Ren's shoulders, looking in Ren's burgundy eyes as they softened into a deep brown to go with his mortal facade. "If we win, it means we have earned her love, and that we have learned to love her back. Think of me, and that is how she will think of me, would you want to treat her so unfairly?"

Ren glanced at the Grela woman. "And she will love me like that?" He seemed skeptical.

Verin took Ren's face in his hands and pressed his forehead to him. "If she doesn't, then we lose. Together, or not at all. Always and forever."

Together, or not at all. Always and forever. It had been their mantra since Verin's mother had taken Ren from Thar and placed him in the quiet solitude of Verin's realm to heal. It would be their mantra until the stars died and the universe, as vast and wondrous as it was, became nothing.

"Is everything all right with you lads?" asked the Grela woman, finally noticing them standing at the edge of her temple's tiny courtyard.

Verin released Ren and turned to her. "We're lost," he said, glancing around.

"Spiritually or physically?" She smiled as she leaned against her broom.

"Probably both," he admitted, his gaze flicking to the temple behind her.

She glanced over her shoulder. "Would you like to come in? I have fresh fruit and water for those in need."

"That would be very kind."

"Come." She motioned them up the steps and through the narrow pillars into the candle-lit space beyond. They followed her, stopping at a straw mat on the floor where she had a pitcher of water and a bowl of ripe red berries. She sat, and they sat, and she poured them water into small clay cups. "I'm Priestess Attara Sarra. And you are?"

"Verin," he said, smiling. He had no fear of giving his true name in this world, as Thar's mortals knew nothing of him.

"Ren," his husband said, and took the cup from her gently. He admired the liquid within. They did not subsist on mortal food, but both could make a good show of it.

They visited Attara for an hour until a couple came to the temple for guidance. Verin asked to be directed to the nearest body of water so they might fish and relax. She pointed them towards a river only a few minutes' walk away.

Two days later, they returned, and she offered them berries and water as before, and, as before, they spoke and parted ways. It went like that for a month before she asked them to stop coming to the temple and speaking with her so familiarly. The villagers were beginning to look at them strangely, and she worried some would accuse her of breaking her vows with them.

So Verin and Ren would meet her as she went about other tasks throughout her day—when she went to the river to fish for dinner, or to collect water for her hut and temple. They would meet her when she gathered herbs and berries from the forest or sticks and twigs for a fire. Soon, she lingered with them longer than necessary as they helped with her menial tasks. Her words became less polite and more personal, sharing things she had no one else to share with. She spoke to them until she began to question being a priestess at all, until her touch on their hands became purposeful and wanting.

And in that time, Verin came to appreciate the way the sun glinted off Attara's silver hair, like all the stars of his realm had gathered to worship on her head. Ren found it impossible to look away when she met his gaze—as if the power he held to transfix and seduce had been imparted on her to use against him. Until twice a week became an impossible thing, because they both longed to be in her company all the days between.

ATTARA SARRA

THE GOD OF Light appeared twice a month to Attara, each time bringing a gift which ever increased in intricacy. He brought her a golden hourglass that, when used, could speed time or slow it down. He brought her a globe that changed the seasons. He brought her a vial that could catch the sun and hold it for a single day. So on and so forth, a cluster of beautiful impracticalities, and she turned them all away.

"What gift do you require that will give me your love?" he would ask, and with each visit there was strain in his voice, an impatience born of petulance. Attara saw Thar as he was, and not as their temple had taught her, and she began to fear the gifts, the question, the word love—until it became a poison on her tongue and in her ears.

Still, she answered honestly each time.

"Time," she would say, and his brow would furrow. Then, he would gather up his elaborate bribe and leave. It was not her fault that he was too dense to understand what she meant.

Once he was gone, Attara went about her duties until she found a reason to leave the temple and wander the forest or down by the river where—every now and then—she would run into Verin and Ren. Eventually, Attara resented the duties she woke to every morning because they kept her from running into the woods to be with them at the start of each day.

At the end of each day, Attara took last prayers and burned them in a copper bowl so that Thar might hear them. She gave the offering of blood from her finger before rushing off through town, towards the river.

Verin and Ren said they lived nearby, but she had never ventured to another village and knew of no huts in the forest belonging to anyone but Grela. Sometimes, she wandered off the path in hopes of finding their little house. Today, after going to the river and not seeing them there, she decided to do just that.

Attara slowed her pace as she navigated the trail, never certain where on it she might meet them, or on what day they would come. She decided to enjoy the walk for what it was, and if she found them on the path, then it would be a happy accident.

The forest was thick with old bawa trees, whose trunks were as round as cows are long, and so tall they might have been mountains. Mulched leaves and brassy needles covered the forest floor. She hated the prick of them beneath her bare feet, but a priestess was not allowed to wear shoes. Priestesses were to be plain, penniless, and entirely reliable on Thar. The only article of clothing they could own was a woven slip. She had added the rope to give her waist some definition and justified it as a tool to help carry out her duties as a priestess—for holding things and tying things and dragging things she might need. Once, she had used it to make a tourniquet on the woodcutter's leg when he hit himself with his own axe, and no one ever questioned her use of it as a belt again.

Attara wove her way through the woods, humming a song her mother had sung to her as a child. She brushed her hands along the bawa trunks and picked at the lichen clinging to the bark. She heard the rustle of feet against the needled earth and turned with a smile to greet Verin and Ren but found, instead, three dark-haired human males with mantles of deer skin and iron knives.

They spoke to her in a language she did not know and even still she knew their intentions. Attara turned to flee and ran into a fourth one. His hand was as big as her head and his eyes were nightmare black. He grabbed her up and slammed her into the bawa tree, crushing her there as his friends felt for valuables. Finding nothing, they threw her down and fell on her. She screamed at them in Grelan, calling out to Thar for mercy. He didn't answer.

She remembered the priestess before her, the woman who had served for less than half her life before being robbed and murdered to grant Attara's prayer of escaping Yur. She wondered if some little girl had prayed for the same thing. Was it her turn to die for another one's priesthood?

Her dress tore. Meaty, calloused hands dragged her flailing legs apart. Attara wished she had not turned down Thar's gifts. Perhaps, if she hadn't, his love might save her now.

Panicked breath burned through her, and she focused her gaze on the canopy of needles brushing blue sky, imagining she was a bird flying away before her first knowledge of man came from the black-eyed one above her. She'd wanted it to be Verin or Ren or both.

Attara felt him brush against the part of her no man had touched, and then… gone. His weight was gone, and something dragged him screaming into the woods. He clawed and grasped at the needle-covered earth before disappearing behind a bawa tree.

A blood-curdling shriek echoed through the forest, sending birds aflight. She had never heard a man scream like that. It ripped through the air from behind the tree, blood splattering on the ground as his thrashing legs went still. The others drew away from her, reaching for their iron knives as Verin emerged from behind the tree, too calm in his approach. His hands were slick and wet, his clothes spattered in red-brown.

Verin's dagger gaze flicked over the men. Attara gathered herself from the earth and went to the nearest tree, crouching there, clinging and shaking against the bark. She could not make sense of what had happened behind the tree. Verin had no weapons or tools, and these men had many. "Run!" she begged, but he only smiled.

One human leapt at Verin, iron knife slicing across the air. He moved, though she did not see it. He was standing as he'd been, and then he was standing somewhere else, near another man, who yelped and drove his dagger up into Verin's ribs. Attara wailed, watching his rich, dark umber skin turn midnight blue and freckled with stars. Verin twisted his head to the one who'd stabbed him, his face morphing into one she didn't recognize. The man leapt away, dagger withdrawing. A universe of colorful light poured from the wound before it sealed shut.

Verin was no longer as she knew him. The handsome,

dark-skinned human became a towering, eldritch beauty with eyes of multicolored nightmares.

Then Ren appeared from behind the bawa tree where the black-eyed man lay still. He wiped a bloody hand across his shirt as his ivory skin bled away to moon-gray. Black horns sprouted through his hair, curling up out of his head.

She fearfully and wonderfully watched as they did away with the humans who had attacked her until they were bloody, indiscernible pieces at her feet.

She should have run. She should have been terrified and sick by the sight. But when they were done, when they approached her and knelt gingerly near her, she flung herself into their arms and cried great heaving sobs.

The world was vast, full of mystery, and she had only ever seen what was within her village. So she did not ask Verin or Ren what they were, and they offered no explanation. They did, however, shed their illusions when no one else was around.

They were ethereal and lovely, and she found herself touching their unusual skin with delicate fingers until they shivered and brushed her lips with theirs. She had never been kissed before, and it woke a burning hunger in her belly.

One day, she met Verin and Ren by the river near the great falls that spilled from the north mountains. She took them by the hand and led them into the water, behind the falls, and to a rocky ledge hidden there. It was where young Grela often took their lovers to share themselves for the first time, and there she shucked her tan slip and asked them to show her what it was to be with a man.

They showed her what it was to be with two.

In their eldritch forms, their mouths explored her body,

kissing places she never knew lips were meant to touch, until her knees became weak and they sank together against the cold granite.

She rested back against Verin's chest, parting her legs as Ren made a meal of her body, tasting her until she trembled and cried out, a wash of fierce pleasure stealing her breath. He came away with a glow in his burgundy eyes, leaning up over her and kissing Verin with the same tongue that had lathed her center.

Then, Ren was inside her, and she felt no discomfort—not like the village girls whispered about when huddled together near a newly married woman. There was only ecstasy. Her fingers tangled with Verin's, and the higher her bliss, the brighter Ren's eyes grew, until he was bucking into her, sharp teeth grazing her skin. Another wall of pleasure shattered down, leaving her dizzy and limp.

Where Ren was a hungry lover who devoured her eagerly, Verin was attentive and patient, as if he had a millennium to explore her. He kissed her, guiding her until her back smoothed against the cold stone, his long form draping over her. Ren laid next to them, his hands clenching hers to the rock.

She felt small and fragile beneath his seven-foot frame, and as his need pressed against her, she feared she wouldn't be able to handle what he offered. Ren kissed her lips as Verin slid in. The warning, sharpness of discomfort shifted to pleasure. Attara moaned at the feeling of being filled so thoroughly.

His hips rocked gently against hers, his multi-colored eyes heavy-lidded with desire. He took his time with her, savoring every thrust and every sharp breath that left her lips, until he curled his hands over her hips and asked if she was ready to tread a line between ecstasy and agony.

She nodded, curling her fingers over Ren's hands as he held her to the stone, and watched as Verin took her in the way only a god could, until she was crying out for mercy and more, until her mind went vacant and her body trembled and the earth felt impossibly far away.

When winter came, they met in her home, after the village had gone quiet and the fires were out. Her hut was in the middle of tall brush and new trees, far behind the stone temple, and her windows were covered in wooden shutters. It was secluded, quiet, but even still, she was afraid of being caught, so they were quiet too.

On those winter nights, they tangled together on her small straw bed, wrapped in wool blankets and torn cotton. Sometimes, she had them individually or together, and sometimes not at all. Sometimes they huddled by the fire, telling her stories of a place of endless night and burning stars, of monsters so beautiful they could make you blind. She wanted to go there, to the place where they were from.

One night, when they lay together afterwards, breathless and sweating, with Ren pressed against her back and Verin curled around her front, she stroked his cheek and kissed his lips and said, "I lo—"

He pressed his finger to her lips, glinting lights growing in his multicolored eyes. "No. Please. Do not say it. Not until I know how I can protect you."

Attara blinked at him. "Protect me? From what?"

His lips trembled, a silver tear sliding down his cheek. He smoothed his hand against her face, brushed fingers through her hair. "I fear what he will do to you when you say those words."

"Who?" she asked, but he kissed her softly. He didn't answer, and Attara felt it didn't matter if she said the words aloud. She'd already said them in her heart. She loved them.

A week later, Thar came to ask his question. He offered her a glowing orb. Godhood in exchange for her love. Again, like all the others, she rejected him.

The God of Light and Life growled, throwing the orb into the sky with a fierce, frightening roar.

"What?" he demanded. "What can I give you in exchange for your love?"

Attara clenched her hands together, meeting the god's sky-colored eyes.

"Nothing," she said. Simple and true.

His brow knotted, lips drawing back with a snarl. He grabbed her, wrapping his large hand around her small neck, lifting her up.

"Nothing!" she cried, writhing helplessly to get free. "Nothing!"

VERIN

WHEN VERIN AND Ren came to Attara's hut in the cover of night, their arms draped around each other, they found it dark and lacking the warm glow of fire from beneath her door. When they entered, she was not waiting for them.

They donned their mortal disguises and went to the temple, the only other place Verin thought she might be so late at night.

Candlelight glowed in the inner chamber. They passed through the porch, between the narrow pillars, and into the worship area, stopping cold just inside.

Ren was the first to go to her—to collect her mangled, unrecognizable body in his arms. She was the color of driftwood, stiff and broken and bloodied. He draped her in his lap, brushing tangled silver hair from her face.

Verin shook as he took a step forward before collapsing alongside them. His disguise melted away, becoming deepest blue and darkened sky. His fingers curled over the tattered remnants of her priestess gown, quaking hands fisting the fabric until the stone beneath them split in two. He turned his face to the sky and roared, "THAR!!!"

Thar appeared in a flash so bright it seemed the sun had risen. His crystal gaze fell on them, eyes widening with shock. He came forward, sinking to the earth. As he hit his knees, Verin rose, fisting hands in Thar's misty clothing and slinging him through the temple's thin porch pillars. The stone crumbled, and Thar crashed into the dirt at the village's border. Before his brother found his feet, Verin grabbed him again, throwing him back to the earth hard enough to crater it. He crushed a hand around Thar's throat and pinned him against the dirt. "You killed her."

Thar held his hands in the air. "Why would I do that?"

"Because she loved us," said Verin through clenched teeth. A deadly growl rumbled out of him before he released his brother.

Thar dragged himself out of the crater as the village woke. Torches and fires flickered to life, and the people emerged from their huts, wandering the edge of the crater, unable to see the warring gods.

"Did she tell you?" asked Thar, frowning.

Verin hesitated. If she had, the game would have ended, and Thar would know. "No," he said. "But I know she did." Because he had stopped her from saying it, because of this, because of what Thar would do when he lost. Had she told him? Had she rejected him? What had she done to earn his wrath?

"I didn't do this to her. I can't harm mortals…" Thar's gaze flashed behind Verin, to Ren emerging from the damaged temple, cradling Attara's body against his chest.

In his hate, Verin had forgotten to hide Ren from mortal

gazes, and they saw him as he was—moon-silver and vengeful. The villagers froze, a chorus of horrified gasps filling the air. Ren paid them no mind as they fled, screaming about the monster who had killed their priestess and destroyed their temple.

"That's a lie," seethed Ren. "Thar can harm those who swear their allegiances to him, who take him as their lord, who devote themselves to him… Priestesses like Attara." He seemed to buckle under his grief, collapsing to the earth with the woman they loved slung over his lap.

Thar scoffed. "I didn't do this to her."

Verin brushed past Thar and went to Ren, kneeling with him.

"Can you bring her back?" asked Ren. Verin's hands hovered over her broken form, fingers gliding over torn and bruised flesh. His frown deepened until it became painful. His heart ached, rending a terrible fissure he thought would never heal. How had he come to care so much for something so frail? So impermanent?

"You… love her," said Thar, frowning. "You really fell in love with her…"

Ren's eyes flashed bright purple. Rising, he glared at Thar. "I'll kill you."

Verin caught Ren's arm.

"You can't and you've tried," said Thar. "Enough of that."

"Can you bring her back?" Ren asked Verin again, bending to look him in the eyes. A silver tear trailed the god's cheek. He shook his head. He couldn't bring her back as she'd been.

Thar rested his hand on his brother's shoulder. "Verin's

powers are volatile in this realm. He could bring her back, but…"

"She would change," said Verin, shuddering as he brushed a lock of hair from Attara's face. "She would be…"

"A monster," finished Thar.

Verin pulled Attara's body against his chest, pressed a kiss to her cheek, and turned to his brother. "You can bring her back," he said.

Thar glanced at her corpse, hesitating. "I can, but… not as a mortal."

"I don't care what she comes back as, as long as it is Attara," said Verin.

"It will be her… but also not. She may not remember."

Verin clenched his eyes. "Please, brother."

Thar frowned at them, eyeing the woman in Verin's arms. "I… did have a gift for her," he said, taking the dead woman from his brother's arms. He held her in one arm and reached to the sky, as if grabbing a star near the moon, and brought a shimmering ball of light to press to Attara's chest. "I give you part of me, Attara Sarra, Priestess of my Temple, so that you may live again, not as a mortal… but as a goddess. I imbue in you the part of me that is the Father and the Mender, so that henceforth, you will be known as the Goddess of First Breaths and Healing."

Attara's body absorbed the light, and her gray, driftwood skin turned luminous, growing so bright Verin and Ren had to shield their eyes. When the light died, Verin saw in his brother's arms a version of Attara that was perfectly alive and perfectly beautiful. Delicate white chiffon swept her curved body, and her silver hair spilled over Thar's arm in a waterfall of starlight. The God of Life and Light stared down at the woman he held, his hand brushing along her flawless cheek.

"You're alive," said Thar, and touched her temple with his finger. Verin saw a spark of light, and then she awoke. Her eyes fluttered open, the color of polished jade, and she touched Thar back in turn, cradling his face as she had done to Verin on so many vivid nights before. Verin's belly twisted at the gesture, and he itched to drag her from Thar's arms, so that she might never touch him as she had touched them.

"I have given you the gift of godhood, Attara," Thar whispered, smiling. "Do you love me?"

Verin shook his head. "The game is over, Thar. It died with her."

"Do you love me?" Thar asked Attara once more. She glanced to Verin and Ren, but it was as if she had never seen them before. Thar guided her attention back to him with a harsh pinch of her chin. "Do you love me?"

She smiled, soft and uncertain. "Yes?"

Ren rushed forward. "You did something to her." Verin caught him. Held him. Ren shook his head with disbelief. "He did this to her! He killed her and he's changed her!"

Thar gave a sympathetic frown. "I didn't, Ren. But I know you hate me and see all things by my hand as vile."

Verin met Ren's gaze. "He did it," said Ren. "You know he did it. She loved you. She loved…"

"You," said Verin, and he held his husband's face in his hands. "I know."

"Kill him," pleaded Ren.

"I cannot," whispered Verin, pressing his forehead to Ren's.

Thar sighed, still holding Attara in one arm as if she weighed nothing—as if she were an insignificant accessory to his misty robes. "I won, it seems?"

Ren shook his head. "Verin… don't."

"What monster of mine would you wish for?" Verin asked, sweeping his hand across his face to smear the silver tears away. He straightened, towering tall and broad before the backdrop of his brother's ruined temple.

Thar set Attara on her feet, and she clung to him, confused and afraid. The urge to go to her—to rip her from Thar and drag her to his black realm—was so strong that Verin's knees trembled with need.

"Jyn," said Thar.

Verin nodded. "Then he is yours."

He lifted his hand, and the world tore open. Verin grabbed Ren by the arm and dragged him through the door as one of Verin's most beautiful creations stepped into Thar's world.

The God of Monsters had made him in the likeness of his husband. In fact, he had made all his Shades in the likeness of Ren—tall, masculine, horned, and brilliant. Verin met Jyn's eyes as they passed, and the Shade seemed as confused and afraid as Attara.

"I am sorry," he said to Jyn before the door between Thar's world and Verin's realm closed.

Ren thrashed and whirled on Verin, striking him in the jaw. "You let him get away with it! He brutalized and killed her so that he could do this! You know it."

"I don't think making her a god was part of his plan," said Verin, with patience born from eons. His rage was tethered, locked in his rattling chest.

"We should have done something. We should have stolen her away. Now she is with him. Do you know what he will do to her? What he does to all things in his reach?" There was horror in Ren's eyes, a knowing Verin didn't understand, even though he had nursed Ren back from the brink of oblivion because of his brother's cruel desires.

"She would not love us if we did that," said Verin. "She would have feared us and hated us." He curled his hands over Ren's shoulders. "Do not take my restraint as weakness or uncaring. I care. I *want* to hurt him… but it will not help us get her back."

"And what will?"

"He has made her a goddess, Ren. In time, she will come to see him as you have seen him, as we know him, and she will abandon him. She may love us again, remember us again—in time. All we have is time. We are eternal, and now… so is she."

VERIN

TWO THOUSAND YEARS had passed since the night Thar took Attara, and for Verin it might as well have been a few weeks. Immortality felt different; time passed differently for someone who had seen millions of years. The older he got, the faster time seemed to move, and sometimes he was glad for it and others he was not. But, at the moment, he was glad.

He stood in a bright, white towering hall with a ceiling made of intricate ribbed vaults, each peek leading to a window. There were no lamps, no sources of light other than what streamed through the arched windows above him.

He followed the hall to a large room, where a lengthy table sat on a dais. The table held twenty chairs, but only one person sat at it. Thar wore his clothes of mist and chiffon, rising from his chair as he spotted his brother's arrival.

"I didn't think you'd accept the invitation," said Thar, holding his hand out in greeting.

"It has been two thousand years since we last spoke," said Verin, glancing around the room. He kept his expression emotionless, but he searched for her, for a glimpse of her. "You and I are too old to let such fickle things come between us, no?"

Thar grinned. "My brother," he said, and lifted a glass of godswine to his lips. Thar motioned to the seat at his right, and Verin slipped into it.

Rare fruits and meat from across the universe littered the table. A multitude of worlds were extinguished and presented on these platters, and Verin hid his disgust behind a crystal goblet of red godswine. Thar was privileged to have a Seeker who could travel the worlds and collect this sacred banquet— privileged to have a mother who doted on him even after an eternity of selfishness.

A bell chimed. A figure emerged from the hall, and Verin's breath caught at the site of Attara sweeping in, white and silver billowing around her like a cloud. Her hair hung straight and silken to her hips, tucked behind her ears and out of her eyes. She smiled at them as she approached, pressing a kiss to the top of Thar's head as she rounded the table and took the chair at his left, across from Verin.

"Verin," said Thar, as he tipped his goblet towards Attara. "You've met my wife."

Verin stiffened at the word but kept the discomfort from his face. He smiled at her, nodding his head. "We met a little while ago."

Her brow furrowed. "I'm sorry... I don't..."

"Memory is a funny thing," said Thar, pinching off a gold grape and tossing it into his mouth. "Especially when one is new to immortality."

Attara glanced away. "You... do seem familiar. I am sorry, I don't remember."

"Wife?" asked Verin. "I apologize for not sending a gift. I

wasn't aware you married."

"It was time," said Thar.

Verin forced a smile. "Next, I'll have a niece or nephew…"

Attara flinched as if Verin had slapped her, her green eyes flicking to Thar before she rose with her plate and went about collecting food from the table. The faceless Glories hidden along the walls behind them could have done that for her, but it seemed she wanted to be busy.

Thar laughed. "I don't think children are in our future, Verin."

By the end of their dinner, Thar was drunk on godswine and rambling about how good Attara was at tending to his world. Some of his people had even gone about building temples in her honor, to worship her alongside him. Thar sounded pleased with the idea, but Verin knew his brother well enough to look at his eyes, to see the jealous cloud building behind the brilliant blue.

When it was time to leave, he shook his brother's hand and turned to Attara. "It is customary to kiss the bride on her wedding day, but as I was not there to see your vows, might I kiss you now?"

Attara glanced at Thar, who nodded and urged her forward with a firm hand against her back. Verin took up her hands and kissed the palm of each one before bending and kissing her forehead. Her hands clenched around his, and he met her eyes, though they didn't seem to see him. They looked beyond him, someplace distant and familiar.

A day later, Verin had the itch to visit Fallemor, Attara's old village. After two thousand years, the forest had claimed it, and all that was left was Thar's broken and forgotten temple.

Verin had visited it many times in the years since she'd died, watching as the river changed its course and the Grela moved deeper into the forest to escape the encroaching growth of human civilization. In all the years he had come, she had never been there when he arrived.

Attara stood at the entrance of Thar's temple, staring at the vines choking the stone. He approached quietly, but she heard him nevertheless. She turned, and the sun hit her hair, a thousand diamonds glittering in the light.

"What brings you here?" she asked, turning her gaze back on the temple.

"I come here every now and then," he said, standing near her. "When I want to remember someone I loved."

She frowned. "Were they mortal?"

"They were," he said, nodding.

"I have never been here," said Attara, tilting her head. "At least, I thought I had never been here…" She looked to him. "You kissed me, and I saw something."

Verin twitched. "Saw something?"

"I saw us…" Her cheeks darkened with rose. "Beneath a waterfall…"

Verin forced his face into placid interest. "Oh? How peculiar."

"There was another with us," she said, her lips pursing. It looked as if she was forcing herself not to smile.

Verin turned to walk away. "A strange dream indeed."

"It wasn't a dream," she said. "I saw it. I… felt it."

"And what did you feel, goddess?"

She skipped to catch up with him. "Don't patronize me. You did something. When you kissed me, you showed me something!"

"I showed you nothing," he said, but that wasn't the truth, and lying to her made his stomach knot.

She grabbed him by the arm. "Why are you here?"

"I already told you," he said. "Why are you? This doesn't look like a waterfall to me, *Minka'nes*."

She blinked at him. "I…" She looked back at the temple. "I dreamed… I dreamed of this place."

"How interesting. You know, not many gods dream. Or sleep, for that matter."

"I do."

Verin smiled. Of course she'd held on to some of her mortal needs. She was a goddess born of death… made by the hands of another.

He reached over and gently removed her grip from his arm. "And what did you dream?"

She was still staring at the temple, though her face had lost its stubborn anger. He looked her over, hands flexing to touch her—to brush her hair behind her ear and draw her in against his chest. Two thousand years without her… Two thousand.

"I dreamed…" Her mouth worked, her gaze flicking back to him. "Nothing."

"You can tell me. I won't tell Thar. We barely speak as it is. I don't… hold much fondness for him."

"Yet you visit him?"

"My mother asks me to look in on him, and I oblige her every now and then," he replied.

"Why doesn't *she* look in on him?"

"Because she is so powerful and massive that her presence

within the space of this beautiful world might devour it."

Attara's mouth gaped. "Is that why she didn't come to the wedding?"

Verin laughed. "I doubt she got an invitation…"

"So… you don't like him?"

"He can be…"

"Cruel?" Her jaw tightened, and she rubbed her shoulder as if it ached.

He forced himself not to ask why she thought Thar cruel. "Your dream?"

She clinched her eyes. "I dreamed he attacked me in that temple… or what may have been that temple. I dreamed he… beat me and broke me and murdered me."

Verin's hands fisted, his jaw tightening, but he kept his face serene. "That sounds terrifying."

She laughed, and there were tears in her eyes as she did. "I suppose it would be terrifying… if it weren't a normal day— negating the death part, as… I can't die."

Verin's gaze fell on her shoulder and how she massaged it. He thought of Ren, and the state in which he'd come to his realm, but Attara seemed completely unharmed. "He hurts you?"

"I should go," she said. "I'm sorry. I shouldn't have said anything."

She was turning, fading from his sight, so he reached out and took her hand and pulled her back into the world. She came back bloodied. Bruised.

His eyes widened, drawing his hand back from her as if she'd scalded his skin. The careful facade she'd painted over her form had faded, and she stood before him as she was—a beautiful ruin.

Gods were not invulnerable. To mortal instruments, they were immune. They could be harmed by them and would heal too quickly to notice. But gods could hurt other gods as easily as men hurt other men—though they tended to heal just as quickly. Attara's wounds were either very recent, or repetitive, or worse…

She touched her bruised face, the necklace of bruising around her neck, down her arms, and then she looked at her chaffed wrists—the evidence of something having been tied too tightly around them.

Verin felt cold rage coil in his heart. He brushed her face lightly with the tips of his fingers, and took her hands, admiring the bloody rings around her small wrists. His teeth clenched tight enough to shatter. They might have, if her drawing away hadn't dragged him, momentarily, out of his rage.

"He uses… a gold chain that makes me feel…"

"Weak?"

She nodded.

Verin snarled. "An Eternity Chain?"

"I suppose, if that's what it's called…"

Verin gripped her hand so she couldn't pull away, and dragged his other across the sky, ripping a black door open. He pulled her through, into his realm, and shut the door behind him.

"Ren!"

Ren appeared in a sweep of black smoke, and before Verin could register his response, he passed Attara's hand into his. "Show her around. Make her comfortable."

"Where are you going?" asked Attara.

Verin smiled. "To say hello to my brother."

38

ATTARA

ATTARA REMEMBERED LITTLE of anything before Thar brought her to his home. She had told him she loved him but wasn't sure why. Once they'd reached his sterile white home, she didn't take back her love. She was home there, in his empty gleaming palace with faceless drone-like servants wearing opalescent skin. He called them Glories. They dressed her and fed her and let her walk Thar's world while they trailed along, all of them invisible to the mortals who lived there. Her life was luxurious and might have been boring if not for the endless state of fear and pain living with Thar brought.

He gave her everything she could want, and married her, and called her his wife, and claimed of her his husbandly rights. But Thar was a sadist and could only find gratification if the object of his desire felt pain.

At first, he had not used an Eternity Chain, but he began to want to see the bruises on her flesh linger, like a watercolor painting on display. So he bound her and hurt her and sometimes he would leave her like that for days or years, she wasn't sure. Time moved so strangely.

She was not the only object of his desire and torment. A beautiful creature resided in Thar's empty palace, and he would hurt them as one. Sometimes, he would hurt them together. Sometimes, he would tell Jyn to hurt her and watch. Eventually, Jyn grew to relish causing pain as much as Thar did.

Attara had wondered if Thar had taken her from some place, because she could not remember a time before knowing him. He claimed to have made her, and that she should be grateful for it. He made her worship him as if she were a priestess in one of his temples, and the prayers did not come so unnaturally to her.

Then, one day, she felt the stirring of a child. She told him joyfully that they might have a son or daughter, and he bound her with the chain and beat her until death felt like mercy. There were six more times in which he placed a child in her belly and beat it out, too fearful of being overtaken by an heir.

Thar had to be worshiped. He had to be the only god his world had ever known—not just because he was selfish and narcissistic, which he was, but because his existence depended on it. If he were not worshiped, then he would petrify. A god could not be killed, but they could be imprisoned.

On one of her outings to his world, Attara came upon a woman in a field struggling with birth and took pity on her. She guided the child into a more productive position and held the woman's hands as she brought him into the world. When Attara placed the child in the woman's arms, the woman asked to what goddess she could make an offering to in thanks. She had replied, "Thar's wife, Attara, Goddess of First Breaths and Healing." The woman told her husband, who told their village, and the next week a small corner of Thar's temple was dedicated to his wife.

Attara began hearing whispers in the back of her mind—prayers from people on Thar's world—all of them asking for help with their upcoming births or for healing. She began to answer those prayers, as many as she could. The small corners she occupied in Thar's temples spread open, and, eventually, they erected whole, separate structures in her honor.

Thar hadn't minded the small corners she occupied because those who came to ask blessings of her also asked blessings of him. But he had despised the competing buildings. Thar was not prone to answering many prayers unless they amused him or brought him something he valued. Attara answered as many as she physically could, so the crowds and offerings made at her shrines were opulent and many—and Thar came to resent her for it.

One day, he'd called her to dinner, and she'd expected him to bind her there and take her life, or hurt her as much as a god could be hurt. Instead, she'd been greeted by his brother, and she'd made a good show of being a good wife in hopes that it might spare her Thar's wrath. His brother was handsome, if quiet. His eyes, an endless universe—a dying star of multicolored madness. When he kissed her, Attara saw a world where she knew only pleasure, and the ache—the longing, dreadful ache—it left behind had nearly buckled her knees.

He left, and she'd almost begged him to take her away.

Thar bound her afterwards. He had beaten and raped her, and he made Jyn repeat the acts until she swore to never answer another prayer. That night, she dreamed of a temple, a priestess's simple garb, and being bled dry on an altar of stone.

Afterwards, she'd looked for that temple, and it was not

hard to find. Thar kept a list of them, and it was in the front, his first temple on his world, crossed out in ancient virgin blood.

Attara had not expected to see Verin there, or for him to care.

And now, she found herself within another realm, in another god's home, defined by their will.

While Thar's opulent palace was sterile, full of white and crisp lines, Verin's was a plain of dark, endless space. She walked the stars, passed a writhing sun, and brushed her hands along the rings of a blue-green world.

Ren regarded her quietly as he followed her around. His eyes were kind, while his face seemed sad. His gaze lingered mournfully on the wounds Thar and Jyn had left behind. She hadn't bothered hiding them because they were already known to Verin.

"I had a vision of you," she said to Ren as they approached a swirling ring of stardust.

Ren tilted his head curiously at her.

"It was the first pleasant thing I've felt in… my whole life, I think. I don't know… I don't remember a time before Thar."

His jaw tightened. Words seemed to beat at the back of his teeth. "Maybe it's a memory," he finally said.

She glanced away, feeling heat rise in her cheeks. If it was…

His fingers danced along the swirl of stars. "What happened in your vision?"

She waved her hand in the air. "It's silly—"

"He hurt me too," said Ren, coming a step closer. "Like he hurt you. I was his once, gifted to him because he was lonely and his mother thought he needed a friend."

Attara felt her heart clench. "You… escaped?"

"No," said Ren. "I was taken away because Thar disobeyed. Then I was given to Verin. Their mother had already made me and had no use for me in her realm. She is omnipresent, eternal, and still had not the heart to put me down like the broken animal I was."

He was near her now, his burgundy eyes aglow. His skin was dull silver, the color of brushed nickel. She touched his horn, traced along its curve back to his temple, through his hair. Her fingers danced along the patches of swirling stars and iridescent tattoos along his brow and cheek and jaw.

Ren shivered, then cupped her hand to his cheek. "Verin nursed me back from destruction. He was kind to me, and after one million years, I felt I could be touched by someone again. So… I let him, and I fell in love with him…"

"Is he kind?" asked Attara, hope swelling in her chest.

"The kindest," replied Ren, curling his fingers around hers.

A shape moved in the dark behind Ren, and a creature emerged. It was many-eyed and many-legged, slick black and writhing. Attara felt a surge of fear. A scream caught in the back of her throat. She stilled as it approached her, watching as it cooed and purred and dipped its head to brush beneath her palm, like a cat. A terrifying, spider-like cat.

"What… sort of god is he?" she asked Ren, stroking her hand along the nightmare's head.

"Some call him the God of Monsters."

"What do you call him?"

Ren glanced towards a black palace on a cold, desolate

moon. He took her hand gently and guided her to it. "I call him husband."

Verin did not speak of Thar when he returned. He did as Ren said he would. He nursed her. Fed her. Comforted her. He allowed her back into Thar's world to answer prayers, and her temples grew while Thar's waned. Ren accompanied her on days Verin couldn't—when the God of Monsters was tasked by his mother to make creatures for her many worlds.

The longer she stayed with them, the more the dreams came to her, until she realized, just as Ren had suggested, they weren't visions at all. They were memories.

After two hundred years residing in the God of Monsters' realm, Attara married Verin and Ren while standing on the dusty rings of a purple, gaseous world.

Fifty years later, her belly grew round with child. Verin doted on her. Ren pampered her. Both protested her going to Thar's world to answer his people's prayers. Their mistake, however, was teaching her how to open the door between worlds on her own.

VERIN

WHEN ATTARA DIDN'T come home as she usually did, Verin went to every temple and monastery dedicated to her name to see if she lingered in one, as she sometimes did. He arrived at *Belina os Toro Attara* as the sun set, expecting to find her mobbed by followers and priestesses. Instead, he was greeted by a great wailing. He followed the sounds of screaming to the courtyard, to a group of priestesses surrounding a figure lying on the earth.

He knew it was Attara. Not because he saw her, but because he felt it in his soul. It should have been impossible to kill a god, but somehow Thar had found a way.

Verin had feared his retaliation, and had asked her to forget his people, to never return to them. He had known, deep in his heart, what would happen if she didn't. But he couldn't stop her. He could not force her to give up something she loved, yet he should have. He should have made her give them up.

Verin stepped through the crowd unseen and knelt next to her. He had lived untold years, had felt rage in many forms, but he had never felt this. He had never felt as if his bones and heart and soul were burning. As if time were spinning beyond his control. He wanted desperately to pull it back, to turn it and bend it to his whim. He had the power to birth a world, to create any manner of being, but he could not save her.

The God of Monsters pulled his wife into his lap, allowing the world to see him as he did. Her priestesses screamed and fled, but he'd wanted them to. He'd wanted them to flee and scream and tell the world about the dark god who'd arrived at the death of Attara.

He brushed her hair back, kissed her lips, and pressed his hand over her belly, over the roundness that was their child. Their child…

Verin roared, and the sky blackened. Darkness poured out of him, a flood of night and teeth and monsters. They gathered around him, purring and growling and shying away from threads of sunlight peeking out from behind the dark clouds he'd conjured. "Every temple," he said, his voice a vicious growl. "Every priest and priestess. Every church or statue to Thar. Destroy them. Devour them all."

Verin's monsters turned and spread out into the world, and he heard their path through the screams beyond the monastery walls.

Verin pulled Attara into his arms and brushed his midnight blue fingers along her cheek. "Listen to me, my love, my *Minka'nes*. You are not dead. You *cannot* die. You are a goddess. You are eternal…" He glanced down at her belly, knowing there was nothing to be done for their child. It had not breathed the life-breath of a god, and that was why he would burn Thar's world to the ground.

He pressed a kiss to her cooling lips. "A god cannot die, born or made—it makes no difference. Their energy can only change. So change. Become something else, so I might find you. So Ren and I might love you again."

But Attara did not change. She grew gray and brittle and dissolved into silver powder in his hands.

A Grela novice—hunkered in a kitchen with her other Sisters—felt a terrible strangeness in her belly. It grew painful as it swelled, until the pain became blinding, and they ushered her to her back. They covered her mouth to muffle the screams, so the dark god's monsters couldn't find them.

A child, grown and birthed in the span of minutes, entered the world with a dusting of silver on her head.

For three hundred years, Verin and Ren waged a war on Thar's world. Verin partnered with the Alykith queen, giving her magic and power over his monsters with the assurance she would conquer the lands loyal to Thar, demolish his temples, and kill his priests.

With every village that fell, with every prayer lost, Thar grew closer to obscurity and petrification—to be frozen and forgotten until the end of time.

Along the way, Verin's kindness for mortals turned to cruelty, and soon it was not enough for the mouthpieces of Thar to suffer, but all those innocently and blindly devoted to him. Until the holy war became a war to end all wars, all people, even Alykith.

Ren tried to drag Verin back from self-destruction, but not even his love could tame the fire of vengeance in the god's heart.

At the border clash between Alykith and Ighten, amid a battle between Shadows and men, Ren spotted a silver-haired woman in the fray. He called Verin's attention to her, but Verin ignored him. There were no more Grela left. Their beautiful tree cities had burned, the entire forest nothing but ash and bones fifty years into this fight.

Ren grabbed Verin's face and forced him to look. Forced him to see through the blood and mud and death, to a woman clothed in holy mail. It blinded him so fiercely he could barely see her, but when he looked upon her face, he knew.

"Attara…"

He called his beasts back, giving an order out to all of them—no one was to harm the silver-haired Grela on the field. Ren begged him to stop the war altogether, but Verin refused. Instead, he ordered Ren to go to her, to protect her from Thar's followers, fearing that once his brother realized she was alive, he would kill her again. This time, for good.

So, Ren went to the Grela, to the one with Attara's face.

When Ren did not return, Verin grew fearful that Thar had taken them both, so he sent Shadows and Shades in search of them. They drew him to a small town near the border, to a ruined stone church at the edge of a narrow, muddy road.

The queens of Ighten and Alykith greeted him. Alykith must have decided that Verin's thirst for vengeance would be their doom, along with Ighten's. The two sorceress queens thought to end the war by ending him.

Verin laughed at them—at their foolish mortal belief that

they could kill him.

But then, Ren appeared. Only it was not *him*, not entirely. He was changed.

Ren didn't seem to recognize Verin, and there was a golden eternity chain around his neck with a pendant of deep ruby. It glowed fiercely, as did the color of his burgundy eyes. Ren struck Verin, and Verin allowed it. He allowed himself to be hit by the man he loved, for fear of striking out and hurting him in turn. He was a god. He could take any punishment Ren dealt.

Ren knocked Verin into the old church. He skidded towards the place where an altar might have been, but now a black hole lay in its wake. He tumbled into it, landing next to the still form of the dead Grela woman.

Verin gathered himself before he pulled the woman into his arms. He did not need to touch her to know she was dead. He smelled her blood around them, painted on the walls in large runes.

Movement above tore his gaze to Ren standing over the hole. A shrill chanting filled the air, the queen's joint voices ringing like holy chimes to burn his ears. Verin moved to stand. The earth held him still.

Crimson, writhing vines sprouted from the blood on the floor and the walls and tangled around his legs and arms, pulling him to kneel. He felt them embed into his skin, wrap around his bones, and chain him to the floor. He roared and then begged for Ren to help him, but Ren did not hear. This was not *his* Ren.

He looked down at the woman he held, at her ashen face, at green eyes staring empty into the void of death.

He'd lost her…

Verin looked up at Ren's face and met a pair of eyes that didn't recognize him.

He'd lost them both.

Movement caught his eye, and he saw a body hovering in the air above him. A dead mortal man with shaggy brown hair. Vacant, dark eyes stared back at Verin, the stranger's arms spreading wide as if to greet him with a hug.

Gods cannot be killed… his brother's voice said to him, into his own mind. "They simply change," Thar finished aloud.

The bloody tendrils pressing into his godly flesh wove their way into his neck and face and mind. They sprouted up from the floor and tangled around the dead man hovering above him. The queens sang their hellish song, and Verin cried out as he felt his soul come untethered from his body. He saw, through the eyes of the dead man, his own body turn gray and shriveled and hunched over the dead Grela woman. And then, Verin saw Thar standing behind the mortal queens, with Jyn at his side.

Jyn held in his hand a gold eternity chain and a ruby matching the one Ren wore. The Shade whispered a word, and Ren moved, dragging the dead body Verin inhabited towards the queens.

Ren threw Verin's useless human prison down before them. They placed their hands on his head, still chanting. Verin felt heat in his cheeks and mind—felt the world close over him and eat him alive.

He knew nothing after that—not of Ren or Attara or of his black realm. Not even his name. He knew only the endless empty darkness of an Ighten prison cell until he escaped.

CASIMIR DROWSKY | VERIN

THE WORLD CAME back to Casimir in a terrible nauseating rush. He was on his back, the lumpy, craggy pieces of altar pressed into his spine. Tenele was partially draped along his lap, and she stirred with him, groaning as the world became real again.

The visions mixed with his memories, becoming a murky soup. It was almost painful how they wormed their way through his head, colliding and consuming him, eating away at Casimir Drowsky and leaving Verin, God of Monsters, in its wake.

The kneeling figure—the body of the Dark God—lifted his head. His eyes parted open, revealing the multicolored lights of two dead stars. But there was nothing there. Not really. Casimir knew this.

Because *he* was Verin, and the body before him was a shell. A place where he should be and wasn't.

Which meant the one in his lap, the woman sitting up and touching her head gingerly—whose smell filled the room around him both new and old—was Attara born anew.

Attara... Casimir's mind turned feverish. Ranemir Stroud... Ren. He was Ren!

And Jyn... *Jyn.*

He wasn't certain why Jyn had brought them here, but he knew the voice in his head now for who it truly was—Thar. Thar was behind *all* of this. His gaze swept to the Red Court Maiden.

"Tenele. Up. Now." Casimir pushed, urging her off his lap and rising. He dragged her to her feet, curling his arm around her waist to steady her. They needed to get out, and he needed to find a way back into his body. He turned his gaze on the kneeling, empty god.

His body.

"What... was that?" asked Tenele, swaying. "My head..."

"Did you see it?" Casimir grabbed her face gently, looking in her dizzy eyes. *Please, please remember me.*

"I... it's all..." She grasped her forehead, curling fingers in her tangled silver hair. "I'm going to vomit."

He helped her sit. "Wait here," he said, and then rushed back to the bones and the god. He touched his own godly shoulders and began tearing the red-colored vines from his flesh. It was strange to be outside his body, to see himself through another man's eyes. Maybe, if he freed himself from this, he could climb back inside. Shift his consciousness from one vessel to another.

He spared a glance back to Tenele and saw a pair of gold eyes glinting in the dark behind her. Living shadows stretched out, wrapped around her arms and legs, and dragged her screaming across the room, up through the shaft they'd fallen through, and into the cathedral above.

41

TENELE RAIDER

WRITHING DARKNESS SLAMMED Tenele onto the cathedral floor hard enough to crack the tiles beneath her and the bones in her limbs—hard enough to shake the last remnants of that dream from her mind. She groaned and focused her dulled throbbing senses on the tether around her wrist. "Rane..."

The Shade of her nightmares wrapped his hand around her throat and squeezed until the next word to leave her lips was a rasp. He lifted her until her feet flailed uselessly in the air. His head tilted, gold eyes observing her struggle. Then, his gaze drifted from her legs, up to her arm, and to the gold chain around her wrist. He curled fingers in the chain, and threads of darkness joined in tearing the thing from her wrist, splintering it into hundreds of tiny fragments and sending the ruby clattering across the stone, into the hole in the floor.

"Thank you, Jyn," said a voice like chimes from the narthex.

Tenele dragged her gaze from the Shade to the large doors at the front of the church. They hung wide open to the dark outside. *Strange…* It had been mid-morning when they fell through the hole. Had they really been dreaming for hours?

Warm oil lamplight lit the nave, and the two Gold Clerics stood over bound, prostrated women. Tenele's heart lurched into her throat. No. *No.* Not her.

"Sinead," rasped the Red Court Maiden through the Shade's strangling grip.

The queen lifted her head, bright eyes widening on Tenele. The Gold Cleric behind her grabbed a fistful of Sinead's corn-silk hair and tilted her head back so he could look into her eyes. A heavy gold collar hung around her neck.

Cold fear coiled like weights in Tenele's belly. Sinead was without her power. That was the only way anyone would ever be able to get her to kneel, to submit to their manhandling…

Tenele's gaze drifted to the woman kneeling with her. She had never seen the Alykith queen, but she had heard stories of a woman whose beauty was as seductive as her magic was strong. Queen Lyra of Alykith knelt, more battered and bruised than Sinead, with a twin gold collar around her neck.

The Cleric known as Tav Holden stepped around Sinead, lifting his gloved hands to his veil and hood. He pulled them away, uncovering a handsome face, cold blue eyes, and platinum hair. Though, even as he revealed himself, his visage changed. He grew taller, his clothes shifting and morphing like mist in rain until it gathered round his hips in a drape. His ivory skin warmed to a pale gold, his eyes turned the color of brightest day, and when he smiled, glittering opals glimmered back.

A wave of nausea rolled through her. She had seen him before. Once in Reagan of the Wood's home, in the compact the witch claimed would show Tenele the face of her death. The other had been in the murky, warped dream beneath the church, where she was the Goddess Attara and he was…

Thar.

RANEMIR STROUD

RANE STOOD IN the middle of the forest because he couldn't stand staying in the shadow of Reagan's home any longer and going towards Whitehall proved impossible.

He had tried to trick it, thinking that if he did a wide loop around the town, and came at it from the other side, he might be able to get back in.

But it had been hard to march through the forest and feel as if his back was being torn apart. Each strike might have driven him to his knees if he weren't indifferent to the pain. It wasn't that it hurt *him*, but it hurt *her*—and that seemed worse than if the lashes were tearing across his own flesh.

Then, the pain eased.

Nine. Nine lashes.

He knew the law, he knew how many lashes there should have been, and nine was not nearly enough for death.

Rane tugged at the chain around his neck, hating it more than he usually did. **Order me back,** he said across their link, but she didn't reply. He felt the dull ache of someone tending her wounds. Gentle hands, unease, and desire. He thought of the priest. He didn't know why. Perhaps it was her mind pushing the image on him, but he saw the handsome man in the dull glow of copper-tinged light. He tugged on the chain a little harder, irritated at how territorial the thought of the priest's hands tending her wounds made him feel. But the thought of the priest… The memory of him was familiar, and the more the desire grew in Tenele the more the territorial fury wavered in him.

Then, pain returned, and terror, and Rane tore apart a tree because he could do nothing else. He was helpless, consumed by her emotions and the rake of torn flesh at her back, until finally he shut it down. He closed the connection he had with her, because it was useless—absolutely useless—if she refused to call him back.

Fury burned through him.

How dare she sideline him? Like he was some fragile creature who couldn't handle a few clerics? Fuck her.

Fuck this feeling she'd wormed inside him.

Rane walked until any human might have fallen over from exhaustion, until the sun faded and the moon rose. Only then did he rest, sliding down against a tree and stretching his long legs across the earth.

He put his mind to work. They had precious few clues to go on, but it was safe to say whoever had conjured the mass of monsters was near or in Whitehall. The church was desecrated, and, judging by the blood he'd smelled on the altar, it had been for over a hundred years—if not more.

Rane thought of the priest, his warm touch—

Touch?

Rane laughed. He should have known. Of course it was

the priest.

Ranemir Stroud was a bound servant of Sinead, but he was still a monster. He'd been stripped down and remade by the servants of Thar, who would sooner stick their bare hands in fire than touch him.

Of course it was the Shade-sympathizing priest with the kind eyes and charming smile… but why?

Why?

What was missing?

Rane opened the link between him and the Maiden again, but there was nothing. Not fear or pain or pleasure. Just… emptiness. He might have thought her dead, but when he tried to turn back for Whitehall, he was still at the mercy of her command. Still alive, then.

The hours ticked away with him monitoring the link for any change. He was still in the same spot when the connection came alive with confusion and bone-chilling terror.

Then, he felt it, the familiar hard tug against the tether binding him to Sinead's magic. He didn't hear the voice summoning him, but he felt its command like a whip across his mind. Rane blinked and stood before his summoner, in the dark, narrow void of a tomb.

Father Drowsky lurked among the rubble, the glow of blue light reflecting on his dirty face. He held the ruby that should have been around the Maiden's wrist.

"It worked," the priest breathed, his eyes awash with tears.

Father Drowsky lunged towards him. Rane snatched him by the throat, eyeing the priest's flailing arms. Rane's brain must have been muddled from teleporting because it seemed as if the priest had tried to… hug him.

Tenele's scent—her blood—permeated the tomb. "Where?" snarled Rane.

"You don't… remember," murmured Father Drowsky, his gaze drifting down to Rane and then the kneeling figure. "Do you know him?" Rane shook his head and tightened his grip on Father Drowsky's throat until the man gagged and slapped at his forearm.

"Where's the Maiden, Priesty?"

Father Drowsky pointed above his head. "She's… Jyn. Jyn has… her. We… need…"

Rane growled, irritated with trying to decipher the man's strangled words. He released the priest, and the man dropped to his knees, sucking in a watery breath. Rane turned to climb out of the tomb.

"You don't remember me," Father Drowsky choked out, a tinge of sadness lying heavy in his voice. Rane bristled at the strangeness of it.

"I remember you, Priest. Why do you have that?" he asked, nodding to the ruby in Father Drowsky's hand.

The priest ignored the question and pointed to the kneeling, seven-foot figure covered in a layer of gray dust and trapped in vines smelling strongly of blood—of Tenele's blood. But it was old. Too old to belong to her. "Do you remember him? Look at him. Do you know him? Ren, please. *Please remember.*"

Ren? The name was a cold caress against his soul.

Rane stared at the calcified being. It was not human, nor was it a Shadow or a Shade… It was something eldritch and otherworldly. "No," he finally said, even if he felt a twinge of… something. Not realization. Not remembrance. But… something. "Who was he?"

Father Drowsky fell near the being and tore the bloody vines from him, roaring as he ripped them away from the figure's arms and legs. The ragged movement jostled the bones delicately laid across the figure's lap, and they splintered apart, clacking hollow against the tomb's floor. The priest wrapped his hands around the being's head, bending to stare into his open, multicolored eyes. "Let me in. Let me in! How do I get back in?"

Back in…

"You're the sorcerer who called the monsters over the border," said Rane, his nails extending into knife-like claws. "Are you here to free this thing as well?"

"This thing?" snarled Father Drowsky. "I'm here to free me!"

"And who are you?"

The priest glanced back at him, his face a terrible wash of torment and sorrow—as if Rane's question had been an ill-gotten knife in his back. His lips parted to speak, but the words caught on his tongue.

"Brother…" A voice like morning chimes called down into the tomb. "Are you down there?" Rane glanced up the shaft, but at the angle where he stood, he couldn't see who the voice belonged to.

"Take this," the priest said as he pressed the ruby into Rane's palm. "Get the Maiden away from here."

Rane stared at the bind in disbelief. It took great effort to curl his fingers over it, to tuck the thing that was his prison into his own pocket. "What the fuck is going on, Priesty?"

"I don't have time to explain to you," said Father

Drowsky, and he turned to climb out of the tomb. "Just... run. Save yourself. Save her." The priest jumped, clutching at the stone above his head, and scurried out of sight.

Rane turned his gaze again on the body kneeling in the tomb. Layers and layers of dust covered the being's dark skin, reflecting the fading blue light threaded through the broken altar. A terrible sinking sensation filled his stomach as he realized who the figure was—the only person it could reasonably be.

Why else would a mad, incomprehensible sorcerer call a legion of monsters down on a small, pointless town on the edge of the border, where the last stand in the Queens War took place—where Alykith and Ighten united to kill a god?

Of course they hadn't killed him. No one could kill a god—not even two of the most powerful sorceresses in generations. They'd trapped him. And now, someone had come to set him free.

So why did it feel wrong to stop them?

43

VERIN

As he climbed out of the tomb, the last threads of Casimir Drowsky blended with who he had always been, and when he stood at the edge of the pit, the shackles of that amnesiac façade fell away. Verin lifted his dark, borrowed eyes to his brother's gilded form and snarled.

"There you are," mused Thar, stroking a hand through Tenele's flowing silver hair. She floated, cradled by nothing but the faintest glow of Thar's power—caught in a perpetual, endless fall. Her eyes were white orbs rolled back in her head, her expression frozen in shock.

"Is this another game?" Verin asked. "Did you lock me away for a few hundred years to see if I could find my way back? How much amusement did you get in watching me fumble while putting the pieces together?"

Thar grinned. "It was amusing, but this isn't just a game, brother. This has purpose."

"And what purpose is that?" Verin asked, his gaze settling on Jyn. The Shade's mouth quirked, his charcoal arms folding across his broad chest. Traitorous creature. "I made you and you betrayed me."

"To be fair," said Jyn. "You gave me away."

"Was it all a ruse?"

Jyn nodded. "Thar whispered in your ear and I guided you here."

"And the attacks along the border? The brands on the bodies. You were looking for her," said Verin, nodding to Tenele.

Thar nodded this time. "Good Queen Sinead hid her well, even in an order dedicated to fighting for me. She was never allowed in mass. Never allowed to use her gifts. Took false oaths to her order and was told a lie about her birth." Thar's cold gaze drifted over to the Ighten queen. The woman knelt, wrapped in silk robes from the night she was bound and imprisoned. Anyone else would have had the mark of fear on them, but not her. She was as solid as stone. "Sinead was right in hiding her. She knew if her blood had bound you, it would also release you."

"Oh, there's a party up here," said Rane as he leapt out of the hole, landing in a graceful stride alongside Verin. He stiffened as he took in the view—his queen on her knees near their Alykith rival, the Maiden trapped in the air, Jyn at the right-hand side of the God of Life and Light. "Again, I ask, what the actual fuck?"

"We were all brought here by Thar," said Verin, because going into any more detail would waste time. And Rane was unlikely to believe him. "He's going to tell us why. Aren't you, Thar?"

Thar smiled, his hand twisting in the air. Tenele's suspended body moved, turning and straightening and floating further out of reach. Verin and Rane took an involuntary step forward, the two men glancing between each other uncomfortably.

"Let her go," warned Verin, and again he felt Rane's uncomfortable side-long glare. He wished he had the time to tell him, to help him see... to show him the realm they'd once called home together as husbands and wife.

"But she's so important," said Thar, and positioned the Maiden over the gaping hole in the floor. "There. Perfect." Thar exhaled a heavy sigh and nodded to Jyn, whose dark shadowy threads of magic swept across the floor, diving down into the hole. A moment later, Verin's body floated out of the void to rest along an invisible surface beneath Tenele's suspended form. "I took your wife and unborn child... Though, I suppose I should call her our wife, because she was mine first."

Verin growled.

"Your war hit me where it hurt, brother," said Thar. "You tried to destroy me by the only means you had, by killing my followers and burning my temples to petrify me into obscurity. It might have worked, if your devastation had not been burning Alykith along with Ighten. The queens realized the war for what it was, mutual assured destruction, and prayed to me for help."

"We devised a way to trap you, and we did. We ripped you from your body and placed you in that shell." Thar looked over the body of Casimir Drowsky, turning his nose up in disgust. "The war ended, and peace came to Ighten and Alykith. But you know what I realized, in the quiet of that truce? War is better for business. A hundred years later, and the prayers have dwindled. You started a war to end me, and in the aftermath, it only made me stronger. I need you to bring that war again, so that the people of this world fear you and flock to my temples. So I will never hunger for their prayers again."

"Wait… Thar's the bad guy?" Rane muttered, looking at Verin. Thar paid him no mind, as if Ren was gone entirely. A sick feeling swelled in Verin's belly. What if that were true? What if he'd burned Ren away...

"Always," replied Verin, soft eyes locking on Rane. *If only you could remember the terrible things he's done—especially to you.*

"I sent Jyn to retrieve your body, but he could not open the tomb, and it was then that I realized what the witches had done. They had devised a failsafe so that not even I could bring you back, if I wished. Only, at the time, they didn't know the truth about the woman I chose as their sacrifice, or that the key they thought destroyed would be born again."

Verin approached his brother. "So you're going to give me my body back, and expect me to wage war for you so your followers will have something worth praying for?"

Thar laughed. "No, I'm not giving your body back to you. You'll just spirit away to your little black realm with your wife and husband and never return. I'm giving it, and all the powers therein, to Jyn. He will become the new God of Monsters." Thar draped his arm along Jyn's shoulders, leaning on the Shade as if they were good, old friends. Jyn's grin turned wicked.

Verin had made Jyn, but he had never been wicked. Had nearly three thousand years with Thar turned him so malicious? He thought of all the terrible things Jyn had done for him as Casimir, knew that it paled in comparison to what Thar might have asked of him. Shades fed on darkness, and

Thar had given Jyn all the darkness he could hope to want.

"Jyn may have my body, but give the Maiden to me," said Verin, even as horror twisted in his mind. He could only think of what the world would become with Thar telling Jyn how to harm it—with Jyn building monsters to ravage it for him. But Verin had seen Attara dead thrice. He could not bear to see it a fourth time. If the world burned, he would have her and Ren and burn with it.

"Fuck that," snarled Rane.

"I'm afraid she's not going anywhere," sighed Thar, turning his gaze up to the woman floating above them. Lamplight glinted off her silver hair. "I made a mistake when I made Attara the Goddess of First Breaths. I gave her the only power I truly had for creation, and as I can't take it back, I need her to give Jyn your body…"

"Alright," said Rane. "Heard enough." He was gone from Verin's side in a blink, reappearing in the air next to Tenele. As his arms wrapped around her, as he almost blinked out of site again, a hand of shadow tore them to the ground.

44

TENELE RAIDER

THE IMPACT SHOOK Tenele awake. She sucked in a breath as she and Rane slid across the nave, his body taking the brunt of blows from the pews they ripped through. They came to rest in a heap of wood at the back corner of the church, near the narthex and the open doors.

She groaned, pushing up to her hands so she could see the being wedged beneath her. Rane stretched, rising onto his elbows, burgundy gaze glinting.

She touched his face, but he pulled away. "You're… here."

"Thank Father Drowsky," he replied, a tinge of hate in his voice.

"I'm sorry. I—"

Rane glanced behind her a second before disappearing from beneath, only to reappear standing as a shield before her. The Shade of her nightmares—Jyn, as he seemed to be called—approached them, shadowy tendrils stretching hungrily towards them.

"Get Sinead out of here," said Rane, glancing back at her. "Run."

"There's no place to run," said Jyn, lifting his hands.

The church windows shattered inward and warped nightmares poured in with the glass. Heavy, malformed bodies thunked onto the tile floors and scurried to them. They were many, in all shapes and sizes. Bipedal. Too many eyes. Too many legs. Teeth like needles and fingers like knives. They screamed or roared or bellowed, the sound loud enough to quake the earth at their feet.

"Go!" roared Rane, and Tenele fled along the back, coming up behind the Gold Cleric with his hands tightly fisted in Sinead and Lyra's hair. The man was too in awe of the beings flooding in from the windows. He didn't notice her approach until she tackled him into the row of pews to his right.

Her hand went to the dagger on his belt as they landed, and she drove it into his throat before he could grab her wrist to stop her. She wrenched the sword from his sheath, grabbed the ring of keys from his belt, and stood. Her body screamed, white-hot agony ripping along her spine, reminding her she'd been beaten and tortured for two days.

She whirled on the two queens. Sinead twisted, scurrying to meet her halfway. "Get out of here," Sinead hissed. "Leave us. Go."

"I'm not leaving you," said Tenele, thumbing through the keys to find the one for the bind on Sinead's neck.

Sinead's eyes watered, their vibrant blue turning murky. "Go," she said, clenching her hands over Tenele's. "I killed you once. Please, don't make me do it again."

Tenele's brow furrowed. She glanced behind Sinead and Lyra, to the God of Light facing off with Casimir. Then, she turned her attention to where Rane battled the onslaught of monsters pouring in through the windows. She felt a ripple of pain bleed through their link, and then he was gone, buried under a mass of bodies.

"Run," hissed Sinead.

Tenele's hand curled tight around the keys. She'd never run from anything in her life and certainly wasn't about to now. Everything in her screamed to get the queen to safety. It was her duty as a Maiden of the Red Court—as an adopted daughter in ceremony and truth. Sinead was her duty—her mother, in the only way she had ever known.

But… She glanced away from Sinead to Rane again. Another part of her drew to him and the devouring horde. It was the same feeling that had sent him away for his own good.

She wanted him safe.

"Tenele," said Sinead sternly. "Go. That's an order. Do you understand me? Go now!"

Tenele's green eyes flashed to Sinead. The Maiden had thought freeing the queen would help them all—that her magic would save them. But Sinead was too hesitant. Too eager to send her away. She was telling Tenele to flee, warning she would die again if she didn't.

Again.

All her life she'd only known obeying—duty and honor and servitude. She had devoted her entire being to pleasing Sinead, to pleasing the High Maidens of the Red Court— unknowingly devoting herself to a woman who had killed her once before, and who had tortured and enslaved Rane, burning out everything he'd ever been.

Ren. His name was Ren.

Tenele pressed the keyring into Sinead's hand and stood,

turning for the throng of writhing teeth.

"What are you doing?" asked Sinead. "Go!"

Tenele didn't answer. Sinead screamed her name as Tenele disappeared into the mass swallowing Rane. She choked up on the sword with both hands, hacking her way into the storm, not even flinching at the teeth baring back at her. If there was one thing she'd learned, they didn't like the taste of her.

VERIN

A CASCADE OF nightmares fell into the room and Verin faced them, lifting his hand and clenching his fist.

Normally, that would have stopped them. They should have frozen as still as black marble statues. Instead, they continued onwards. A spike of rage rushed through him. He took another step forward, his voice lifting into the air. "I am your master. I am God of the Dark, the Father of Monsters, and you will heed me."

Still, they ignored him.

Thar winced. "Dear brother… The power to control them lies in your body, not your voice."

Verin snarled, touching the gold ring on his middle finger, lifting his hand. Casimir had used it to call Jyn and other monsters. Surely it would—

"Jyn conjured them for you. They are his to command. Jyn was never under your control, Verin. He is mine, as he was mine the day you gave him to me."

Verin whirled on Thar, leaping towards him. "I will make you nothing!"

"You have no power here," said Thar, allowing Verin's very human hands to wrap around his glimmering throat. They were so much smaller than the hands he was used to—much weaker than his godly form. He spared a glance at the floating, calcified corpse.

"If you want it back, you'll have to kill her," said Thar, his voice the low rumble of an organ. "She wouldn't be gone forever. She comes back. The gift of creation means she can never truly cease to be…"

Verin shook his head. There had to be another way. There was always another way.

"I have missed you, brother. Your visits and our games. Let's get your body back…"

Verin squeezed his hands around Thar, glancing away from his body to Tenele as she disappeared into the fray. His heart dropped to the pit of his stomach. "Her life is still a game to you, isn't it?" Thar had given Attara godhood and still treated her as some trivial human to toy with.

"I'm eternal," sneered Thar. "All I have are games."

46

Tenele Raider

ENTERING THE THICK of monsters was like walking through a black fog. They moved quickly, fluid and light on their feet. She struck them, using the gold-lined holy sword to rend flesh and sever limbs.

As before, the monsters paid Tenele little attention unless she actively sought to harm them, and even then, their attacks were to wound or deflect and not kill. She continued to hack her way towards Rane... at least, in the direction she assumed he was, where the Shadows congregated like a thick matting of fur and blood and teeth.

She sliced through one, and it split off into two independent creatures—one fleeing for safety, the other driving into her shoulder hard enough to spin her like a top. When she righted herself again, Jyn blocked her path.

Gold eyes glowed, his pearly white teeth glinting with a smile caught between a snarl. "*Minka'nes,*" he said, bowing his head ever so slightly. He stretched his arm out, a tendril of shadow solidifying into a long, black blade in his grip. "I need your blood."

"What does that mean? *Minka'nes?*" asked Tenele, flicking the edge of her sword slightly towards him. She bit down the lick of fear dancing along her spine when his gold eyes fixated on her waist, where his Mark had once been, and where Rane's now stained her skin.

Jyn's sharp smile unfurled into a wicked grin. "Sweet goddess," he said, disappearing in a rush of swirling shadows passing by. When they were gone, Jyn was gone with them.

She felt something brush up against her back, felt warm lips along the edge of her ear. "Drop your sword, *Minka'nes,*" said Jyn, his voice serpentine and bottomless, a chasm to be lost in. She felt her grip on the sword's hilt loosen, but she didn't release it. "Let. Go. Tenele." And she almost did.

Almost.

"Scared to fight me?" she asked. "Have to resort to that silver tongue of yours? This isn't a nightmare, *Jyn.* I'm not so feeble-minded when I'm awake." She spun away from him, swiping the sword out as she did. He blocked it with the long sweep of his black blade.

"I do miss your dreams," he said. "The taste of your fear..."

"The next thing you'll taste is gold in your belly and blood in your mouth." She dove for him, shoving away the screaming agony of the lashes across her back, the dull ache of weariness in blood-starved muscles. She pushed it all down, as she'd done many times before, to some dark place she could draw from later. But no matter how much she pushed down the weakness of her mortal form, she was mortal, and he was not.

As they danced through the chaos, becoming a sleek ripple of clanging strikes, she felt Rane's clenched hold on their connection open unwittingly. A wave of agony washed so strongly over her she stumbled in its wake, clattering to her knees.

Tenele tore her head up. "Rane!" She stumbled to her feet, following the pull of his magic, of the tying thread of power linking her soul to his. "Rane!"

She saw him, crushed against the cathedral floor, claws ripping at his spine. His burgundy gaze flamed with rage when he found her.

"Get off him!" She swung the sword down at the bitter creatures while Rane wrestled up from the floor. When he was on his feet, the smallest of creatures still clung to him, their tiny teeth pinched in the skin of his arms and neck. He ripped them off and tossed them away.

"I told you to go," he said, voice blackened by irritation.

"I don't take orders from you," she replied as he stepped closer. He thrust his hand behind her head, grabbing the creature that had slinked up behind her by the jaw. He threw him out the stained-glass window behind him, shattering the remnants of Thar's perfect face.

Rane loomed over her, wrath pouring off him, but also… Fear. Concern. Hurt. The emotions bled through the link, twisting up inside her.

"You sent me away."

She nodded. "To protect you."

Beasts rose up around them, circling and coiling into a writhing cyclone of death, placing Rane and Tenele in the eye of their storm.

"Let me save you," said Rane, the glow in his eyes softening. He stood impossibly close, his chest flush against hers.

She traced his sharp jaw with the tips of her fingers,

thinking of the dream she'd seen in the crypt beneath the church. "Ren," she said softly, whispering the name against the drowning song of snarling beasts.

Rane blinked at her, cocking his head. Perhaps he hadn't heard, or he had but didn't know the name anymore. She didn't truly know it either. What Tenele knew was that she had died three times at the hands of Thar, and that she was unlikely to avoid the fourth. How could anyone outrun a god?

"You're not so bad, you know," she said softly, smiling. "For a Shade." She rose to the tips of her bare toes and kissed him, letting herself enjoy the taste of him—blood and all. It was pleasant. Pleasurable. And she imparted that feeling into him, fed him.

The cyclone narrowed, until the wall of teeth and claws gave them little more than a foot berth, and then a charcoal hand stretched out from amidst the throng. Gold eyes glinted in the blackness as it curled around Tenele's arm. She glanced down at the clawed fingers before turning wide eyes on Rane, reaching to grab hold of him as the hand dragged her into the nightmare sea.

RANEMIR STROUD

RANE SAW THE dark hand wrap around Tenele's arm, and just as he reached to hold her fast, she was gone. Her brilliant, holy sword clattered to the chipped stone floor, and the mob of monsters collapsed over him. Their weight crushed him to the granite, teeth and claws ripping at him.

He felt her fear. Tasted it.

He roared at the things above him, focusing his energy into porting out from beneath them. He managed to only take a few with him as they landed in a heap of broken pews in the north transept.

The thing over him had many appendages, and they coiled like snakes around Rane's arms and legs, tangling him in over himself. Rane's claws became swords, and he shredded the limbs he could reach, his burgundy gaze hunting for Tenele, torn between trying to free himself and finding her.

He had to find her.

Rane dragged his eyes up to the church rafters, several feet above the God of Monsters' floating, empty vessel. The Shade clutched Tenele's back to his chest. A second later, he tore her belly open. Blood fell, dripping and plenty, onto Verin's soulless body.

Rane roared. He thrashed through the tangling beasts, slicing and carving and tearing. Black blood and sinewy flesh covered him by the time he reached the altar. His mind ached with exhaustion, burdened with rage and horror. He attempted to port up to her, but the energy to do so had burned up with his last escape attempt. So he tried to leap. As he did, a golden hand caught him by the ankle and tore him down to the stone.

He cracked against the floor, shattering slate and mortar. His head flashed with pain and for a moment, he was blind and deaf to the world.

"Begin, witches," Thar commanded the two queens. "Or I will raise your kingdoms, slaughter your people, and tell the ones who are left that the wrath of their god is on you."

Rane rolled, sweeping his dizzy gaze up the aisle to where Sinead and Lyra knelt. The god swept up his hand and curled his fingers. An invisible force drew them forward, their knees skidding across the ruined floor. The collars at their necks clinked open.

"Begin!"

For the briefest of moments, Sinead glanced at Rane. There was pity in her eyes. He had never seen pity from her. Never felt mercy or guilt for what had been done to him. But he saw it now.

"Don't," murmured Rane.

"Stop!" The priest flew up from the floor, diving towards Thar. His mortal hands wrapped around the god's neck, but Thar only laughed at him. He grabbed a handful of Father Drowsky's hair and tore him back like a fly, turning him so that he could watch Tenele die.

Sinead and Lyra began their song. Their chant swept the room, a cold, invisible hand brushing the dust away and taking hold of the threads of life leaking out of the Red Court Maiden. The red drips stretched and tangled, the blood becoming a rope, and then a netting of living, pulsing vines tangling around Verin's body. They grew over Jyn, too, until he and Tenele were cocooned in her death.

Though, she wasn't dead yet. Rane felt it in the burning of their bond. Not dead.

Dying.

He struggled up from the floor, dragging his knees beneath him.

Thar cast him an amused glare. "Still a fighter, aren't you, Ren. Burn everything else away, but you can't take that out. That's what I loved about you. I could tear everything down, mutilate, and ravage you, but you still fought me."

Rane snarled. "I don't know what the fuck you're talking about, dick. But you got it right." He stumbled up to his feet and then launched himself at Thar. Thar dropped Casimir, catching Rane in the same instant with his opposite hand. Just as Casimir's feet connected to the ground, the priest dove for Thar, leaping onto his back. Thar tore him off, throwing him into a pillar hard enough to sever his spine.

For a long minute, Casimir didn't move. He was still as death, and Rane thought he might actually be dead—that he *should* be dead—but then he gave a sharp gasp and jerked to life. The priest's gaze widened. Hardened.

Rane dug his claws into Thar's arm, shredding flesh until the hardened, apathetic look in the gilded deity's face melted with pain. Thar slung Rane away, cracking the pillar just above Casimir's head. The priest rolled out of the way as Rane flopped onto the ground where he'd been.

Thar turned his back on them.

Of course he did. He was a god. They were insects. He had no fear of them. There was nothing they had that could stop him.

Tenele knew this.

That was why she didn't run.

There was no escape.

"The chain," said Casimir, grabbing Rane by the collar and hauling him up. He grabbed at the chain around Rane's neck, snatching at it. "This. Off."

"It doesn't come off..." Rane's gaze darted to Sinead. *He* couldn't take it off, but she could.

Rane reached into his pocket, dragging out the ruby the priest had pressed into his palm. He shoved it into Casimir's hand, meeting the priest's dark eyes.

There was something in Casimir's gaze that set Rane's blood on fire. A force tugged at the back of his mind, a scrape of blades against his thoughts. The dull ache in his head became a consuming agony and a need to know *something*— Rane wasn't sure what. If the world weren't crumbling around him, if Tenele wasn't dying in the arms of her tormentor, he might have begged to know.

The two said nothing, because nothing needed to be said. The priest seemed to know what he was thinking.

Rane turned and rushed Thar from behind. He leaped, tangling his arms around Thar's neck and chest, digging claws into his flesh and locking himself there. He wrapped his legs around Thar's waist and pulled, attempting to cleave open the deity's ribs.

Thar thrashed and danced, his hands curling to grab hold of Rane, and as they spun, Rane's gaze locked on Sinead. "QUEENY!"

He loosened one hand from Thar's chest and grabbed at the chain around his neck.

Sinead's gaze tore from Tenele above them, down to his hand. Her blue eyes glittered, and her lips moved. He didn't hear the word. It was a silent whisper. An answered prayer. The chain around his neck snapped open.

The world rushed through Rane. Sensations he had never known—or he had known once and forgotten—filled him. It was almost too much—too distracting—and for a second, he hovered uselessly above the God of Light and Life, the Eternity Chain clenched in his hand.

"Ren!!" roared Casimir.

The name called forth a realm of stars and midnight fire. Endless night and blissful ruin. Peace and hope and love. But it was all a tangled web of half-formed emotions, a blip of imagery moving too chaotic and fast to discern, but it was enough to shake him. To wake him.

Rane ripped his other hand free of Thar's chest, and as he collapsed down to the earth, he jerked the chain around the God's neck. The metal stitched itself back together, links interlocking.

Thar grabbed at his throat, opal teeth bared.

Casimir lifted his hand, ruby clutched tight in his grasp, murder keen in his eyes. "Kneel."

Rane loved the sound of his voice—the terror of authority

laced in a single word. He almost knelt himself, just for the pleasure of obeying—which was wholly unlike him. Instead, the God of Life and Light dropped to his knees.

48

VERIN

VERIN APPROACHED HIS brother, clutching the ruby in his hand so tightly it threatened to crack. Thar snarled at him, and Verin could tell by the twitch in his muscles that he was trying desperately to move. To thrash and hit and use his magic. The Eternity Chain held him fast.

Kneel. It had been one word, but Verin's implied desires were woven into it. Kneel. Don't move. Don't breathe. Don't speak. Thar fought against every unspoken commandment.

Verin cast his gaze to Sinead, Queen of Ighten. "Release her."

Sinead nodded, all too eager to do just that. She and Lyra said a word, and the vine-like tendrils of power tangled around Tenele, Verin's empty vessel, and Jyn snapped. Jyn and Tenele fell toward the earth. Rane rushed by leaps and bounds and caught her before she broke against the altar's rubble.

Sinead rushed forward, and Verin followed. They gathered around the pale Maiden cradled in Rane's arms.

Verin reached out to touch her, but Rane bared his teeth. He tried not to feel as though Rane had driven a knife through his heart. Ren didn't remember.

He might never remember.

To Rane, Verin was Casimir Drowsky, a pretender of a priest. The thought that his husband may never remember or love him again was the worst sort of pain.

The Ighten Queen's hands smoothed over Tenele's blood-drenched abdomen, a pale light glittering beneath the monarch's skin. She whispered a spell, and Verin watched as Tenele's wounds stitched themselves shut with glimmering magic threads. Not healing, but close enough.

Rane felt at Tenele's neck, fingers brushing her skin, pressing to the pulse beating faintly. There was relief in his eyes, and he curled the woman against his chest.

Verin turned his attention to Jyn, who was splayed and unconscious across Verin's empty midnight-blue body. He turned his dark eyes on Sinead. "Was enough blood spilled to put me back where I belong, Mortal Queen?"

Sinead's lip curled.

"Surely you see now who the real monster is?"

"Both of you are monsters," Sinead replied. "We are just the ones caught in your maws."

"You think you know monsters," scoffed Verin, his borrowed eyes glittering in the firelight. "But you know nothing of the monsters someone will build if they find a way into that body." He thrust his finger towards his lifeless form. "Put me back in."

Sinead shook her head. "Even if I wanted to, it would be her life. I will not do it again. I will not bend to a god and murder what I love. She was my friend once. Now, she is my daughter. I will not do it. I don't think I would even do it to save my kingdom anymore." Her eyes grew misty as they turned on Thar's still form. "Raise it if you will. Kill us if you must. I will not be a pawn anymore."

Thar said nothing. He couldn't. But a cold glint shimmered in his sky-blue eyes.

The rubble behind Verin shifted, and he turned to see Jyn waking. Only, Jyn's body was still as a corpse. The one moving was his own. Verin's empty vessel collected itself from the rubble, his multi-colored eyes gleaming bright. Shadows collected, gathering as a robe around him.

The midnight figure brushed fingers over his arms, one at a time, and trailed them along his shoulders and chest, up to his neck and face. He ran them through his living, writhing hair, and smiled. "It... worked."

Verin rose. "Jyn—"

Jyn lifted his arm and a burst of darkness swept across the rubble, sending them tumbling into the nave. Verin searched the black fog for Ren and Tenele. He picked out his own multicolored eyes roaming in the dark. The mist parted, and Verin saw Jyn hovering over Tenele's prone form.

Verin bolted, clamoring across the floor until he covered part of her, holding up his hands to Jyn. "Stop."

Murder sizzled in Jyn's borrowed eyes, a hatred Verin didn't understand—not fully. But Jyn had been with Thar for nearly three thousand years, and Verin could only imagine what had happened to him. Even so, that didn't explain Jyn's hatred of Attara. Unless…

"Jyn, please. Don't. She isn't to blame. What happened to you is not her fault. It's mine. It's *mine*. I gave you to him."

Jyn's gaze shot to the ruby clutched in Verin's hand and

then drifted to where Thar still kneeled, unmoving, on the floor. Jyn snatched Verin up by his collar. A second later, they were standing over Thar. A moment after that, the three of them were gone from the church entirely.

TENELE RAIDER

TENELE STARED OUT over Loight from her seat near the windows, watching a flock of pigeons sweep across the city. Midday sun filled the room, bathing warm and gold across the quilt laid in her lap, a sharp contrast to the autumn chill outside the windows.

"How are you feeling today?" asked Sinead from the door. Tenele hadn't heard it open, or perhaps, the monarch hadn't used it at all. She had other ways of entering rooms.

"I made it to the chair by myself," said Tenele, turning her face back towards the view.

Sinead slipped into the armchair next to Tenele. It had become her place in the weeks since arriving back in the capital.

Weeks… They'd been home weeks, but everything up until a few days ago was a blur. Sinead had recounted little of it, insisting she rest and mind her own health before worrying over the affairs of state. It wasn't until Tenele threatened to drag herself down the hall and discover the truth herself that Sinead had bothered to sit and speak.

Sinead had gained freedom in Whitehall after weeks of being imprisoned by the Church of Thar. The charge, they had said, was conspiring with a creature of Verin. In reality, it had been Thar himself who took her, disguised as a Gold Cleric. He'd convinced the Church of her blasphemy, bound her, and brought her to Whitehall. Upon returning to Loight, she rounded up the High Priests, arresting and replacing them with ones closer to her inner circle. She had thought of disbanding the church entirely but hesitated in making an already dangerous situation more volatile. Thar had not come to seek his vengeance, which meant he was bored of them, had gotten what he desired all along, or was still a prisoner of an Eternity Chain.

They would cross that bridge, Sinead had said, when they had to.

A heavy silence settled between them as Sinead plucked at the embroidery on her gown.

"Who was my mother, really?" asked Tenele, her green gaze flicking to the startled queen.

Sinead shifted uncomfortably in her seat. She must have known the question would come eventually, though.

For Tenele, the visions she'd received of her past lives as Attara and Elir—the warrior who had served Sinead, and the one the queen falsely claimed as her mother—had faded like dreams after waking. She caught glimpses of them, half-formed and blurred by distance. Perhaps they were so hard to remember because she was not Attara or Elir. Tenele was an iteration of them—a copy of a copy, diluted by mortal blood. She had not woken as Attara, like Casimir had woken as Verin, because she was Tenele and only Tenele.

Sinead sighed, pressing her fingers into her temple. "She was a priestess at *Telana Toro Attara*."

"Did she die having me?"

Sinead shook her head. "No, she didn't."

"So why didn't she… raise me?"

"She was traumatized by the birth. It was unexpected. She had never been with a man, and you grew inside her and were born in the span of minutes. When the Church notified me, I sent for you. When I saw you, I knew. I didn't understand, then, how it was possible. But I knew you were Elir. The woman who birthed you was human and died at the ripe age of ninety-three. The Sisters of First and Last Breaths made her a saintess."

Sinead glanced away. "I killed my best friend to save my kingdom, to save our world. Lyra and I both thought we were doing the right thing. We bound Rane, and killed Elir, and then we locked Verin away." Her eyes grew misty, and a tear rolled down her cheek. "I lived with such guilt. Terrible dreams of her—you. I killed the incarnation of a deity. The Mother, the Goddess of First Breaths and Healing. But more than that, I killed a woman I grew up with, a woman I thought of as a sister. Someone I loved very deeply. I tried, in some way, to atone for it by raising you."

Tenele frowned. "You sent me away."

"I did," said Sinead. "For your own protection. The Priests were asking questions. They wanted to anoint you as my heir, which meant a public ceremony within the grand cathedral. Oaths, and christenings. Thar would have known you were alive. Until then, you were a secret. Thar can only see those who pray to him, and even to those he pays very little attention. But he can control those who have taken oaths to him. I didn't want him to find you. I didn't want him to control you. Attara was the wife of Thar, and instead of welcoming her into his arms when he found her in Elir, he had me slaughter her—slaughter you. I wasn't sure what his feelings were towards you. I only knew I didn't want your blood on my hands a second time."

"So when the priests asked you to anoint me as heir, you sent me into the Red Court."

"Far from the capital, from the main cathedral, and the many eyes and mouths of Thar," said Sinead, nodding. "The High Maidens at the time knew… Elir had fought alongside them. They were her friends. They vowed to protect you, as I wished to protect you. So we inducted you with blasphemies instead of oaths. Desecrated the church at Lastower so Thar could not see into it. We hid you as best we could. So well, that when he wanted to find you, he killed every single Maiden to do it."

Tenele glanced away, feeling a swell of sadness at the memory of the women who had lost their lives because of her.

Sinead coughed, shifting uncomfortably again. "Rane isn't eating. He hasn't had anything since we first arrived, and if he hadn't been totally mad with hunger he likely would have refused that too." Tenele's gaze shifted back to Sinead. A flush of crimson darkened the monarch's cheeks and she refused to meet the Maiden's eyes. "I've given him the usual fare, and he refuses it all. Sends it away." Sinead spoke as if she'd dropped a tray of hors d'oeuvres off at Rane's door, and not a person for him to fuck or torture.

"Oh," said Tenele.

Sinead shifted again, very much the mother who didn't

want to discuss her daughter's love life. "If he goes on much longer, he'll shut down. Calcify or die. Though I'm not sure if he can die."

"He isn't a Shade, is he?"

"Well, I don't know, exactly, what Ranemir is."

"Ren," said Tenele. "He was Ren once."

"Once," said Sinead hollowly. "I thought—"

"You thought you were doing what was right," finished Tenele, slowly rising out of her chair. She cast the quilt aside and stepped closer to the window.

"I gave Rane a room in the East Tower, the one that we don't use anymore. He is free to come and go as he wishes."

Tenele smirked. "Your priests must be thrilled."

"The new ones are very happy with their appointments and have little reason to question my ruling. Besides, it helped when I told them the granddaughter of Attara was bound to him."

Tenele stiffened, twisting back to face the queen. "Well, that's not confusing at all considering I am… I am…"

"Attara."

Tenele's jaw set so tight it hurt. "Partly. Maybe. Once."

"I don't think it's wise to go around telling the world you're the reincarnated, very mortal version of a fertility goddess with an ex-husband who wants you dead."

"So it's better to say I'm her grandchild?"

"I needed a lie to protect Rane but also to protect you. You're Marked, Tenele." Sinead glanced at Tenele's side. "And it's not fading like most Shade's Marks."

"Because he isn't a Shade."

"So, we need a reason to justify the Mark, and why Rane

doesn't need to be kept in a dungeon, and why you're… with him." Sinead rose from her chair. "Thar knows of you. There is no reason to keep you or your healing gifts a secret. So, let's use them to write a better story, one that protects you and Rane—you and Ren."

"And what story are we writing?"

"It's already written. A child of the gods tamed a Shade and saved Ighten when Verin rose from the dead. It's the story I told when we returned. It's the story spreading across Ighten, and it's the story that will follow you until the day you die."

"Again," Tenele snorted.

Sinead frowned. "Again."

"How did Rane take the story? He isn't much for being tamed."

"Well, he's on a hunger strike. But I feel that has more to do with you than me."

"What do you mean by that?"

Sinead scowled at Tenele. "Please don't make me say it aloud." Sinead turned for the door. "There is one more thing, an addition to the story."

"Oh?"

"Verin is back, in some form or another. Whether it is him driving his body or not. Our kingdom—our world—is in danger. The Red and Black Courts are gone, and they can no longer protect my people. So I've forged a new one. A court of two. A court of impossibilities, of moon dust and nightmares. Monster and monster hunter. I have given the proclamation and signed the law. From now until we are no more, you and Rane are the Silver Court."

"You do love colors, don't you?"

Sinead smirked. "I thought of calling you the Godkillers."

"Oh, that does have a better ring to it."

Sinead waved her hand dismissively. "Too late. I already signed and sealed the papers."

Tenele laughed, and Sinead with her. Sinead edged towards the door, pausing as she opened it to look back at her Maiden. "You should, when you're feeling better, see Rane. Preferably before he starves himself to death."

RANEMIR STROUD

THE EAST TOWER of Loight's palace was the oldest, and the least used. It was, in theory, the perfect place for Rane, other than the dungeon room he'd spent the last one hundred and fifty years occupying. He thought he should feel grateful for the windows, for the freedom, but all he felt was a sickening, gnawing hunger.

The room was mostly round, except for a small section on one side that held a flat wall and a door. The door was hard mahogany, reinforced with steel. It was new, he surmised, because the brick and mortar around it wasn't aged like the rest of the tower. He suspected the queen had changed the door out for something she could lock, if necessary.

He had the last room at the top of a lonely tower, with an annoying number of stairs. No one would venture up unless they needed to, and he was unlikely to venture down without a reason. In some ways, it was more isolated than his dungeon room.

His bed sat against the curved wall opposite the door, a heavy wooden monstrosity with tall posts draped in crimson fabric. Other than the bed, there was his table from the dungeon, the board game with its pieces scattered across the tabletop and floor, and a throne-like chair near a dead fireplace.

The room was frigid, and his breath fogged in front of him, though the temperature bothered him little when he was this numb. All he could think about, all he could dream about, was silver and starlight and sin.

He sat in the high-backed chair, drumming his fingers along the arms as he watched the woman Sinead had sent—the second of the day and the fourteenth since they'd arrived back. She was lovely, smelling of rose and lust, and he should have wanted her.

His stillness made her nervous, which was odd given that he had had her once before, over a month ago. She shifted from foot to foot, waiting for him to rise from his chair, to claim her on the table as he normally did. He hadn't the energy to rise, much less have her, even if he did want her.

Which he didn't.

"Will I still get paid?" she asked, and he nodded, flicking his hand towards the door. It groaned open, some unseen force pulling it towards them. She fled, and he was mercifully alone.

The problem with his hunger was that it had wanted the woman, and he did not. He'd never experienced such a disconnect with his body. He wondered if humans had the same issue. Did they crave steak when they only had porridge?

Not that Tenele was a steak or that others were porridge.

Well, perhaps that wasn't far from the truth. She was a goddess trapped in flesh, who tasted like divinity and bliss, who was familiar and warm and nothing like he'd ever known. Or... rather, that he remembered knowing.

He didn't remember who Ren was. He might never. But she had known him as Ren, and perhaps the part of him that was Ren still longed for her.

Was it love?

He didn't know. He wasn't sure, exactly, what love was.

But he knew longing—had known it for weeks now. He would know it for weeks longer, if she chose not to see him when she was well enough. Their work was done, after all. They'd succeeded, in some measure. Sinead was back on her throne, war with Alykith had been averted, and they knew who had called the monsters over the border. Their alliance of convenience was no longer necessary; their relationship no longer hinged on survival. He doubted he would ever see Maiden Raider again.

Good riddance.

She was insufferable.

And beautiful.

And his.

He thought of his Mark on her skin, longed to run his fingers over it. He followed the link connecting him to her, opened it like parting pages of a book, and felt her. She was tired. Winded. As if she'd been running.

For a second, his heart lurched in his weary chest, and he feared she was in trouble. But there was no fear. No pain. Just irritation.

His door groaned open wide, and Tenele stood in the light glinting through the windows of the tower foyer. She was panting air into her lungs, gripping the handle like a vise.

"Too many fucking stairs," she said, sneering. "If you expect me to climb those often, you're in for a rude awakening."

His lips parted. His throat went dry. Though he didn't require water, and drank wine for the fun of it, nothing would quench this thirst.

He arched a brow as she slipped into the room, closing the door behind her. She rested back against the wood and steel. She wore a violet-colored dress, similar to the one she wore when they'd first met. Her silver hair was braided, falling over one shoulder, forgotten threads of silk fluttering around her face. Her green eyes pierced him, and he was lost.

"You look awful," she said, swaying towards him. The ache in his throat grew worse. "Sinead says you're not eating."

He forced a sharp smile to his lips, waving his hand dismissively in the air. "I just ate."

"Bullshit," she whispered. "I felt you open that link. I felt your hunger like knives in my belly when I got to the door. Besides, your would-be meal was arguing with the servant on the stairs about payment when services weren't rendered. She was lovely. I could invite her back and you could have a meal of us both."

He dragged a shaking hand over his face. "You are the worst Red Court Maiden to ever live, Tenele Raider."

She slipped into his lap, sitting across his legs. He swallowed hard, hating how his body responded so easily to something so innocent. "Technically, I'm not a Red Court Maiden, it seems. I never actually took the vows."

"Well, apparently I'm not a Shade," he said, fingers brushing the satin running down her arm. "Seems neither of us are who we thought."

"Which begs the question," she said, leaning over him. "What are we?"

"Don't you remember?" His hand traveled up her arm, and down her side.

"A fog of images. It faded like a dream, and maybe it was. Maybe none of it was real, though Sinead thinks otherwise. She knows who we are, even if we don't."

He frowned. "And she kept it all locked away."

"To protect us from a god."

"To protect you." His burgundy gaze settled on her. "So, if you're not a Maiden, what are you?"

"A Lady," she said, smiling.

"Hardly," scoffed Rane.

"And you? What are you if not a Shade?"

Rane smiled, sharp teeth glinting in the light. "A monster, obviously."

She took his chin in her fingers, tilting his face up ever so slightly. "Hardly," she said, and kissed him. Warmth flooded him, a momentary dampening to the near maddening ache to have her. He hadn't noticed how his other hand—the hand not touching her—had cracked the arm of the chair by holding it too tightly. "Hungry?"

"Beyond reason," he said, voice heavy.

"How would you like your meal, Lord Stroud?"

"*Lord?*"

She smiled, wicked and bright, and every bit of restraint he had burned to nothing in its wake.

He was on his feet, arms curled under her, carrying her to the table. It was nearer than the bed. Rane laid her across the top, kissing wild and needful. His hands fisted the bodice of her gown and tore, the fabric shredding like paper. She yelped, and he growled. The lacing of the corset beneath snapped like spider silk, baring her breasts to the cold air. His lips found them, hot lashes of tongue across her skin, drinking in flesh to quench his thirst.

While his lips devoured her, his hands grabbed fistfuls of gown and raked upwards, shoving until the violet satin gathered above her hips.

He kissed downward, tearing the rest of her dress open until he saw the pink, fresh scarring on her belly. He paused, breath catching. It was so new. Barely healed. She was barely healed.

His eyes dragged upwards to her flushed face and jade eyes. "You should be resting."

"We can rest after," she said, desire weighting her voice.

"I don't want to hurt you," he murmured against her belly, tracing the scar with his tongue.

"You won't." She grabbed one of his horns. "Please."

She pulled him back up, and his lips melded with hers. His hands tugged on the laces of his trousers, freeing himself.

"I'll be gentle," he murmured against her lips, though he wasn't certain that were true. He was starving, and she was here. After weeks of wanting, she was here *and* his. His length pressed to the wet, endless heat between her legs and he groaned, slipping inside.

She gasped, nails scraping along his back. Her pleasure rippled through his Mark, through his magic. Rane fed on it, drank it like the sweetest wine. He buried in as far as he could possibly go, savoring the taste until she rolled her hips against him, impatient. Pleading.

Rane knotted his fingers in her braided hair and tugged back, exposing her throat. His teeth grazed her skin as he drove into her, forgetting gentleness and patience. Hunger won out. It always did.

Her voice echoed off the rafters of his pointed tower, a song of pained delight. It was delicious. Exquisite. She was the finest thing he'd ever made a meal of—would ever make a meal of.

Rane's hand found his Mark on her side, black as ink and endless. A void. A hollow in her soul he filled. His.

She was his.

"Come for me," he whispered, hand slipping around her throat. He watched Tenele writhe beneath him, watched her grasp for something to hold onto while he fucked her into oblivion. He enjoyed the sheen of sweat on her skin despite the cold, the helpless, overwhelming pleasure on her face. She reached back and grabbed the edge of the table, and he smiled with cruel beauty.

Their eyes locked.

He thrust, sharp and vengeful. Claiming.

His.

She came with a silent scream—mouth open, back arched, legs tangled around him. He felt it, a drowning pulse of agonizing bliss that filled him while he filled her. He came apart, shuddering into her, grunting her name with helpless abandon.

Rane drooped over her, resting his hands on the table, admiring the spent and dreamy look of her.

"So much for gentle," whispered Tenele, closing her eyes.

"Is that a complaint?" He dipped his head to kiss her neck, her lips, her cheek. He nuzzled into her hair. Lavender. She always smelled of lavender.

Tenele, his voice said into her mind.

Tenele grinned at the sound of her name, her legs tangling a little tighter around his waist.

A while later, when he was certain his legs would carry them both, he gathered her in his arms and took her to his bed. He made love to her again, long and slow, until she trembled and begged for the mercy of release—which, of course, he granted.

Rane wasn't certain who he had been, who he was, or who he would be tomorrow. He only knew one thing above all others: Tenele Raider was his, and he was hers, and only the gods could tear them apart

51

Atul Hajaris

He was Atul Hajaris, Crown Prince of Hajara, or at least that was what he was told. He did not remember yesterday. He did not remember the week before. He did not remember his name, or his family, or his kingdom. He knew nothing but darkness until his eyes opened, and a procession of worried faces grew nearer. They called him by this name—Atul—and fretted over the wound in his head.

Dead, they'd said. He had been dead for a day. An entire day. By the miracle of some god, he was back.

Though, not entirely, he supposed. Since he did not remember who Atul Hajaris was.

He stared into a gilded mirror, looking at a pair of vivid blue eyes. They were the color of the sky, a strange and bright color to be set in such dark skin—a deepest caramel, with hair as black as midnight. It was long, drawn back with a bronze clasp. He was handsome, if he said so. Beautiful, even. Unnaturally so.

He traced the contours of his face, the sharp line of his jaw, the high points of his cheeks. He wore makeup, dark painted lines to highlight his already striking eyes.

They told him this was his face, but it was that of a stranger. He had never seen this face before, but he knew no other.

The candle near him flickered. A wind, slightly colder than the desert's night air, blew in through the open doorway. There were no windows or doors to keep anyone out. The room simply spilled through pillars onto a balcony. The only separation was a set of sheer curtains. They ruffled apart, and shadows leaked in from the night.

His heart caught in his chest as they collected and grew and solidified into a being. He was midnight blue, hair a writhing mass of darkness, and eyes a multicolored collection of stars.

"Do you like it?" he asked, and Atul swallowed, stepping back until he brushed the wall.

"Like what?" he asked.

"Your new body."

Atul tilted his head, glancing around the room. Perhaps his head injury was worse than they'd thought. He had died— had been dead for a day…

"Thar is so small-minded. He never realized what was right under his nose," the being said.

"Thar?"

The creature lifted his hand and snapped his fingers. An eternity's worth of knowledge crept from the farthest reaches of Atul's mind to sit forward, to remind him of who he was. He doubled over, vomiting across the floor.

When he wiped his mouth and stood straight, Verin remembered.

He remembered agony, and Jyn performing an endless torture of tests to see all the ways he could be harmed and not die. He proved quite resilient. The last thing he remembered was a cauldron of acid. It turned out that not even a cursed body could survive that.

But a god could not die. They transformed.

"You were aimless, floating. But Thar never realized your body held the power of creation, just as Tenele. Except you create monsters. I have given you a monster for a body. Atul Hajaris, Crown Prince of Hajara, bastard son of Thar. He had inherited your brother's love of sadism. His back, sadly, ran into someone's hand yesterday, and he toppled down the stairs."

"Give me my body, Jyn," hissed Verin.

"You and Thar played games for eons. It's my turn to play a game with you."

"Where is Thar?"

Jyn's smile transformed into a frightening grin. "Enduring. He'll be along to play soon enough. When he's learned. When he's mine."

Verin stiffened. "Jyn, I… I am sorry. I am sorry about Thar. I don't know what he did—"

"He liberated me," Jyn seethed. "And butchered me. He violated me and brutalized me and made me brutalize the woman you love until I learned to enjoy it. Until pain became pleasure. Until hurting someone became a hunger. He made me a monster more than you ever could, and I thank you for it. Your reward, father, is this life. The life of a prince, in a game you won't even know you're playing, until it's far, far too late."

"What game, Jyn?"

Jyn pressed a finger to his lips—"Shh. The game starts

now."—and snapped his fingers.

He was Atul Hajaris, Crown Prince of Hajara, or at least that is what they told him. He did not remember yesterday. He did not remember the week before. He did not remember his name, or his family, or his kingdom. He knew nothing but darkness until his eyes opened and he stared at himself in the mirror. They called him by this name—Atul—and told him he was to conquer a kingdom and take a silver-haired bride.

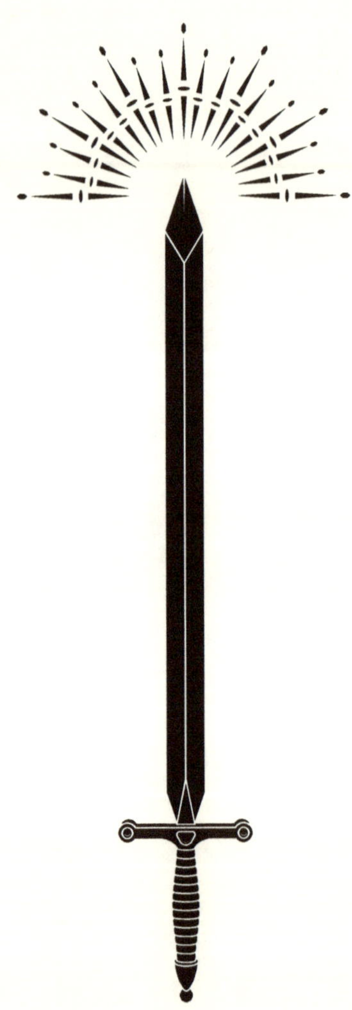

AUTHORS NOTE

ABOUT THIS CRAZY STORY:

The characters of Tenele and Rane first appeared in some form on a play-by-post RPG site in 2005. Tenele Raider has always been Tenele Raider, but Ranemir Stroud started off as a completely insane vampire rip-off of Alucard from the Hellsing anime. When his owner abandoned the forums whilst in the middle of a big story arc, Soran Nightblade (Kathy) took him over… and the rest his history.

In 2019, Kathy and I got together with the idea of working on a project involving Tenele and Vlad for NaNoWriMo. The first quarter of this book was written in collaboration with Kathy. Vlad underwent an overall. In a matter of days, he was stripped of his vampiric powers, given gray skin and horns and fed a victim's life force instead of blood. His personality stayed relatively the same. Demons can be as ornery as vampires.

Life is life, and Kathy and I didn't get to finish collaborating on the story together.

In February 2023, I was feeling some burnout with my

novel series, but had the overwhelming urge to write something I was comfortable in. I picked up the story Kathy and I started, and obviously lost my mind. I wrote seventy thousand words in a month. In secret, of course, because I was terrified I'd hurt Kathy's feelings if I told her I continued it without her.

And, because I'd had an itch to explore writing "spicier" books, I'd made some changes to Rane's character. He no longer fed on someone's life force. He fed on pleasure and pain.

Eventually, I got up the courage to mention to Kathy that I may or may not (I had) picked up writing our collaborative story again, and then ask if she'd be okay with the idea of me finishing it. She was, and here we are.

Thank you, Kathy, for always being a wonderful friend. Thank you for stumbling on my writing in 2005 on Fiction-Press.com. Thanks for following the link in my bio to the random website I built, and playing in the world I made. Somehow, by some stars aligning, by a twist of fate or the hand of God—who knows—we became friends, and it changed me. Saved me.

In 2005, I was a very strange, very lonely and imaginative girl in a town of four hundred and fifty people. That year, my father talked my grandmother into buying us a computer. That year, I learned to code by reverse-engineering websites, and figured out how to launch a forum, and made a story-based game. Somehow, out of all the people in the world, we found each other, and wrote stories together both online, and in real life.

THANKS TO...

As always, thank you to my encouraging friends and

colleagues at Duksbound Books. Thank you to my editor, Cari Dubiel. I am forever indebted to you and your help with all of my writing projects. Thank you to G.A. Finocchiaro for helping with the digital formatting of Of Silver & Sin. Thank you to Aly Welch for stepping outside your comfort zone to help proofread this book.

To my family...

Never, ever tell me you read this book. Love you bunches.

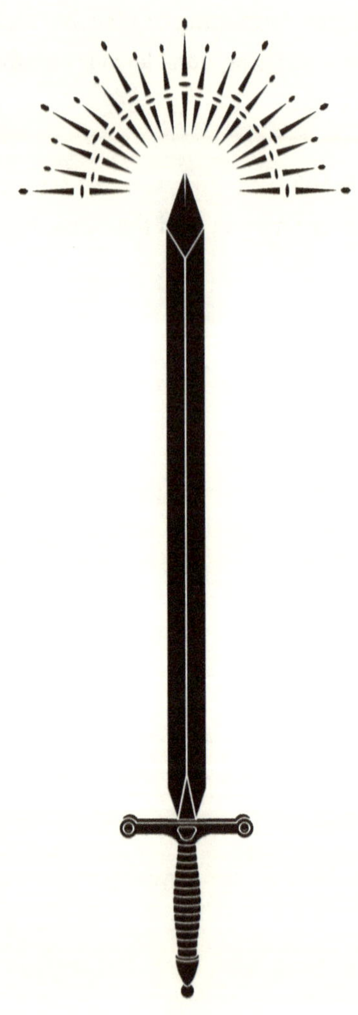

9 798989 747849